THE
SERPENT'S
SECRET

KIRANMALA AND THE KINGDOM BEYOND

THE
SERPENT'S
SECRET

SAYANTANI DASGUPTA

Illustrations by

VIVIENNE TO

SCHOLASTIC INC.

To immigrant parents and children everywhere—
who imagine an idea called home into being
through the telling of stories.

And to my own immigrant parents—
who told me stories, believed in my stories,
and keep helping me imagine my way home.

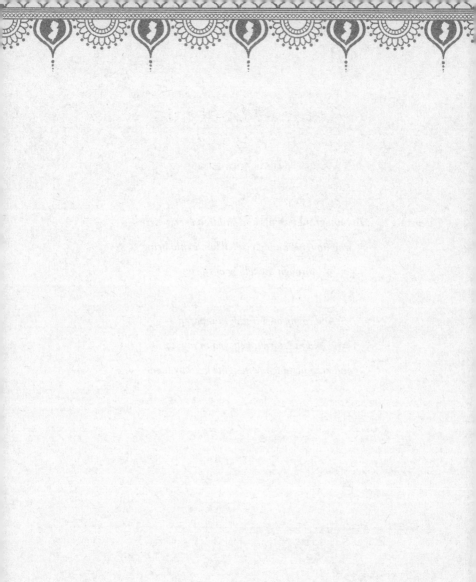

Table of Contents

THE
SERPENT'S
SECRET

CHAPTER 1

A Monster Visits Suburbia

The day my parents got swallowed by a rakkhosh and whisked away to another galactic dimension was a pretty craptastic day. The fact that it was actually my twelfth birthday made it all that much worse. Instead of cake or presents or a party, I spent the day kicking demon butt, traveling through time and space looking for my family, and basically saving New Jersey, our entire world, and everything beyond it. Not that I didn't have help. But I'm getting ahead of myself. I'll tell you that part soon. First, let me back up a little.

My life pre-rakkhosh incident had been pretty ordinary—I spent most of my time at school, hanging out with my best friend, Zuzu, at her family's diner, and helping at my parents' store. There were Zuzu's grandma's spanakopita and Baba's stockroom inventories, doing homework and avoiding my next-door-neighbor-slash-archnemesis, Jovi, and her giggly gang of popular girls. Regular old sixth-grade stuff. Nothing that really prepared me for interdimensional demon slaying.

I guess Ma and Baba had tried to warn me, in their own goofy way. Ever since I was a little girl, they'd told me awesome stories about rakkhosh: these carnivorous, snot-trailing demons who liked to speak in rhyme while chomping on innocent villagers. Ever heard of Jack's giant, the one who wants to grind Englishmen's bones to make his bread? Well, add some horns, fangs, and talons to Mr. Fee-Fi-Fo-Fum, and you're getting close to picturing a rakkhosh. But no matter how real giants or demons or goblins seem in stories, nothing can prepare you for seeing one on your doorstep, right?

But that's exactly what happened to me on my twelfth birthday. Which, because fate clearly has a twisted sense of humor, also happens to be Halloween.

I'd always hated having a Halloween birthday. When I was younger, it was because everyone was so busy gearing up for trick-or-treating, they usually forgot it was my special day. Worse still, my parents never let me hide behind a superhero or monster mask. No matter how much I tried to be like every other witch or zombie or caped crusader in the neighborhood, my parents always had other ideas.

"Maybe this year I could be a pirate," I'd suggest, holding out some scarves and gold hoop earrings.

"Or a ghost?" I'd beg from under an old bedsheet.

But every year, my parents insisted on the same costume. A costume that made me stand out more, not less.

"Darling piece of the moon, you must be an Indian princess!" they would enthuse. "You are, after all, a real Indian princess, and here is the single day that you can actually look like one!"

When I was in the first or second grade, the other kids thought the shiny silk saris my mom wrapped me in on Halloween were cool. They believed me when I told them the bangles and necklaces I wore were made of real emeralds, diamonds, and rubies. But there are only so many years you can fool your friends—or yourself—into thinking you are a real Indian princess, banished from your fairy tale and hiding out in a suburban split-level in northern New Jersey. No matter what your crazy parents insist. Pretty soon, the rest of the world starts catching on.

"Doesn't your dad own the Quickie Mart on Route 46?" Jovi asked one day when we were about nine. "What kind of a king owns a Quickie Mart?"

She'd been snapping her gum and tossing her perfect blond hair and giving me this look like I was less than dirt. I had wanted to disappear into the floor right then and there.

When my mother heard, she gave me some typically loopy advice. "My royal daughter," Ma had singsonged, "none of us is just one thing. Life is a process of learning to recognize our many faces."

"Besides which, your friends are right; no king worth his throne would own a Quickie Mart!" Baba had boomed from behind our store's Giant Gulpie fountain. "Go tell your classmates that even kings and queens have to work hard when they move to a new country. And remind them, your father does not own a Quickie Mart; he owns a Royal Farms Convenience Emporium!"

"And if they still don't believe you," Ma added from the aisle where she was restocking the meat-flavored jerky, "tell them we're not your real parents. Tell them you're the daughter of an underworld serpent king and we found you when you were a baby floating in a clay pot down the River of Dreams."

I guess every kid whose family is from somewhere else thinks their parents are weird. But with mine, it wasn't just their language or their clothes or their food. It was something more—like my parents never really appreciated the distinctions between fact and fiction, science and mythology, dreams and reality. But it wasn't until that fateful twelfth birthday that I really understood why.

CHAPTER 2

The Princess Curse

The day began just like any other October morning in Parsippany, New Jersey. No ominous portents of doom, no noticeable rifts in the time-space continuum, not even a multicar, tractor-trailer pileup on the Jersey Turnpike. Just an autumn sky ribboned with tangerine clouds that tumbled in and over one another, like a bunch of orange-flavored cotton candy. But if you were looking carefully (which I wasn't) and had watched enough sci-fi television to know (which I probably had), you might have seen a tornado-shaped shadow hidden in all those clouds, something that looked like an intergalactic wormhole.

But like any Dorothy at the beginning of her adventure, I was pretty clueless back then. I had no idea that soon I wouldn't be in Kansas anymore (okay, New Jersey, but you get where I'm going with the metaphor).

The morning of my twelfth birthday, I totally slept through my alarm. It was Zuzu's phone call that woke me up.

"Feliz cumpleaños! Joyeux anniversaire! Most felicitous of birthdays, Princess Kiran!" The voice shouting over the house phone was *way* too chipper for that early in the morning. Not to mention the extra chipperness of her shouting in multiple languages.

I made a little gagging sound. Zuzu knew perfectly well that I was allergic to anything remotely princess-y. It was probably because of my parents' obsession, but I couldn't stand princesses of any culture. Whether in saris and bangles or tutus and tiaras, the thing that really got to me about princesses was all that self-righteous, Pepto-Bismol-pink-coated prettiness. And of course all that waiting: waiting for princes to come, waiting for fate to change, waiting for rescue to swoop in. Just thinking about it made my throat feel like it was closing up.

"It's my birthday, and you're going to make me choke on my own bile." I squinted my eyes against the morning sun, wishing for the quadrillionth time that my mother would let me have curtains on my windows. But she'd somehow gotten it into her head that it was healthier for young people to sleep in the moonlight.

"Oh, I think you'll survive that, Princess Pretty Pants." I imagined Zuzu pushing her hipster-red glasses up her pert nose. "But Ms. Valdez might impale you with her protractor if you miss the math test today."

Gah. I finally registered the time. "Oh, man, I'm totally late!"

"Ahde! Schnell! You better hurry, babe!" Zuzu chirped. "But don't you fret, this is going to be the wildest birthday ever!"

I had no idea then just how right she would be.

Forget a special birthday outfit; I threw on my favorite pair of jeans and a black T-shirt, and quickly braided my dark hair so that it covered the weird scar I had on the back of my neck—one of the two that my parents swore were nothing more than big birthmarks. I tied a bandanna over the even uglier scar, the one on my upper arm that looks like a pair of saggy glasses, and then, for double protection, threw on my favorite black hoodie. I ran down the stairs, ignoring the odd expressions on my parents' faces, their strained birthday greetings, even the elaborate breakfast of puffed luchi bread and potatoes Ma had made for me.

"Kiranmala—" Baba began, but I cut him off.

"You know . . ." I snuck a few chocolate cookies from the pantry into my pocket. "I was thinking, tonight, for trick-or-treating, I might go as a vampire."

"There is not enough fiber in that, darling." Baba's sharp eyes hadn't missed my contraband breakfast. "Roughage is very necessary for good digestion."

Ignoring Baba's worries about my digestive system, I shoved a cookie in my mouth, then slipped on my favorite shoes—bright purple combat boots Zuzu and I had found at the thrift store. I threw my backpack on my shoulder and hoped Ma wouldn't yell at me too much about not eating the food she'd made.

"You don't have to buy me a vampire outfit, maybe just some fake plastic teeth?"

My mouth was all thick with chocolate, and I wished I had time to pour myself something to drink.

"What is this vampire-shmampire?"

Ma handed me a glass of lactose-free milk as she asked this. I was expecting the milk to be accompanied by a "you better eat a proper breakfast" death-glare, but Ma seemed too tired to scold. There were circles under her caramel-colored eyes, and the normally tidy bouffant on her head was a bit lopsided.

"Oh, you know what a vampire is." I bared my teeth, doing a bad impression of an old movie monster. "I vant to suck your blood."

Baba shook his finger in mock jocularity. "A vampire is a second-rate monster, if you ask me. Now, a rakkhosh—*that's* a monster with some chutzpah!" My father loved using expressions he learned from his customers. "Suck your blood? A rakkhosh will suck the very marrow from your bones and then use your finger as a toothpick!"

His laugh, which jiggled his paunchy belly as usual, seemed a little forced. While this all struck me as weird at the time, I just chalked it up to my parents' baseline weirdness.

"My piece of the moon, my garland of moonbeams," Ma began as she took my empty glass. "There is something . . ."

She was going to start in on the whole Indian princess routine, I knew it.

"Don't worry about the vampire thing, Ma, it was just an idea." I turned the front door handle, ready to jet. "I'm going to be late for school."

"Kiranmala, wait," a voice called, but I didn't respond.

I stood on our porch, looking out over our totally bare front yard. The contrast between our rickety fixer-upper and all our neighbors' McMansions hit me. Everyone else on the street had manicured lawns with pruned hedges and flower beds. Us? Barely skeletal hedges and raggedy trees. I blushed, remembering how Jovi had once asked if lawn maintenance was against our religion.

Out of the corner of my eye, I saw the school bus turn onto the street.

"Princess . . ." Baba called.

"In the name of the Garden State Parkway, how many times do I have to tell you guys?" I jogged down the front steps. "For the last time already, I am *not* a princess!"

Ma looked stricken and I wondered if the words had come out harsher than I intended.

The regret nipped at me, but I didn't have time to make nice like a good daughter now. "Look, I have to go, okay?"

That was when I heard the bus door open behind me with a whoosh. I sensed more than saw the kids on the bus taking in my family scene—Baba in his ratty, too tight kurta; Ma in a blinding, bright yellow-and-green sari, her bare, ringed toes peeping out from beneath the frayed hem. I felt the heat of mixed emotions flood my cheeks. Why couldn't they just be like everybody else?

I rushed to get on the bus. But in my hurry, I tripped in the snake ditch—the long, shallow trench that Baba kept dug around our yard to protect us from Parsippany's non-existent cobra population.

I could hear kids on the bus snickering and kept my head down as I took my seat. I only looked up as the school bus pulled away to see both my parents standing in the driveway. I couldn't hear them, and through the thick pane of glass, their faces looked strange and distorted.

CHAPTER 3

Tricks, Not Treats

All day long, the guilt churned in my stomach. I couldn't shake the memory of my parents' anxious expressions. What had they wanted to tell me? Well, maybe this would convince them to let me have a cell phone, like every other twelve-year-old kid in the universe. I planned my argument all day at school with Zuzu, who was obsessed with languages and loved using long, complicated words to get her way.

"Mobile telecommunications are a critical component of modern society," I rattled off as I opened the front door that afternoon. But I stopped mid-argument. The house was strangely still.

Ma and Baba never both worked on my birthday. At least one of them was usually waiting inside the door to ambush me with food and presents. Where were they?

I took off my boots and crossed into the kitchen, noticing the back door was propped open at an odd angle. I knew that the hinges were old, but this was ridiculous. One more item to add to the list of things that needed fixing. I shut it the best I could behind me, and stepped back into the house.

That's when I noticed that Ma's normally spotless kitchen was a mess. The kitchen chairs were this way and that, with one upside down near the door, like someone had knocked it over as they ran.

My heart started beating so loud, my head felt like a drum. I'd seen way too many television crime dramas not to think that maybe someone had broken in.

"Hello?" I called, my voice cracking. I eased a knife out of the countertop butcher block.

But as I took a quick turn around our small house, there was nothing else out of place. Even Ma's small jewelry box was where it should be on her bedside dresser. I returned to the front hall, confused.

Where were my parents? How had they forgotten about my special day?

What I saw by the front door made me feel a little better. On a rickety folding table rested a covered tray of home-made rasagollas and sandesh with a note that read:

For the dear trick-or-treaters
(gluten-free, nut-free, and made with
lactose-free milk obtained humanely
from free-range cows)

Classic! I laughed shakily, putting down the knife. I was letting my imagination get the best of me. Nothing could be wrong if my mother had remembered to make homemade Indian sweets for the neighborhood kids. It was one of her Halloween traditions. The problem was, cloth grocery bags and old pillowcases aren't made to carry around the syrupy, round rasagollas or molasses-sweetened cakes of sandesh she handed out to unsuspecting trick-or-treaters. But it would never have occurred to my parents to just give out store-bought candy. Another example of their overall cluelessness.

I was about to grab a sticky rasagolla myself when I spotted something else lying on the floor. A birthday card, half in and half out of an envelope. It was Baba's typical sense of humor—a bright neon pink and sparkly card meant for a baby. On the front was, what else, a crown-wearing princess under the words *Daughter, you're 2!* Only, Baba had taken a Sharpie and written a number *1* before the *2* so that it read *12*. Har-*dee*-har. Again, typical Baba. But why was it on the floor like this? Wiping my syrupy fingers on my jeans, I picked it up.

Inside the card, under the words *Have a Spark-a-licious birthday!*, was a scrawled message, so unlike Ma's normally precise handwriting.

Take heart, dear daughter.

We were hoping for the last dozen years that it would not come to pass. But it has happened—the magical spell protecting us all has been broken on this, your twelfth birthday. Forgive us for trying to shield you from the truth. Now there is too little time to explain.

Whatever you do, do not let any rakkhosh into the house. Trust the princes to keep you safe, but more importantly, trust yourself. We leave here some extra rupees and a moving map in case you find them of use.

But I beg you, do not try to find us. It is far too dangerous. We go

now to that dark and terrible
origin place where all spells meet
their end.

(Oh, and make sure to take your
gummy vitamins every morning.)

Darling piece of the moon, the
first thing you must do is to find—

The note broke off there with a big, ugly inkblot, as if she'd
been startled by something into stopping mid-sentence.

I shook the envelope, and out fell a small wad of colorful, unfamiliar bills—the rupees Ma had mentioned. But
the other thing in the envelope wasn't a map at all—just a
yellowed piece of blank paper.

That was it. They had always been odd, but now my parents had totally gone off the deep end. I called their cell phones and the phone at the store. When I got only voicemail, I started to really panic. If this was some kind of a bizarre Halloween trick, it wasn't funny. All that stuff about princes and rakkhosh—what planet did Ma and Baba think we were living on?

I felt myself start to tear up, and bit the inside of my cheek to stop the waterworks from spilling out. Along with dressing and acting in ways that were unnoticeable, it was another of my self-imposed rules for making it through middle school. There was no crying. Not ever. Tears were like a door to a scary room inside myself I'd most definitely rather keep closed.

I took a big breath and tried to calm down. *Weeping is for wimps.*

I was about to call Zuzu at her parents' restaurant when the doorbell began to ring nonstop. It was the little kids—dressed as fairies and animals and superheroes—out with their parents before it got dark. In a daze, my head still swirling, I handed out the messy sweets.

"Gee, thanks!" said a little boy dressed as Robin Hood. "This is a lot better than the dentist lady next door. She's giving out toothbrushes!"

I shut the door with shaking hands, my heart tight in my chest. Dusk was settling onto the neighborhood. Where were my parents? What had happened to them? Why had they told me not to try and find them?

Just then, the doorbell rang again.

Standing on the front porch were the strangest trick-or-treaters I'd ever seen: two boys, about my age, maybe a little older. They looked like brothers. The smiling one was so handsome he almost melted my eyeballs. The other one was taller and broader, and looked a little bored. The funny thing was the way they were both dressed—in flowing shirts and pants in the same sparkling fabrics as Ma's saris. They were wearing silk turbans and shoes with curling-up toes. Each had what looked like a jewel-encrusted sword tucked into the sash around his waist. The handsome boy's sash and turban were red, and the taller boy's were blue.

"Blast you, little brother; she's probably been eaten already," the boy in blue was saying as I opened the door. "You just had to stop for that Giant Gulpie, didn't you?"

"That Giant Gulpie is the only reason we made it here at all," argued his brother. "You never want to ask for directions, you stubborn rhinoceros."

But I didn't have time to make sense of all that, because

at that moment, the boy in red looked straight at me with his movie-star eyes.

Now, don't get me wrong. I'm not one of those boy-crazy goobers whose rooms are wallpapered with posters of floppy-haired boy bands. And I don't fill my school note-books with my initials and the initials of some cute boy surrounded by a goofy heart. It's not that Zuzu and I don't have a few celebrities whose pictures we like to look up on websites like Cute Boys Do Dental Hygiene Too. (I mean, who doesn't like to see their favorite TV star flossing his teeth for the cameras?) But until that moment when I opened the front door, I'd never met someone so handsome in real life.

"Are you ready, my lady?" the boy must've been asking, but something had gone all wonky with my hearing, so he just sounded like one of the teachers in a *Peanuts* cartoon— "Waa waa waa waa waa." Boy, was he good-looking. I felt a shiver, the kind I might describe in a note to Zuzu with little asterisks around it. *shiver*

The boy looked at my dark jeans and black sweatshirt, furrowing his brows. Not that it made him any less pretty. "Brother Neel, I don't believe the lady is ready."

Then the other guy—whose name was Neel?—reached out for the tray of sweets in my hand. He popped at least two rasagollas in his mouth, not even worrying about the sticky sauce dripping down his chin. Gross.

"You're supposed to say 'trick or treat,'" I said primly, then immediately wanted to kick myself. Two cute boys come to my door and the first thing out of my mouth is, "You're supposed to say 'trick or treat'"? How uncool was I?

"It must be like a costume, Lal." Neel winked while licking syrup off his fingers. "No one wears boring clothes like that for real."

An uncomfortable heat rushed over my face. "What are you, the fashion police?"

Even though I amazed myself by coming up with a smart answer in time, the tall boy's statement stung. Here was another rich kid with fancy clothes, I thought, making me feel bad about what I could afford to wear. And what about them—Lal and Neel? Weren't those the Bengali words for red and blue? And they were dressed according to their names? How fashion forward was *that*?

When Neel reached out to pick up more sweets, I slapped his hand away. Hard.

"Yo, easy, *Prin-cess!*" The way he said it, all sarcastic and dragged out, made me think he was making fun of me. Obviously, I was the furthest thing from a princess in his mind.

I felt a pricking behind my eyes and I blinked the moisture away like crazy. Then, as if the atmosphere was reflecting my mood, the air became filled with a putrid, garbage-y smell. What *was* that?

I turned my back on Neel and his mocking eyes, and appealed to the handsome Lal. "Am I ready? Am I ready for what?" I put my hand on the door.

But the boy in red didn't answer. Instead, he took out his sword—which suddenly didn't look like a costume sword at all. It looked shiny. And sharp. Before I could react, he grabbed my wrist and tried to yank me out of the house toward him.

Now, if I wasn't as streetwise as I am (I've been to Manhattan *five times* and ridden the subway *twice*), I might have made the mistake of thinking this was some kind of dream come true. But I'm a Jersey girl, and Jersey girls are no dummies. I knew perfectly well that no matter how handsome someone is, you can't let them start grabbing at you. Seriously, I've seen a lot of made-for-TV movies in my time, and those serial killers are always super good-looking.

"Get off me!" I said in my loudest anti-attacker voice. Every muscle and nerve in my body felt taut—ready to fight. I shook him off, and pulled myself back into the house. I weighed the serving tray in my hand, ready to clobber him in his gorgeous head if I needed to.

"That, my dear lady," Lal finally said. "Are you ready for *that*?" He pointed at something behind me.

It was then that I realized that Lal wasn't the one I had to worry about.

Someone in a snarling monster costume had slammed through the half-open kitchen door. The creature was at least ten feet tall, with warty green-black skin, enormous horns and fangs, and beady eyes that squinted as if it couldn't see very well in the light. It drooled a stream of thick saliva on Ma's clean floor. The costume was freakishly good. Too good. My hand went loose and a bunch of sweets slid to the floor. Neel grabbed the falling tray before it crashed down.

My heart hammered so loudly in my ears, Lal's next words came from miles away.

"It's a rakkhosh, my lady! Come for tricks, I fear, not treats!"

A rakkhosh. A *rakkhosh*? Not somebody in a costume, but a real demon—straight out of one of Baba's folktales? Right here, in my kitchen, in Parsippany, New Jersey?

I tried to scream, but the room had gone all wickety-wockety, like one of those paintings of melting clocks. My bones were molasses.

The monster crashed blindly around the kitchen, ripping off the refrigerator door with its razor-sharp nails, crushing the cabinets with its huge feet. It was kind of hunched over, but its horns gouged long holes in the ceiling, and plaster flaked down on its already beady eyes.

"My parents told me not to let a rakkhosh in the house," I heard myself squeak.

The demon was tossing back dinner plates like they were pieces of popcorn. It then started chomping on the still-plugged-in toaster, making sparks fly everywhere.

"Hate to break it to you, but it's too late now!" Neel took out his sword too, but he looked less worried than his brother. He filled his pockets with the sweets that I'd dropped on the floor.

I barely had time to grab my birthday card, with the money and map, before the brothers shoved me out of the house. The last thing I saw before they slammed the front door behind them was the demon emptying my fruit-flavored gummy vitamins into its ginormous mouth.

Finally, I shrieked.

"Oh, man, my mom is going to kill me!"

CHAPTER 4

A Demon in the Front Yard

Things got seriously weirder after that. I ran out of the house, my feet barely shoved into my untied boots. The first thing I saw were two winged horses standing in a corner of the front lawn, snuffling at the few lone strands of grass Baba hadn't killed. There was a medium-sized white one with snow-colored wings and a larger, dangerous-looking black one with feathers the color of a raven. Their wings were muscular and wide, sprouting right out where you'd imagine their shoulders would be. Both horses pawed the ground near Baba's snake ditch. They whinnied nervously. Apparently, they didn't like snakes either.

Some little trick-or-treaters on the sidewalk gaped at the winged horses, giggling and pointing, but their parents ignored the animals—as if the horses had some kind of

grown-ups-can't-see-me spell on them. Even as the adults
sauntered by with their little ghosties, firefighters, and
goblins in hand, a group of high schoolers dressed as punk-
zombie-rockers stopped in front of the house to squint at
the winged horses, blinking as if they weren't really sure
what they were looking at.

"Wicked horse costume, man!" a boy with mascara and
a nose ring shouted as we came rushing out of the house.
"Hey, who's in there?" he yelled into the white horse's nose.

"Unhand our horses, sir!" Lal yelled as Nose Ring tried
to pull one of the midnight feathers off the stallion's wings.

The pack of costumed boys broke out laughing. "Check
out the loser! Look at that getup! Fresh off the boat!"

Lal stopped in front of the boys, growing as red as his
turban. "You uncouth hyenas!"

"Enough already with the posh accent!" I thought I
heard Neel mutter. In a louder voice, he called, "Let it go,
Lal!" Neel and I hadn't stopped running, and now he shoved
me onto the back of the black horse, which snorted and
shifted under me. "We've got more important things to
worry about right now!"

The crashing sounds coming from the house were getting louder. For a second, I thought about how upset Ma
would be at the mess when she came home. But then I

remembered I had no idea where she and Baba were. Had the rakkhosh taken them before I got there? What was it that Ma wrote? Something about a protective spell being broken on my birthday? Was all this really happening? My stomach clenched, and I felt my tear ducts doing something suspicious, until I reminded myself: *Blubbering is for babies.*

Lal put away his sword and rolled up his sleeves. He circled Nose Ring with his fists raised, like an old-fashioned boxer. "We are the princes Lalkamal and Neelkamal— guests in your land from the Kingdom Beyond Seven Oceans and Thirteen Rivers. You have insulted us, and I must ask for satisfaction."

Princes? Ma's note said something about trusting princes. The truth was, I guess I'd already decided to trust the boys— right after I'd figured out they probably weren't serial killers. Why else would I be sitting on the back of a winged horse, waiting for Lal to finish his duel with a teenage zombie?

The horse under me whinnied and stamped its feet, and I was grateful that Neel had its reigns firmly in hand. But Lal wasn't paying either of us any attention.

"You are unarmed, so I challenge you to fisticuffs! Hand-to-hand combat!"

Lal's dark eyes glinted at his opponent, as if he had nothing better to do than fight a mascara-wearing high schooler. As handsome as he was, I had to admit, Lal wasn't the most practical person I'd ever met. And why did he talk like an old-fashioned hero when his brother didn't? It was like he was playing some movie version of a prince. I almost expected a little glint of light to cheesily spark off his front tooth. Like: *ching*

"Hello? Could we move it along? Being chased by a demon here?" I muttered. Neel gave me a sideways glance.

"Haoo, maoo, khaoo!" The crashing sounds were louder now, and I could hear the demon's cries very close to the front door of the house. The horses skittered and neighed, and I held on as tightly as I could, but kept my attention on Lal and his opponents.

"Man, that's a wicked scary haunted-house tape!" Some of the high school boys looked nervous and started backing off.

Only Nose Ring stayed. He hacked and spit at Lal's feet. The goober hung on a lone blade of grass, shimmering like a disgusting jewel.

"I demand satisfaction!" Lal yelled. He circled the boy, his fists still up. Despite how ridiculous he was being, anger only made Lal more hair-meltingly handsome. While I got my fill of Lal-flavored eye candy, Neel swung himself up on the ever more agitated black horse.

"Hold tight," he ordered over his shoulder. "I bet you don't know how to ride and I don't want you rolling off and getting pancaked."

My skin prickled at Prince Neel being so close. Not just because he was a boy, and I wasn't sure I'd ever sat that close to a boy, but because he was an obnoxious boy. A boy who thought he was all that and a packet of samosas.

"Why can't I ride with Lal? I bet he's more of a gentleman!"

"Oh, sure, he's more of a gentleman, and better at being royal too." Neel raised a dark eyebrow. "But you better believe I'm the better rider."

Uck! Obnoxious and an egomaniac! I was about to zing off a good response, when I heard a cracking noise—like an iceberg breaking off a glacier.

I looked up just in time to see the entire wall around my front door collapse. The horse flapped its wings and bucked in fear. I had no choice but to hang on to Neel's waist for dear life.

"Time to go, little bro!" Neel hollered, barely keeping the animal on the ground.

The rakkhosh pushed through the wall of my house as if it were tissue paper and held one of the pillars from the front porch in its hand. Bricks and mortar fell on the demon's shoulders, but it brushed them away like raindrops. When its beady eyes finally focused on the far end of the lawn, the demon lumbered in our direction, the pillar raised like a club over its head. Each step made the ground shake.

"Mommy!" Nose Ring was halfway down the street, running at full speed behind his already disappeared crew.

To my left, I heard a thin, high-pitched voice. Oh no!

"Look at the scary monster costume, Daddy!" A little mermaid approached the house with her suit-wearing father.

"Run!" I shouted at the dad, since I was pretty sure he couldn't see the rakkhosh.

The father stood frozen, as if he wanted to run but wasn't sure why. I shouted at him again, and by some instinct, he grabbed his daughter and started sprinting down the sidewalk. The girl's smiling face bobbed over her father's back, her tiara hanging crookedly from her head. "But I want to see the monster eat the prince, Daddy!"

Lal was paying no attention to the rakkhosh that was gaining on him by the second. Instead, he shook his fist at Nose Ring's departing form.

"Run, you lily-livered lamprey! Run from my wrath!"

Even with a looming demon, a near-eaten neighbor girl, a spooked horse, and a rude riding companion on my mind,

I noticed that some of Lal's dark curly locks had come loose from his turban. *sigh*

The advancing rakkhosh was drooling so much goo from its mouth now that strings of the frothy stuff were sticking to the tree stumps and bare bushes it passed. It eyed Lal, licking its lips.

"Dirty socks and stinky feet!" the demon screeched. "I smell royal human meat!" Bristle-like hairs stood up on its arms and nose.

Wow, rakkhosh really do rhyme! I thought in passing, before my mind became more appropriately preoccupied with my imminent death and dismemberment.

Handsome or not, this royal wack job was going to get us all killed. Trust the princes, Ma had said, but we'd all have to survive first.

"Come on, Lal!" I yelled. "Let's get out of here!"

The white horse was just as scared as the black one. Its eyes were big and its breath came out in audible whooshes through its nose. But it wasn't going anywhere without Lal. The loyal animal opened its wings and took a few steps toward its master. It shook its mane, as if asking him to get on its back. The black horse bearing Neel and me shuddered, dashing this way and that, barely under Neel's control.

The demon's black tongue lolled from between his fangs. "How he'll holler, how he'll groan, when I eat the mortal prince's bones!"

"Seriously?" Neel mused. "That's the best meter he could come up with?"

The horses whinnied in fear and warning.

"Lal!" I screamed. The rakkhosh's fingernails were inches from his head.

But just then, Prince Lal did something fairly high on

the Richter scale of stupidity. He launched himself off a tree trunk, did an Olympic-level double back somersault in the air, and landed on the demon's head, gripping its two horns like motorcycle handle bars.

"Me thinks, sirrah, you need to go on a diet!" Lal announced. He tried to stab the monster with his sword, but the rakkhosh's thick skin stopped the blade from going in too far.

"This prince is like a little fly!" cried the demon, swatting at Lal. "*Me* thinks it's time for him to die!"

"Aren't you going to go help him?" I yelled at Neel. He just sat there in front of me, watching the spectacle.

"Aw shucks, he's just showing off." Neel reached into his pocket and scarfed down a couple more of Ma's rasagollas.

I shrieked as the monster's fist managed to connect with Lal's head. The prince slumped forward, unconscious, and then began to slip off the rakkhosh's neck. Only his red sash, which had gotten tangled up in one of the demon's horns, saved him from crashing down to the ground. Prince Lalkamal hung upside down from the thrashing monster, his perfect face deathly still.

And then I don't know what the heck got into me.

"Well, if you're not going to help your brother, I will!" Pushing off Neel's back, I slid from the dark horse and ran at the rakkhosh. Unfortunately, I only reached the monster's waist. I grabbed Lal's sword, which had fallen from his limp hands, and stabbed the hairy demon in the foot.

"Let him go, halitosis-head!"

Some instinct told me to plunge the sword into the soft spots between the demon's toes. I was scared, but felt something else besides fear coursing through my veins. Something brave and strong and heady. Like I'd been fighting rakkhosh all my life instead of doing inventory on two-liter soda bottles and pine tree–shaped car deodorizers.

"Princess smells like yummy pickles!" the demon snarled. "Stop it! Stop it! Ooo, that tickles!"

I felt the monster grab my hood. "You best not rip my favorite sweatshirt, you drooling toad!" Sure enough, as the monster lifted me up, I heard the material start to tear.

I hung from the monster's fingers ten feet above the ground. I kicked my legs, swinging my sword in a wild arc. Lal, still hanging unconscious, was suddenly very close.

"Here, horsey! Come catch your master!" I sliced through Lal's tangled sash, freeing him. The unconscious prince plummeted toward the earth.

Luckily, the monster was too occupied with me to worry about Lal, and too shortsighted to see the winged horse that swooped up, catching him on its snow-white back.

"Good job, Snowy!" I could have sworn the horse smiled at me as it flew back toward where Neel and the black horse still stood at the far end of the lawn.

As the rakkhosh lifted me face-high, it was hard not to faint at the smell coming from its mouth. Holding my breath, I took aim at its teeny, bloodshot eye and stabbed the sword forward with all my might. Unfortunately, sword fighting wasn't on the curriculum at Alexander Hamilton Middle School, and my aim wasn't exactly perfect. I looked in horror as Lal's weapon lodged itself right in the middle of the monster's bulbous nose, resulting in yellow streams of rakkhosh snot streaming out of both nostrils.

"Barf!" I yelled as the monster's sinuses drained all over me. "Neel, anytime now, some help would be awesome!"

If it was possible, the monster looked even more furious. "Princess mean, but she'll be sweet! Princess meat is good to eat!"

I was done for—abandoned by my parents, covered in rakkhosh snot, and about to be eaten. This was the worst birthday ever!

CHAPTER 5

Home and Abroad

The rakkhosh lowered me toward its toothy mouth.

Just then, something glinted by me with a swish. It grazed my arm and cheek before getting stuck upright between the demon's lips. My right sleeve was sliced open. The side of my face felt on fire, and not because I was blushing. I realized what it was. Neel's sword.

"Gaak!" The monster thrashed around, grabbing its mouth. In its confusion, it dropped me, and I fell toward the hard ground. *If only my dad hadn't savaged all signs of life from our lawn*, I thought as I plummeted to my doom, *maybe there would be something there to cushion my landing.*

"Yagh!" I yelled, or something like it. "Yeek! Yegads!"

Somebody's strong arm grabbed me around my waist. It was Neel, flying up on the back of his black steed. He threw me in front of him, swinging me over the horse like a sack of potatoes.

Now, if you've never flown on the back of a winged horse like that, I don't recommend it. It's not just the ungraceful butt-in-air aspect, it's the mouthful of sweaty horsehair you get in the bargain. Technically, I guess Prince Neel swept me off my feet. Actually, it was the exact opposite of the gallant rescuing you read about in fairy tales.

There was an awful wailing and crashing, which I learned later (I was still doing a face-plant in the side of a horse at the time) was the rakkhosh—with one sword protruding from its nose, one trapped in its open mouth—flailing around. Finally, it tripped over a tree trunk and fell with a shaking crash to the ground.

"Somebody's gonna have a terrible migraine!" Neel drawled as he dismounted.

I managed to slide ungracefully off the horse, holding my aching ribs. It was a relief to see the demon lying across my lawn, out cold.

"I was doing fine there without you, Mr. Late-to-the-Show!" I snapped at Neel. "You didn't need to swoop in at the last moment and do the whole princely rescue shtick."

Neel gave me a hard look that made my face warm. Then he looked at my torn sweatshirt and my now exposed right upper arm. He raised his eyebrows, but only said, "You're welcome."

Humiliation washed over me. I hated people seeing my scars. I tugged the torn material over the freakish mark and glared back at him, imagining little daggers coming out of my eyes.

With a most casual air, Neel walked up to the rakkhosh, plucked his own slobbery sword from the monster's mouth, and then retrieved Lal's sword from its nose. He handed the weapon to his brother, who was just waking up.

"Werewevictoriousbrother?" Lal slurred.

"Yup." Neel got super busy cleaning off his slimy sword on a leafless hedge. "You completely kicked that demon's butt, Bro." Then he glanced up at me. "With a little help from this one."

"Whatever." I mopped up the blood on my cheek with my sleeve. I didn't like being called "this one" almost as much as I didn't like getting nearly decapitated with a sword. Even by somebody who saved my life.

Neel put his sword into a sheath I hadn't noticed on his back, and petted his horse's sleek nose. It was like he'd totally forgotten about the rakkhosh. And why was he lying to Lal and not taking credit for defeating the demon?

"Aren't you going to . . . uh . . . kill it?" I asked in a low voice. Whether adults could see it or not, how I was going to explain an unconscious demon on our front lawn was beyond me.

Neel shook his head. "Yeah, I'm not really into the whole rakkhosh-killing business; that's all a little too show-offy for me." He nodded at his brother. "There's only room for one storybook hero in this family."

I saw something twitch in Neel's face—what was that, jealousy? But that couldn't be right. Neel was bigger and tougher than Lal and definitely—by most people's standards anyway—cooler. Maybe it was that Lal was more movie-star handsome? But that didn't seem right either. Boys were weird.

"Come on, let's go!" Neel urged. "That demon ain't going to sleep forever."

I bit my lip, suddenly super unsure.

"Lady." Lal's words were gentler than his brother's. "I know this is all confusing right now, but you need to trust us."

I remembered Ma's letter, but I hesitated, looking from one brother to the other, and then finally down at myself. As I did, I realized I was a mess. The scratch on my cheek was still bleeding a little, my now one-armed, hoodless sweatshirt was covered in demon snot, and I was pretty sure

I smelled like a skunk after a hard night partying with some dung beetles.

Neel dug a grubby-looking handkerchief out of his pocket, but I shook my head. I didn't meet his eyes, but swiped at my face again with my sleeve.

"I'm not a damsel in distress, you know; I can take care of myself." Despite my words, my voice sounded shaky.

Neel's mouth quivered a little, somewhere between a smile and a smirk. "Fine, suit yourself."

"You must hurry and pack a few things," Lal urged. "We should be on our way to find your parents."

A cloud parted within me. Ma and Baba!

"Are they okay? You guys know where they are?"

"I thought you didn't want our help," Neel reminded me with an annoying raise of one eyebrow. "I thought you could take care of yourself."

"Brother, for shame!" Lal scolded.

"That's right." A flash of anger shot across Neel's face. "The shame of the family, that's me."

"That's not what I—" began Lal before I interrupted the brotherly interchange.

"Could we get back to the part where you guys tell me where my parents are?"

"They have passed through the mouth of the beast into that other place," Lal said.

I really, really hoped this "mouth of the beast" thing was some kind of metaphor. My heart hammered as I thought about the demon's lolling tongue, its enormous teeth.

"Are you trying to tell me they got *eaten* by the rakkhosh?"

"No." Neel turned his back to me as he tightened his horse's saddle. "Not literally eaten."

"How do you get eaten un-literally?"

"They have been transported into another dimension." Lal spoke like he was reciting something he'd memorized. "These protective spells—like the one that was over your family—they are very unstable once they reach their expiration date."

I knew he wasn't talking about spoiled milk. "It's my twelfth birthday," I blurted. But the brothers nodded, like they already knew that. Everywhere in my body felt shaken and scared and raw. I needed some answers—now.

I made my voice as firm as I could. "What. Happened. To. My. Parents?"

"You wouldn't understand. It's too complicated to explain . . ." Neel grumbled.

"Imagine"—Lal pointed dreamily to the sky—"when a star is dying. It grows bigger, then smaller, and finally it implodes into a black hole."

Okaaay. No matter how stupid Neel thought I was, I knew about black holes. I'd been to the planetarium. I even loved watching that public television science show with Shady Sadie the Science Lady.

"But what does that have to do with my parents? Or spells? Or rakkhosh?"

"The spell that was protecting your family has, well, run out of gas," Lal stammered.

"Gas?"

"The spell's begun to lose power," Neel said. "As it gets closer to imploding, it first shoots the matter within it—your parents—into a new place, a new dimension."

I struggled to form a question. "But . . . I'm still here."

"It must have been placed over them specifically, or it could be there's an additional spell protecting you," Lal said. "Anyway, an expired spell also makes everything around it unstable—in this situation, the boundaries between the various dimensions."

"Which is how the rakkhosh came into your world," interjected Neel. "We've been tracking him since he got your expired spell scent. There'll be more where he came from if we don't get you out of here."

My head was spinning. Spells. Dimensions. Black holes. And my . . . expired spell scent? Like, eww!

Then I remembered something I'd learned from Shady Sadie the Science Lady's show, as well as endless reruns of that old outer space program, *Star Travels*.

"But nothing can survive inside a black hole, not light, not matter . . ." My words tapered off as my voice was seriously wobbly. I coughed.

"You are unfortunately correct. Most of what you understand to be black holes manifest in other dimensions as demons—terribly greedy rakkhosh—who gobble up everything around themselves," Lal said.

"Think of them like giant galactic vacuum cleaners," Neel added totally unhelpfully.

The vivid image made my throat feel even more like it was closing up. I let out a terrified squeak. He was talking about my parents being hoovered up by some outer-space-phenomenon-slash-hungry-demon. This was no joke.

"But enough with the astronomy lesson," continued Neel. "All you need to know is that there's still some time before the spell completely collapses and goes

all . . . celestial stardust. Which is why we'd better boogie."
He pointed me toward the house. "Now."

The princes stayed by the horses and the snoring demon
on the lawn while I rushed through the disaster movie that
was once my home. The bedrooms were still intact, and the
bathroom worked, even though it had a new skylight courtesy of demon renovations. I threw on a fresh T-shirt and
hoodie, then tossed a toothbrush and change of clothes in
my backpack. I tried to call Zuzu, but only got her family's
voicemail.

"The Tomopolous family is visiting Mount Olympus
right now. The Mount Olympus Diner and Bowl-o-Rama,
that is! Come to the heart of Parsippany to strike the best
baklava this side of Delphi! And if you'd like to leave a message for Marina, Costa, Athena, Alex, Frankie, Niko, Zuzu,
Grandma Yaya, or Zeus the dog, do so after the beep! Opa!"

What was I supposed to do? Tell her a demon had broken into my house? That my parents were trapped in an
imploding spell? That I was about to fly off with some
princes to rescue my family from an intergalactic demonic
vaccuum cleaner?

In the end, I fudged the truth.

"This is a message for Zuzu. Uh, this is Kiran. Hi, everybody. Listen, we, uh, have some unexpected out-of-town

guests. From, uh, really far away. And I . . . um . . . I need to do something for my parents. Something really important. We'll be back . . . probably in a few days. I guess . . . um . . . you could tell 'em at school, and . . . collect my homework." I was getting a little choked up, so I thought I'd better end the message. "Don't worry, I'll be . . ." The recording cut me off before I got to "okay."

I stared stupidly at the phone in my hand. Now what?

"Hurry up, Prin-cess!" I heard Neel yell. "The big guy's gonna wake up soon!"

At the last minute, I shoved Ma's red-and-gold wedding sari into my pack, along with her small jewelry box. My eyes fell on a framed family photograph on Baba's night-stand. It was taken in front of the Convenience Emporium. My mother was reverently holding a statue of the blue-skinned Lord Krishna as a fat baby, a stolen dab of butter in his hand. Right next to her, my father sported a T-shirt we carried in the store embossed with a New Jersey Turnpike emblem. And I was in between them with a Giant Gulpie in my hand, smiling like a loon.

"I may not have always been the perfect daughter," I muttered, "but I swear I'll get you back."

I threw the photo in my bag and raced out the door.

The rakkhosh was still on the ground, but rubbed its

closed eyes with its enormous hands. I held my breath and ran by.

"No time to be lost, my lady!" Lalkamal urged. "It's time to go home!"

"Come on, get a move on!" Neel waved me toward his horse. "Let's get out of this place!"

I felt a last pang of hesitation. "Wait a minute!" I looked from brother to brother: one smiling, the other frowning. "This"—I gestured to the rubble in front of me—"*is* my home!"

"Does she not know?"

Neel scowled. "I guess not."

"Know what?"

"This is not your home, my lady," Lal said. "You are from a place far away, a Kingdom Beyond Seven Oceans and Thirteen Rivers."

"We don't have time for this, dude," Neel urged. "Just grab her; let's go."

"No one's grabbing me!"

Behind me, there was a groaning noise as the demon started waking.

"My lady, you have always known you were different?"

I nodded.

"Perhaps even, not of this world?"

I stared.

There was a low-pitched moan from the direction of the demon. Both horses were flapping their wings and stamping in fear.

"Oh, wake up!" Neel snapped. "No one ever told you about how they found you in a clay pot floating down the River of Dreams?"

"What?" My eyes widened. "How did you . . ."

And then he said it.

"No one ever told you that you were really a princess?"

There it was. The truth. Staring at me right in the face this whole time.

(Yeah, you don't have to say it. I know it's a little ironic in light of my previous attitude toward princesses in general.)

"Hai, mai, khai!" The ground rumbled beneath my feet.

"Run, Princess Kiran!" Lal yelled.

"I'm riding Snowy," I called, sprinting toward Lal's white horse. This time, it definitely winked at me.

The horses had just launched off the ground when I looked down and saw the frothy-mouthed demon bolting toward us. It stood on my front lawn, shrieking as we sailed higher and higher into the night sky.

CHAPTER 6

The Transit Corridor

I was flying.

No. Way.

I was *flying*.

Cool wind whipped through my clothes and hair as we glided into the night. Despite everything, I was in awe. If I were to reach out, I could pluck the very moon from the sky and put it in my pocket. The houses below me were like teeny toy villages, but I wasn't freaked out. Instead, I laughed out loud. Even the stars seemed to be twinkling at my pleasure.

"It is most wonderous, is it not?" Lal pointed out a few constellations. "You know, every one of those stars is a spell."

"Are we riding into outer space?" Despite our lack of pressurized space suits and oxygen tanks, it didn't seem like an unreasonable question to ask.

"Alas, no. Just a different dimension."

Oh, well, *that* explained it perfectly.

Not.

I gulped in some crisp night air, feeling strangely new. My parents were missing. My house was a wreck. I was flying off to who knows where. The situation sucked, to put it mildly. But I'd faced down the scariest Halloween monster I'd ever met, and I hadn't hidden or backed away or anything. I'd acted. I'd fought. I'd done something useful and brave. And that part of it felt kind of, well, amazing.

As we rode, I found myself actually relaxing, if that makes any sense. It was super easy to talk to Lal. Turned out, he was a great sky-tour guide, and kept pointing out things like cloud formations, flocks of Canadian geese, a shooting star—which was a spell being cast, he explained. After a while I couldn't see the ground below us. The funny thing was, I wasn't scared of falling—not at all. I got the feeling I'd always lived up there with the sky and the stars. Maybe it was all that curtainless sleeping in the moonlight, but it felt comfortable and familiar, like the moon itself was looking out for me.

Lal even let me take the reins. Neel was right; I'd never been on a horse before (riding lessons weren't exactly in our family budget), but Snowy was gentle and responded right away to my touch. A good ways ahead, Neel's black horse—whom I'd started to think of as Midnight—bucked and snorted as he galloped in the air. I could only see his vague outline by the thousands of twinkling stars that lit the way.

Lal caught my gaze and sighed. "My brother is so much better than me at almost everything."

Lal's words startled me, because they were tinged with that same wistful jealousy I thought I'd seen on Neel's face back on my front lawn.

"That's not true." I stumbled over my words in my effort to be reassuring. "You're brave, and nice, and very ha— um, I mean, very princely." I almost said the word *handsome* but stopped myself barely in time.

"You think?" I couldn't see Lal's face, but he sounded nervous. "I've been working on it, the princeliness, I mean."

"Oh, it's going really well!" I said in a rush. "You have excellent manners and perfect posture and great . . . erm, diction!"

"Many gracious thanks, my lady!" Lal said stiffly. Then his voice lost its confidence again. "But I don't think I'll ever be as smart and strong as my brother."

Wow. Neel was a lot more of a bully than I thought. I

couldn't believe he would make Lal feel so bad about himself. Way uncool.

We rode for a while longer in silence, until I started to yawn something fierce.

"Sleep, dear princess," Lal said, taking back the reins. "It is a long distance to the Kingdom Beyond Seven Oceans and Thirteen Rivers."

"And we'll find my parents there?" I rested my exhausted head on Snowy's mane. I could hear the horse's breathing, steady and low, like a waterfall—and imagined I could even hear the river of his blood flowing in his veins. I was asleep before I heard Lal's answer.

The dawn was already breaking when I opened my eyes. My butt was sore from spending all night on a horse's back, and I had a wicked charley horse in my left leg. I imagined it was like being on an overnight flight—except without the stale air and packaged peanuts.

Lal was saying something to me, pointing to the ground below, but the wind whipped his voice away. I shook my head, not understanding, until he repeated, "We have arrived! The transit corridor!"

The horses flew toward the ground, like planes preparing for a landing. My ears popped and I did the trick of swallowing hard. It didn't work. (I've read you can also chew gum, but I didn't have any, or, like, hold your nose and blow, but I was afraid that would risk unplanned boogerage in my hand, so I didn't do that either.)

After hours of riding separately, Neel pulled his horse up next to Snowy, and now the two winged horses flew side by side, whinnying at each other.

"Your parents are beyond the transit corridor, Princess," Neel yelled. "To get to them we'll first have to get you through the checkpoint."

"I suppose you possess the appropriate documentation?" Lal asked near my ear.

"Documentation?" I gulped. The horses were coming down fast. And all I could see below me were dusty rocks and red earth.

"You know," Lal clarified, "an Earth exilation notification, a royal-to-nonroyal cover pass, a tweet from the president?"

"Um." I closed my eyes as the horses finally landed in a vast canyon. The red-brown ground was dry, without a sign of any tree, bush, or shrub. More bald than our front yard even, and that was saying a lot. Weirdly shaped outcroppings of stone, and a giant mesa-like mountain marked the eerie landscape.

Where were we? Something about the spires of red rocks seemed familiar, like I'd seen a picture of this place before.

"Are we in . . . Arizona?" I asked when we finally dismounted. I stretched my aching legs. Snowy pawed the ground like he was stretching his legs too.

"It's the biggest non-wormhole transit point to other dimensions in the U.S." Neel looped Midnight's reins loosely in his hands. "Even though the local government doesn't like it."

"So what kind of papers do you have, lady?" Lal asked again. "You'll need them to get through here."

Why were they so obsessed with my "documentation"?

"I have a birthday card from my parents, and . . ." I don't know why, but I hesitated before telling the princes about the map. "Yeah, just the card."

"A birthday card?" Neel snapped. "Who travels with just a birthday card? How are we supposed to get you past the transit officer without getting snacked on?"

"Princess Kiran will prevail. Have faith, Brother." Unlike Neel, who looked totally rested, Lal seemed a little tired after the long ride. Not that it made him any less handsome, but his fourth eyelash from the right definitely looked less curly than the others. Or maybe it was that I'd gotten to know him a little better and could see him more like a regular person.

Lal peered at me with a hopeful expression even as Neel continued to scowl, biting his nails.

"You must be good at riddles?" Lal asked.

"Riddles?"

Zuzu's brother Niko was obsessed with dumb jokes and riddles, and was always trying them out on us, but I couldn't see why that would be helpful.

I squinted against the harsh sun. It was like we'd ridden all night and landed on some alien planet. There was nothing here. Just rocks. No train station, no airport, no subway platform. Not a soul—animal, human, or even monster. Where was this transit thingy the boys were talking about?

Neel stomped off, kicking red rocks and making a mini dust storm as Lal continued, "Please—you must be familiar with puzzles and logical games?"

"A bit," I admitted.

"All this way, and Princess K-pop gets eaten by the transit officer because she has no papers!" Neel shouted to no one in particular.

"Chill, dude! She won't be consumed by the officer, all right?" Lal said in a voice so different than his usual cultured way of talking that I realized how much of an effort he put into his princely accent. But I didn't have time to worry about that now, because I really didn't like what I was hearing.

"Consumed? Who's going to consume me?" Why did the boys keep putting me and *consumed* in the same sentence?

"No one, no one will consume you!" But Lal was looking worried too. Which wasn't comforting. "The transit corridor is the place where, in passing from one world to the next, the officer checks your papers, makes sure all is in order."

"Like the security lines at an airport?" I took a swig from the water bottle Lal supplied. The water was warm and metallic and did nothing to make me less thirsty.

"Oh, sure." Neel ground a good-size rock to dust under his heel, making me wonder about his workout routine. "If airport officers were ten feet tall and had a taste for human bones."

"The transit officer is a rakkhosh?" My stomach spasmed. I might have discovered some secret demon-fighting gene in myself, but it didn't make them any less scary. In fact, all the confidence I had felt last night seemed ground to dust this morning, like the stone under Neel's foot.

"Not a rakkhosh precisely," Lal said, "but a sort of an unusual fellow who has, er, been known to eat individuals without the proper documents."

"He's been known to *eat* people? Are you kidding me?" My head ached. It was all too much—my parents' disappearance, the surprise trick-or-treaters, the demons, the spells, the risk of death and dismemberment at every turn. Besides which, I was *hungry* and *thirsty* and had just had a really crappy birthday, all in all.

I felt like the last day had been one of those superfast, upside-down roller coasters at the amusement park. (I actually really hate those—once I yuked corn dogs after riding one. Zuzu didn't help by laughing her head off.) Only now I felt sick and I wanted to go home.

"I'm sorry guys, I can't do this anymore." My voice shook and I swiped furiously at my nose. "I mean, killer demons? Different dimensions? Black holes? I'm just an ordinary kid from New Jersey. I can't deal with all this!"

Lal's face softened and he looked like he was going to say something nice, but his brother cut him off with a furious exclamation. "Don't be such a 2-D!"

I whipped around. "What did you call me?"

"A flatfoot, a ruler, a 2-D!" Neel ground out the words like they were curses.

Which maybe they were, by Lal's reaction. "Brother, please!"

But Neel kept going. "People from your world think that everything is so easily measured and explained—that everyone's exactly the same, paper dolls in some two-dimensional universe! Well, it doesn't work that way, all right? Not everything makes sense and not everything in life is fair. The quicker you figure that out, the better off you'll be!"

My fear was quickly turning to fury, but still, I squirmed inside as I thought about Neel's words. Maybe I did want everything to be easy and the same. How many times had I wished my parents would just give me a straight explanation for something? How many times had I wanted them to be like everyone else? And now they were missing, and maybe if I'd actually believed all their crazy stories, I would know how to get them back.

"You can't just decide to forget who you are because its inconvenient, Princess," Neel barreled on. "Life doesn't work like that. It's messy and complicated and everything's not always peaches and unicorns. There's dangerous things out there, things none of us understand. But you don't just quit the first time you get a little scared!"

"I am not scared!" I shouted. But I was. I'd almost just

been eaten. My parents were missing. And I'd just realized my whole life had basically been a lie.

"What do you know anyway? I mean, peaches and unicorns? What are you, like six years old?" My face felt positively radioactive.

Neel grabbed at my dusty sweatshirt. "Don't you want to see the people you know as your parents again?"

"They *are* my parents!" I flung his hand off my arm. "And I'm going to get them back no matter what it takes! What have you done to them?"

"Nothing! Of course we have done nothing!" Lal stepped in between us. "We were sent by them to help you. As my brother has said, they're beyond the transit corridor. The officers tend to close the corridors on a whim, so it would be best if we could pass through now." Lal gave Neel a warning look. "All your questions will be answered on the other side."

"Sure, right, if she's not made into an appetizer!" Neel glared at me.

I glared right back. I had no intention of being eaten, no matter which course of a meal. All the worry and confusion I'd felt just a second ago was now replaced by a new resolve, and a strong desire to punch Neel in the nose.

"Trust yourself, Princess. When you're faced with a task that seems too big, it's all you can do," Lal said quietly.

"Okay." I took a big breath. Even if Neel was more annoying than anyone I'd ever met, these princes obviously held the key to finding Ma and Baba. "Let's do this."

Lal, Neel, the two horses, and I picked our way over the rocky ground. As we approached the base of the high mesa, Lal turned to me. I noticed Neel still wasn't meeting my eyes since we'd argued.

"This ancient mountain is known by many names. But we call it Mandhara—the mountain of concentration. It divides our dimensions, but it also unites them."

"The mountain of concentration, got it."

"You have to know within yourself, for certain, that you are committed to climbing it, committed to this journey," Lal explained. "Or else you will never reach the cave on the summit."

I stole a glance at Neel. He was shading his eyes and peering upward. I did the same. From where we were standing, I could barely make out the top.

All righty, a mountain that would go on forever unless I was set on climbing it.

I took a big breath, nodding at Lal. "This is how I get my life back, huh?"

"Yes, Princess Kiran. This is the first step in finding what you seek."

"Just Kiran is fine." I rubbed my aching neck.

"All right, Just Kiran, we should be going now," said Lal with such a sweet smile I couldn't correct him, especially in front of his judgy big brother.

"Onward and upward, I guess."

We climbed for what felt like hours in relative silence except for an occasional whinny and a grunt from me as I stubbed my toe on a stone. The sun was up, but the higher we got, the more the desert winds ripped through us, biting at our skin. My bones ached and my stomach growled. I wished I'd stuck some sandesh in my pockets too.

"Why don't we just have the horses take us up there?" I panted. It was so much higher than it looked. The animals were doing well on the hard rocks, but neither of them had unfurled their wings.

"It is a winged horse no-fly zone." Even though that didn't exactly clarify the situation, I decided not to ask any further. I didn't want Neel to call me a 2-D again.

I also didn't ask why it was taking so long to get to the cave. Probably something to do with my concentration or commitment. Was I ready to face my real identity? Was I ready to see the place that I came from? The truth was, I didn't really have a choice. Turning away from this journey would mean forgetting about my parents and letting them die. And there was no way that I was willing to do that.

I tried to focus my mind, visualizing getting to the top. It seemed to work, because all of a sudden I could see the plateau of the mesa. And on the top, a dark cave. But a few yards before its entrance, something very strange blocked the way. After no indications of civilization whatsoever, we suddenly faced two roped-off lines going in different directions. They were the kind you see in front of theaters or in airports—waist-high metal pillars with black vinyl ropes hooked to them. The lines were marked with large signs. The first one read:

Those upstanding royalty, citizens, animals, and demons holding papers (this way)

While the second said:

All the rest of you good-for-nothing undocumented scoundrels (this way)

No one else was visible for miles, but the roped lines threaded their way over the ground in front of the cave.

Who'd put them there? And who was here to check which way I went? But my question was answered as the princes headed toward the right side, and a disembodied voice barked, "This line is for those with papers *only!*"

Lal and Neel fished inside their pockets and pulled out papers, which they waved around in front of them. Then Neel reached over to each horse's saddlebag and pulled out what must have been the horses' official papers.

I took a big breath and headed all by myself toward the left-hand line, the one for "undocumented scoundrels."

"This place could use some immigration reform," I grumbled.

"We'll meet you on the other side, Just Kiran!" Lal called with a nervous smile. "No matter what happens, answer honestly, and do not be afraid."

Neel gave me a hard look. "And if that doesn't work, for the Goddess's sake, run like crazy!"

CHAPTER 7

The Transit Officer

For a few minutes, we threaded our way through our individual lines. It was slow going. The ropes herded you this way and that—like the lines in an airport—so you couldn't walk straight but had to keep turning left, right, left, right.

At each corner, there was another ridiculous sign. The first read:

**Drink all your liquids. Take off your shoes.
Hop on one foot.**

I looked over at Lal and Neel, and saw that they were hopping away, curly toed shoes in hand. I slipped off my combat boots and did the same. Until I came to the second sign.

No drinking of liquids. No bare feet. And unless you can provide evidence of being part toad, kangaroo, or jumping juju beast, stop hopping!

I put my boots back on and kept walking, until I came to the third sign.

All bows and arrows, knives, whips, maces, clubs, swords, and magic wands must pass through the X-ray machine. No nunchakus, poisonous darts, or firearms permitted.

And then:

P.S. If your arms shoot fire, that's okay. But you will be liable for anything or anyone you accidentally set on fire. And you must provide your own fire extinguisher. If you do not have your own fire extinguisher, one will not be provided for you.

Miranda rights for people with fire-shooting arms. Now I'd seen everything.

Up until this point, I'd been able to see Lal, Neel, and the horses turning this way and that in their own line. Now they disappeared behind a huge boulder, probably to have their weapons X-rayed. My heart sank to see the last flick of Snowy's tail.

I realized I must be getting closer to the guard's station, because the next sign read:

Do not sneeze, cough, snot, or drool on the transit officer. If you must, use conveniently located spittoons for the appropriate deposition of your bodily fluids.

And then, in smaller letters:

A spittoon is a spit-bucket, you illiterate swine.

I remembered being covered in the rakkhosh's reeking snot. I looked around for a spittoon, but didn't see one. I continued walking until I saw the next sign.

Any rakkhosh, khokkosh, magical beast, or half human caught eating a spittoon will be

**prosecuted. Any human caught eating one
will become very ill. And probably die.
(Stop eating the transit spittoons, we
know who you are.)**

The line came to an end a few feet away from
the entrance of the cave. In front of me was a podium—the
kind of stand Principal Chen used during auditorium
assemblies at school. On it was a teeny tiny bell and a sign
that read:

**Ring here for transit officer.
Be not afraid. (If you can help it.)**

I looked around the deserted hilltop and down into the
rocky valley. I wasn't anywhere near Alexander Hamilton
Middle School or Parsippany anymore. I felt very small and
very far away from anything I knew. What I would give to
see a familiar face. Even giggly-mean Jovi's.

The wind shrieked around me, lifting my hair with jagged fingers. I shuddered.

There was nowhere to go but forward. I had to get to
my parents before they got sucked into some alternate
dimension or black hole or spoiled spell or whatever. I

couldn't—wouldn't—even imagine the alternative. As weird as they were, they were my weirdos, and nothing in the universe could ever be right without them.

With a courage that came from somewhere deep but still unfamiliar, I picked up the petite bell with two fingers. Then I shook it.

I didn't hear anything, so I shook it again. It wasn't until the third shake that a deafening gong-like noise from the bell startled me into almost dropping it.

In a few seconds, the ground beneath me began to shake. And then the most horrible-looking creature emerged from the darkness of the cave. I sucked in my breath.

The transit officer wasn't as tall as the rakkhosh had been and looked nothing like that hairy, warty demon. Instead, it had a face like a cross between a lion and a rooster. On its head were a ginormous crown and three curved horns. Beneath its googly eyes and hooked nose was a toothy mouth. I took in the giraffe's neck, the man's arms and chest, the porcupine's quill-filled tail. And I saw the spike-covered club that the creature dragged behind it on the ground. I swallowed hard. Then it . . . *smiled* at me? *double gulp*

The beast shouted:

*"Fear not, fear not, fear not! You won't be maimed or
    shot!*
*Truth be told I can't hold my own against one so strong,
    I'm a bag of bones!*
*Sharp horns have I, but I use them not, my joints are
    old, my muscles shot.*
*I have a club with spiky ends, but I won't hit you, my
    dearest friend!*
*Come closer, chum, into my cave. You're tasty, young,
    and far too brave!*
*Are you afraid? Are you insane? Do you want me all
    your blood to drain?*
*Myself and I and my nine boys, we'll grab your legs like
    two stick toys.*
*You're such a doll, you're such a dear, we'll eat you up if
    you have such fears!"*

It took a forcible effort to shut my mouth, which had
dropped stupidly open during the officer's speech. I couldn't
think of anything to say. The creature's words and expression seemed—if not *pleasant*—at least not actively harmful.
On the other hand, I'd rather not meet the transit officer's
nine mini-mes, and having my blood drained as a punishment for being afraid didn't seem like an ideal plan either.

"Um . . . are you the transit officer?" I finally asked.

"No papers, eh? That's such a shame." The creature's eyes went buggy. "Well then, we'll have to play a game."

"What kind of game?" I wondered if the princes were through their checkpoint yet. Would they rescue me if the game this overgrown chicken was thinking about involved having me for lunch?

"Answer these, my pretty, please!" The officer clucked. "What's black and white and—"

Really? Was this a joke?

"And read all over?" I finished. "A newspaper!" My fifth-grade teacher Mrs. Ury had actually taught me that one—*red* and *read* were homophones—when you spoke them aloud they sounded the same and that was the root of the joke.

The creature seemed so sad, I actually felt sorry for it. "Try another one," I encouraged.

"What has four legs in the morning, two legs at noon, three legs in the evening—"

"Man!" I practically laughed as I blurted out the answer. It was the old question that the Sphinx was supposed to have asked the Greek hero Oedipus. Human beings crawled in the morning—hence the four legs—they walked on two when they were grown, and then walked with a cane when they were old. I'd seen that one on a documentary I'd watched at Zuzu's house about the ancient Greeks.

The transit officer was pacing around now, stomping its giant rooster feet. I was careful to stay out of the way of its porcupine tail as it moved back and forth. But something like hope was blossoming in the pit of my stomach. Maybe I'd make it through this test and be able to rescue Ma and Baba after all.

"I reach to the sky, I touch the ground, sometimes I leave, but I'm always around?" The officer's chicken wattle wobbled in agitation.

This was an oldie but goodie from one of Niko's joke books.

"Yeah, I know that one too; it's a tree," I said. "Listen, don't get upset. It's not your fault. Can I go now? I bet my friends will be worried about me."

This was obviously the wrong thing to say, because the officer's bloodshot eyes narrowed in my direction. My heart gave a jerky leap.

"Friends?" it spat. "Kik, kik, ri gee! You've got friends, have you? Oh my, oh gee!"

I licked my dry lips. "They're not really good friends."

"Those were just practices, my pretty, my sweet," the

officer huffed, baring its yellow teeth. "If you don't get this one, I'll eat your feet!

> *"The ocean's pearl, a grain of sand*
> *More precious than all the gold in the land*
> *Life would be flat, life would be bland*
> *Without this diamond in your hand."*

I bit the inside of my cheek. I hadn't heard this one before. And now the transit officer was angry with me. I wondered even if I were to get the answer right, would it ever let me go?

"The ocean's pearl?" I stalled.

"Kluk!"

"Life would be flat?"

"Kik ri gi!" the creature crowed. It was suddenly looking much happier. "Into my stomach with thee!"

"Wait a minute, wait a minute, I'm thinking," I protested. "Besides, I probably don't taste very good."

"Princesses taste so very nice! I won't even need a spice!"

At the officer's words, the childhood nursery rhyme about "sugar and spice and everything nice" popped into my head.

"Hold on." I grinned. "I've got it!"

"No, you don't! All lies and stuff! Princess makes a big old bluff!" But the officer looked worried. Its spiny tail swished in the rocky soil.

What's from the ocean, like a grain of sand, a diamond in your hand? I got a flash of a day trip I had taken with my parents last summer to Atlantic City: the surf, the sand, the gritty taste of the waves on my lips.

I smirked confidently at the officer. "Salt."

"Kik ra koo!" The beast's googly eyes rotated wildly. "Into my gizzard with you!"

"Wait a minute. Stop! That's not fair. I got the right answer; it's *salt*!"

The creature banged its club on the side of the cave, causing a small avalanche of stones. I ducked, covering my head with my hands.

"That's not fair, that's not right! I won't let you go without a fight!" The officer stomped its foot. Its cheeks were now wet with enormous tears and gurgling noises came from its beak.

Before I had a chance to say anything else, the transit officer lay down on the ground, kicking its arms and legs.

"What will my supervisor say," it wailed, "now that I've let you get away?"

It was having a monster of a tantrum. For a minute, I was tempted to give the giant rooster a time-out in its coop. Ma would have never stood for such bad behavior.

"If the princess gets me fired," the officer shrieked, "who will feed these boys I've sired?"

"Shh! Stop crying so loud!" I urged, trying to edge by the flailing monster.

Just my luck, all this yelling was going to wake up his entire family of younger, stronger, monstrous offspring. And I really didn't feel like getting divided up as an after-school snack among this guy's nine hungry kids!

CHAPTER 8

The Bizarre Bazaar

Waa hoo hoo!" the creature cried, its face on the ground. "Boo hoo kik ri goo!"

"It's okay, don't cry! Shh!" I whispered, scooching past the hiccuping and snotting transit officer. My heart was beating like crazy in my throat. Would I get away in time?

When I heard the sound of yawning coming from the cave, I stopped trying to be quiet and just flat-out ran as fast as I could.

"Cluck! Cluck! Clacket! What's all the racket?" someone called. I didn't wait to see if the officer would answer, but kept running until I was well out of sight of the transit corridor. I ran so fast my gym teachers would be very proud. Even Mr. Taylor, whom I had accidentally—and completely nonfatally!—injured once. I only stopped to catch my breath when I was sure I couldn't hear giant monster chicken sounds cackling behind me anymore.

After a few minutes of no younger versions of the transit officer chasing me down, I finally let myself relax a little. I was safe. At least for now.

As barren as the previous landscape had been, I was shocked to see the change on the other side of the mountain. I was overlooking a lush valley intersected by several rivers whose source was a snowcapped peak in the far distance. Beyond that peak, I was pretty sure I could see a sparkling ocean dancing with the serene blue sky.

I was finally here, in the Kingdom Beyond Seven Oceans and Thirteen Rivers. Now, just to find the princes and get on with rescuing my parents. How much time did we have to get to them before the spell "expired"? I had no way of knowing.

Going up the mountain had been a hard scramble over sharp rocks. Now I ambled down a grassy slope. I took off my sweatshirt and tied it around my waist, enjoying the warm sun on my skin. My skin. I reached for my bandanna to tie it over my scar. But then I remembered I didn't have one. I'd changed clothes at home before we'd left. Crap. I never went anywhere without long sleeves on, or else something to cover up the weird, U-shaped scar on my upper arm—like a strange, saggy pair of glasses. I felt relieved that

I'd been wearing my sweatshirt during the trip from New Jersey, so Lal and Neel hadn't seen my hideous blemishes all hanging out there in the open the whole time. Of course, Neel had already seen my arm scar once, and I'd be lucky if he ever forgot that awful sight. I'd have to find a scarf or something to tie over it before I found the brothers, or at least just put my hoodie back on.

It had been late fall on the other side of the mountain, but here it seemed to be spring. There were riots of blossoms on all the trees that gave the valley a festive air. A family of bottle-green dragonflies zoomed past my face, and fat bees feasted on the wildflower carpet beneath my feet. As I walked farther down, I realized there was another surprise waiting for me at the bottom of the valley. I was no longer alone!

A few yards in front of me was a marketplace. The bazaar was right next to a babbling stream from which I could see fish leaping out, their golden bodies catching and reflecting the sunlight. I crossed over a little bridge and onto the dusty main path through the center of the market. Off of it, countless little alleyways zigzagged this way and that.

The buildings lining the main street seemed to be built by the same architect as those ramshackle alleyways, because they zigzagged too. They were slapped together haphazardly, with the top floors at slight angles to the bottom floors, so that nothing exactly lined up. Entire rooms seemed to be added on as afterthoughts and stuck out like pimples from the upper stories of some buildings. A twisted little pink house leaned so heavily on the patched green one next door it seemed to be riding piggyback. Bright saris and other laundry waved at me from the flat rooftops. On one crooked clothesline, I saw rows of colorful bills, each clipped with a large clothespin, as if someone had just washed out his life's savings. Everything looked odd and precarious. The entire place seemed to be thumbing its nose at any principles of sense or gravity.

Looking for the princes, I scanned the faces in the crowd, which were both unfamiliar and familiar at the same time. Brown skin, black hair—it was a strange feeling to be around so many people who looked like me. Like I'd somehow come home to a place I never knew I belonged. But none of the faces belonged to Lal or Neel.

"Have you seen two brothers—one in red, one in blue?" I asked a rikshaw puller, who looked at me blankly.

"Ride? Ride? You want a ride?" the man asked.

I asked everyone I could as I made my way down the bustling street. Most people ignored me or just shook their heads and kept going. The crowd pushed me this way and that, and I had to shove my way through with my elbows sometimes. I walked past men with overloaded pushcarts, sleeping cows and water buffalos, footpath stalls selling everything from shoe polish to tooth powder to mountains of dizzying-scented flowers.

"For you, lady!" Someone dropped a thick white-and-pink garland around my neck. The scent was heady, the color of the pink flowers blinding.

"No, I don't think so." I returned the garland as politely as I could, then sneezed. The pollen count on these things was probably through the roof.

"You should learn to smell the flowers." The merchant shook his finger at me.

The market was starting to feel less like a homecoming and more like an overload on all my senses. I hadn't made it five steps before I was accosted again.

"Don't diet—buy EZ Fit glass bangles!" a roly-poly lady in a polka-dot sari bellowed. She balanced a flat basket on her head. "Changes to fit your changing body!

"Hey, slippery," she barked, poking me in the arm with her fleshy finger. Ow. "You buy some bangles from me."

When I shook my head, she plunked her reed basket on the ground and crouched beside it. The folds on her belly jiggled as she worked so that she looked like a big bowl of polka-dot Jell-O.

"I really don't think—" I began, but she pretended that

she couldn't hear me. The woman dug through a sparkling array of green, magenta, turquoise, and gold bracelets until she found what she was searching for.

"I have your color!" she insisted, pulling out a dozen silver and pink bangles that she slipped on her own robust arm. As she slipped them off, she grabbed my arm and began shoving the huge bracelets over my wrist. Strange thing was, they shrunk to fit me perfectly.

"Uh, no, thanks." I pulled the bangles back off and dropped them into her basket with a clatter. "I don't like pink."

"It's not a crime to like pretty things." I caught the lady peering at my scar, and I put my hand over my arm to cover it. The bangle seller shrugged her beefy shoulders, heaving the basket on her head again. "You should eat something, maybe then you wouldn't be so grumpy."

"I'm sorry, they were very nice," I began. "Maybe in a different color . . ."

But she was already hawking her wares again. "EZ Fit bangles—for the generously proportioned and the skinny-butt offspring of slimy snake creatures alike!"

What the heck did that mean? I got the feeling that maybe the bangle-selling lady wasn't exactly the sharpest knife in the drawer.

On the other hand, maybe she was right about one

thing. I was pretty hungry. Maybe if I ate something, I'd feel less overwhelmed. As if on cue, my stomach moaned. I looked around at the signs on the shopkeepers' stalls.

FRIED DRIED COCKROACHES. ALSO PILLOWCASES—DEEP-FRIED OR NOW, FOR YOU HEALTH NUTS, STEAMED.

As ravenous as I was, neither item seemed particularly appetizing. I stopped by a stall that was selling kati rolls— egg and meat with onions and chilis, folded into fluffy parathas, and then rolled up in a paper carrier. I inhaled the first one in about three bites and then bought three more with Ma's rupees, eating as I walked. I rolled my eyes a little as they filled my mouth and stomach with spicy goodness. As I finished the last one, ineffectively wiping my oily fingers on the oily wrapper, something caught my attention.

Lazy? A slowpoke? Running from a rakkhosh? Try Mr. Madan Mohan's motivational motion device! (PATENT PENDING)

Huh. I had certainly run from a rakkhosh, and there was nothing to say I wouldn't do so again in the process of rescuing my parents. This seemed like something I should investigate.

"Mr. Madan? Mr. Mohan?" I called from the counter.

From the back of the stall emerged a little man whose curling moustache was at least the length side to side as he was tall. He could barely peer over the counter, and stood on his toes to do so with an air of suspicion.

"It's Mr. Madan Mohan, Esquire!" he snapped. "Well, what is it? I haven't got all day!"

"Well, Mr. Esquire, I wanted to see your"—I paused to read the sign, not wanting to offend the shopkeeper again—"motivational motion device."

"Hmm. I was just going to oil and curl my moustache," Mr. Madan Mohan, Esquire, muttered. "What use have you for it anyway?"

"How can I know what use I have for it if I haven't even seen it?"

"Then it'll be just as well you come back tomorrow. Or better yet, next week." The man took out a metal rod and began to pull down the corrugated shutters in front of the shop. "Maybe next month, there's a good girl."

I was getting irritated. "If you're not willing to show it, how do you ever expect to sell it?"

"Sell it?" Mr. Madan Mohan, Esquire, put back up the shutters with a snap. "For money? Why that's a splendid thought! Why didn't I think of that myself?" The little man reached over the counter and pumped my hand. "There's a reason that you're in the business that you're in!"

I snatched back my arm. "I'm not in any business! *You're* the one in business. I just wanted to see what you're selling—in case I need it to run away from a rakkhosh!"

"Yes, of course you do! Why didn't you say so before?" His moustache quivered.

I rolled my eyes. Someone needed some lessons in basic capitalism. But before I could turn away, the tiny shop-keeper came out of the stall with the most amazing contraption.

CHAPTER 9

The Motivational Motion Device

A wooden frame balanced on Mr. Madan Mohan's shoulders, and from the back of this frame rose a long stick extending beyond the man's head. From this stick, parallel to the ground, was what looked like a fishing pole whose end dangled just beyond the man's nose.

"What *is* that?"

"Just see!" He took a bag of potato chips from his pocket, attached it to the end of the fishing pole, then let the line out a little farther from a handle he held.

Even though he had just put them there himself, Mr. Madan Mohan, Esquire, went a little crazy at the sight of the potato chips. Glassy eyed and drooling, he started chasing the chips farther and farther down the street, as if not realizing that all he had to do was reel them in.

"Wait! Wait!" I ran after the little man.

He was so fast, it took me a few seconds to catch up with even his short legs.

"*This* is your invention? A fishing pole with a bag of chips at the end?"

"What do you know about it?" The shopkeeper seemed ready to keep running, so I grabbed the potato chips from the pole. This incensed the little man even further.

"Thief! Thief!" he shouted, his face purple.

"Wait a minute! Take the bag!" I thrust it at the man. "I didn't steal anything from you! I was just wondering why anyone would need chips if they were running from a demon. I mean, wouldn't that be motivation enough?"

"But they're vinegar and chili flavored!" he said, as if this explained it all. Then his face turned purple again and he continued to shout. "Thief! Thief! You're part of that band that stole my moustache last week!"

Mr. Madan Mohan, Esquire, yelled so much that a small crowd gathered. I tried hard not to laugh.

"This girl has stolen my moustache!" The man pointed a spindly finger at me.

A portly police constable pushed his way forward of the group. "Brother Madan, calm yourself. When did this theft occur?"

"Last week!" the little man shouted. "Yesterday! Tomorrow!" With each word, his moustache twitched and danced.

The crowd rumbled, and I felt my amusement congeal into fear. I heard someone hiss the word "stranger."

The constable wrote down the shopkeeper's accusations in a tiny notebook. In fact, the notebook was so tiny, he had to keep flipping pages with each and every word he wrote. "Last"—*flip*—"week"—*flip*—"yesterday"—*flip*—"tomorrow." He mouthed the words as he wrote, sounding them out.

"Wait a minute!" I protested. "No one stole it—your moustache is right on your face!" But my heart was starting to gallop. What was the punishment for theft in this place? Jail? Whipping? Being forced to eat gross snack foods? Something worse?

"Don't believe her!" The little man shook his fist. "She's a practiced liar! She came to sell me her rakkhosh-slaying invention!"

"I didn't!" I protested. "I wanted to see *your* invention!"

"You see? A liar through and through! First she tells me she doesn't like vinegar and chili chips and now that my moustache is on my face!"

"You don't like vinegar and chili chips?" The constable took a step toward me. I put my hands up, and tried to back away, but the people behind me pushed me forward.

"Look!" a shrill voice piped up from the crowd. It was a round-eyed boy in too-big clothes, and he pointed at the shopkeeper. "His moustache *is* on his face!"

It was like a miracle.

The shopkeeper touched his considerable facial hair. "So it is! She must have snuck it back when I wasn't looking!"

The police constable frowned. "Consider this a warning, young lady! Moustache theft is a serious crime!"

Mr. Madan Mohan, Esquire, was making witchy fingers in my direction, but I ignored him, and eventually he started back for his shop. He placed the bag of chips at the end of the fishing line and once again chased it until he was out of sight.

The crowd that had formed around me began to thin. I took a deep breath, willing my heart to calm down. That was a close one.

Someone tugged at my elbow. "You are wanting something to help you fight a rakkhosh?" It was the boy with the big eyes. Just like his eyes swam in his face, his slim body swam in someone else's enormous shirt and pants. "Come into my father's shop, please."

He led me to a stall filled with weapons of every variety. There were rows of glittering swords, their handles inlaid with scrollwork and precious jewels. I picked up one, but it was so heavy it practically bent my wrist all the way back. Remembering how hard it was to control Prince Lal's weapon, I returned it to the rack.

"What are these?" I pointed to a glass shelf full of bottles and powders.

"Hot oil for pouring in a demon's ear," the boy explained. "Snuff for making it sneeze. A tack to put on a sitting chair. Tricky chewing gum to glue its jaws together."

I didn't want to ever again get close enough to a rakkhosh to pour oil in its ear or put a tack on its chair. And how I was supposed to convince one to chew gum, I wasn't sure at all.

"What about these?" I ran my hand over a beautiful bow and a set of arrows of light ash. When I pulled it, the string of the bow sang a note pure as a bell.

"Sister, you are knowing to use a bow and arrow?"

I nodded. Archery was something they *did* teach at school. And despite that unfortunate accident—where I hit Mr. Taylor, the assistant gym teacher, in the thigh with an arrow—I actually loved it. Whenever we were given a choice between sports, I always chose archery. When everyone else was practicing their spikes, lobs, or dribbling, I'd been practicing aiming an arrow at a target. (And trying not to injure any more teachers, no matter how tempting.)

The bow and arrows came with a featherlight quiver I slung over my shoulder next to my backpack.

"What are these?" My attention was captured by a pair of cuffs with a swirling snake-shaped design on them. The big white orb in the snake's mouth made it look like the serpent was trying to swallow the moon. I couldn't take my eyes off them.

"Those are for protecting an archer's arms from the bow." The boy glanced at my arm. Was he staring at my scar? "There is a legend . . ."

I made a quick gesture I'd per-
fected from years of being stared at
by curious kids. I turned my right
side away from him, tugging the
T-shirt sleeve down.

"I'll take them all."

I was just paying for the weapon and
cuffs with some more of Ma's rupees
when a familiar whinny made me
turn around.

"Snowy!" I threw my
arms around the winged
horse's neck. He

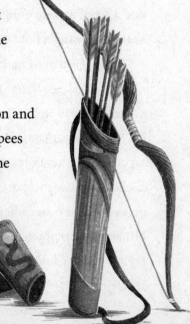

chewed on my shoulder, which I took to mean he was glad to see me too.

"Just Kiran, we were so worried!" Lal bowed low. "We are so delighted you are alive!"

I felt all fizzy soda-pop on the inside. It was good to see some familiar faces.

"It took you long enough!" Neel muttered. But underneath his glowering brows, I could see a hint of a smile.

All right, I'd made it past the transit officer, bought a bow and arrows, and finally found my princely tour guides. Time to get this rescue on the road!

CHAPTER 10

The Merchant of Shadows

"It is an excellent weapon," Lal said, handling my new purchase. "The bow is supple but strong, and these arrows will fly true."

Lal's words made the whole warrior-princess thing super real. I might be good at aiming at a target during gym, but would I be able to fight off another real-life demon? If I was honest with myself, the answer was yes. Growing up, I'd always had the feeling there was something special out there, something more, with my name on it. That it would involve battling rakkhosh, I never would have guessed. But still, it was like my heart had been caged up this whole time, and now I had finally set it free to beat as loud and brave as it wanted.

"Those armbands." Lal touched the snake cuffs on my

forearms. Then I saw his eyes widen as he spotted my scar peeking out from under my T-shirt. "Princess, the design—"

But Neel cut him off. "There's one other thing we'll need before we go."

"My parents . . ." I began.

"We suspect they have been taken to a well of dark energy—the place from where all rakkhosh originate," said Lal with a reassuring hand on my shoulder.

"Ma said something about the dark and terrible place where spells end," I remembered aloud.

"They should be safe there for a little while," Lal continued. "But in the meantime, we must make sure that we are well prepared with all we need."

I didn't have time to ask more questions, because Neel was urging us along. He led us toward a dingy little stall all the way at the end of the market. As we approached it, the horses fought their harnesses and stomped their feet. Maybe I was imagining it, but it was as if I could feel the fear coming off their skin in waves.

"I know how you feel, buddy," I whispered into Snowy's ear. The animal rolled its eyes back and shed a few feathers in its agitation.

"What is this place?" I asked Lal.

"My brother is determined to make a purchase from Chhaya," Lal said as he tried to control an increasingly aggressive Midnight, "the purveyor of shadows."

The shelves lining the walls of the little shop were covered in row after row of bottles. They were large, small, round, slim, some in deep colors of red and blue and green, others in clear glass, still others frothing and bubbling under their lids.

An old woman in a tattered sari stood behind the counter, leaning on a knobby cane.

"Why are you here, my prince?" she hissed. "Surely not for what I am selling!"

"Chhaya Devi." Prince Neelkamal joined his hands together before her in a gesture of respect. He added the word *devi*, which means "goddess," at the end of her name—so that her name became "the shadow goddess."

I hung back with Lal, helping him control the skittish horses. I caressed Snowy's nose, whispering to him. He exhaled puffs of hot air on my hand, while opening then folding his wings, as if he wasn't sure whether to fly away without us.

The old crone peered at Neel with one sharp eye. The woman's other eye, rheumy and diseased, focused directly at me. I could feel her gaze boring into the mark on my arm.

"You have brought this princess back home from exile?"

Neel nodded. "We're going to face many challenges, and I think we might need help from both the darkness and the light."

My skin broke out in goose bumps. I hardly noticed Snowy chewing nervously on a strand of my hair.

"That is your mistake, Prince! And that will be your downfall!" the crone snapped, waving her cane. "You think of good and bad as something separate? There is no darkness without light, no light without darkness." The old woman coughed—a horrible, hacking sound. When she caught her breath again, she continued, "Unless you accept that, you will fail in this quest, my crown prince."

"You know I'm not—" Neel began, but the crone cut him off.

"I know no such thing."

Next to me, Lal took in a shaky breath. His face was pale and now he looked as frightened as the horses. Even though I didn't know what worried him, it was my turn to pat him reassuringly on the shoulder.

"You must see and accept the face of your shadow self, but never lose yourself in the darkness," the old woman was saying. "If you do that, no one can fetch you back."

Neel looked a little shaken by the crone's words. "I

won't ... I'm not ... I mean ..." He snuck a look in my direction. "I understand."

"You understand nothing! You are like one forever asleep in your selfish misery!" she spat. "But you will understand before this quest is over. You will awake and see or perish trying!" The old woman hobbled over to a tiny purple vial with a pointed cork. The vial seemed to be full of a pulsating, swirling energy.

"Take this shadow—it took me weeks to capture the spirit of the old banyan tree. Its roots are many and deep, its branches curious and reaching." She cackled to herself. "But Chhaya is patient, more patient even than the oldest tree in the oldest grove. I waited until the banyan's shadow began to creep out over the earth. And then I caught it in my bottle!"

Catching the spirits of trees in bottles? Visiting the goddess of shadows? I shivered. I was definitely not in New Jersey anymore.

The old woman handed the vial to Neel, who seemed careful not to touch it. He wrapped it in a cloth pulled out of his pocket and tucked it away again.

"How much shall I give you?"

"Do not talk to me about money!" the old woman spat. "You know what I want in return."

Lal gasped. "No, in the name of our royal father, please don't promise it!"

Neel didn't even acknowledge his brother's presence. "I promise," he said to the crone. But the fist by Neel's side was clenching and unclenching.

Then Neel turned on his heel and strode toward us. "Close your mouths; you don't want mosquitoes to fly in, do you?" he snapped, grabbing Midnight's reins. "Let's go."

We were all quiet. I mounted Snowy, sitting in front of Lal like I'd done before. Neel gave me a hard stare, but said nothing. I'd never known it was possible for someone to look both angry and lonely, but that's how he looked to me.

The horses seemed more than willing to take off after our visit to the merchant of shadows. They beat their strong wings on the wind, as if to put as much distance as possible between them and the old woman's shop.

I was feeling impatient now. We'd gotten to the transit corridor; I'd made my way past the transit officer and managed to find Neel and Lal in the bazaar. It was time to get on with my goal: to find my parents in this dark well thingy and bring them home.

"Where is this place my parents are trapped?" I asked over my shoulder as soon as we were airborne. "And how do I get them out?"

"To tell you the truth, um, Princess, I mean, um, Just Kiran, from the point of view of exact latitude and longitude, calculating for planetary rotation and, of course, head- and tailwinds . . ." Lal hesitated.

I had a bad feeling in the pit of my stomach. Worse than when I threw up corn dogs at the amusement park. And it wasn't the altitude.

"Spit it out," I shouted over the wind.

"Well, the truth is, we don't exactly know where your parents are."

"What the what?" I snapped around so fast I almost slipped off Snowy's back. "You told me they were in that demon wellspring!"

Lal grabbed my arm and the horse adjusted itself to stop me from almost plummeting to my doom for the second time in two days.

"Yes, erm, but, well, ah." Lal had the grace to blush. "That's probably true. Only, there are a lot of, um, such wells all over the kingdom and beyond."

"Are you kidding me?" My mind was racing. The princes had lied to me—they lied!

"I am terribly regretful . . . we let you believe we knew more precisely where they were," Lal mumbled. "We know they are somewhere here in the Kingdom Beyond Seven

Oceans and Thirteen Rivers. Or perhaps very near. We'll . . . well, we will just need a bit of help finding the exact location."

"Is that so? And why should I believe you?"

Neel pulled Midnight next to us. "Come on, stop being such a—"

I shouted over him, poison daggers in every word, "Don't even *think* about calling me a 2-D!" I was so angry, I could practically feel the fangs coming out.

"Whoa!" Neel countered. "Look who's getting her turban in a bunch."

"I'm not wearing a turban, or hadn't you noticed?" I snapped back.

Neel looked over at my long hair, which was, as usual, in pinned braids at the back of my neck. "I noticed."

I felt my cheeks start to burn. I looked away from Neel, but not before I saw that one evil eyebrow rise. Argh, he was impossible!

Neel cleared his voice. "Look, we don't exactly know where they are, but we're going somewhere we can find out."

"Where's that?"

Lal pointed to the ground below. "Home!"

CHAPTER 11

The Royal Stables

We were far away from the green valley with its strange bazaar, and had arrived in a place equally as breathtaking. There was a forest to our left, with cackling monkeys and cawing birds. Out of the corner of my eye, I saw a herd of brown-and-white-dappled deer run by. Rising majestically to our right was the most awesome palace I had ever seen—not that I'd seen any in real life, but it was more beautiful than any movie or storybook castle. Its spires were golden, studded with diamonds, sapphires, and rubies. Its walls were silver and bronze, with carved decorations in them. Each carved panel on the palace walls seemed to tell its own story. Scenes showed a festival, a wedding, and . . . yup. Two turbaned princes setting off on a journey mounted on their winged horses.

"We've got to find Minister Tuni. He'll probably have some useful ideas about where we should start looking for Just Kiran's parents." Lal's words melted me a little. Even though he'd lied, he was obviously still willing to help me find my family.

"Let's, ah, get the horses settled first." This suggestion of Neel's was made with a funny, teasing tone.

"If you insist, Brother." I was curious to see Lal squirming a little.

I wasn't sure what that was about, but Snowy and Midnight seemed to like the idea. As soon as we dismounted, they trotted off in the direction of what must have been the palace stables. The stables were like twenty times nicer than my house—even before it got totaled by a demon with a sinus infection. The walls were made of bronze, with pillars of marble, and images of flying horses were carved into the outer walls.

"Hurry, Princess! I wanna show you my favorite place in all our kingdom!" Lal dashed off, forgetting at last to act like a fancy prince.

Even though I was still annoyed at him, I couldn't help smiling. Unlike his brother, it was so easy to see what Lal was feeling. And right now, the handsome prince was happy to be home.

"Come on, he wants you to meet Mati." Neel frowned at me as he said this, as if irritated that I was still there. At that, all my fear and worry transformed back into anger.

"So do you *ever* smile?"

Neel raised that eyebrow again. "Only when I have something to smile about."

He really should change his name to Mr. Smirky Cool Guy, I thought. If Lal was always trying to be princely and proper, at least he was actually nice underneath that fake accent. Neel, on the other hand, kept trying to make himself unlikeable. And boy, was he doing a good job of it.

"You really think highly of yourself, huh?"

"You're really nosy all the time, huh?" Neel countered.

"I wouldn't call wanting to know the truth about where we're going or where my parents are being nosy." I felt my face heating up and my voice rising. "You're the ones who lied to me."

"Well, I'm so sorry this rescue isn't going exactly according to your schedule, Princess. Would you rather we just didn't help you and let you get on your way alone?"

"You know that's not what I meant!" I snapped. "But you could have told me the truth back in New Jersey!"

"Would you have come with us if we told you we didn't know exactly where your parents were?"

I had nothing to say to that. We'd left Parsippany in such a rush, escaping from that rakkhosh. But if I'd really had time to think it through, would I have gone off with two princes I didn't know, who didn't even know how to find my parents? Probably not. And where would that have left me? Alone and no closer to rescuing Ma and Baba.

We walked in a tense silence behind Lal to the palace stables. The big double doors had been hastily shut after the horses had trotted in. A little light shone from in between.

"May I come in?" Lal called through the half-open door.

"No, you may not," answered a musical voice from inside. A girl's voice.

I glanced at Neel, who muttered, "It's the custom here," without meeting my eyes. "You never—*never*—say you invite someone through a door."

Before I could ask any more, the ornately carved doors of the stables flung open.

"My princes, you are home!"

Standing before us was a sturdy, capable-looking girl with shoulder-length dark hair. She was dressed like the boys, in loose pants and a flowing top. She had on knee-high boots and held a broom in her hand.

"Princess Just Kiran, I am honored to introduce you to

my very best friend." Lal grinned ear to ear. "Except my brother, of course! This is Mati!"

Mati joined her hands. "Namaskar, Princess Just Kiran, welcome to our kingdom."

"Um . . . hi." I awkwardly namaskar-ed her back. Even with all the stuff I'd discovered about myself in the last day—that I could fight demons, that I really was a princess—I still didn't like meeting new people that much. I could never think of what to say. Except with Neel, of course, but His Royal Pain-in-the-Heinie was obviously an exception to the rule.

I stepped through the stable doorway and took in the surroundings. The place was sparkling, and smelled like . . . the closest thing I could think of was the smell of freshly washed cotton—like when Baba pulled me out a shirt straight from the dryer. And what was that other smell? Was it honey?

"This is nectar from the bees in our forest." Mati pulled out a silver pitcher and poured a rich golden liquid into Midnight and Snowy's troughs. "It's the best food for a pakkhiraj horse."

"A pakkhiraj?" I repeated.

"The name for this type of flying horse." As Mati moved from trough to trough, I noticed that she dragged one of her feet a little. It was barely noticeable, but one of her shoes had a thicker sole than the other, making up for the shorter leg. "Didn't Their Royal Highnesses tell you?"

"Cool it with the royal highness stuff, Mati," Neel ordered. He had taken off his jeweled turban and collar, and his dark hair was sticking up on end. "We've known you for way too long to take that kind of beetlejuice from you."

"Mati is the daughter of our stable master," Lal explained. "A wise teacher who taught all three of us to ride, to use weapons, to care for animals, and many more things."

"She's like our little sister. She's a lot tougher than she looks." As he passed by her, Neel playfully messed up Mati's hair, to which the seemingly mild-mannered Mati threw the nectar pitcher at his retreating head. It hit Neel's shoulder and bounced harmlessly to the stable floor.

"Nice! Your throwing arm's improving!" Neel examined a big blob of nectar on his shirt, and took a taste. "Maybe you'll make it as a bowler in the royal cricket league after all!"

"All credit goes to you for giving me so much reason to practice my aim, Your Royalness!" Mati stuck out her tongue, then lobbed a horse brush at him, which Neel caught with a laugh and a bow.

This was a different side of Neel than I'd seen before. With me, he just seemed irritating and self-centered and maybe even a little dangerous, but with Mati he seemed almost like a nice person. Almost.

As I thought this, I looked over at Lal, and noticed that he wasn't joining in his brother and Mati's teasing. He made big eyes and gaped a little at Mati, then caught himself and studied a nail in the floor, a beam on the ceiling, and, finally, a little thread on his sleeve. In fact, he made such a big show of looking everywhere but at Mati, it was totally obvious that was the only person he wanted to look at. If the girl noticed, she didn't say anything, but kept throwing random stuff at Neel. Suddenly, the reason for Neel's earlier teasing of his brother became clear. Had we all been at school, I would have passed a note to Zuzu in class with the word *AWKWARD* written in big curly letters.

"Unlike some people, I still have work to do." Mati shook her finger playfully at Neel, and moved over to the white horse.

"Excuses, excuses." Neel tossed the horse brush back at her. "You'll never fulfill your potential as a cricket star with that attitude."

I felt a pang of jealousy at how comfortable Mati was with the princes, how much she *fit* with them. They were all so relaxed in one another's presence—there was no arguing, no lying, no calling one another 2-Ds or anything else.

Instead, everyone seemed to just be so happy and, oh, I don't know, *at home* with each other.

As Mati worked, she radiated such a sense of purpose and competence that I could almost feel it. Snowy nuzzled her cheek, leaving a nectary trail on her neck. "There you go, my handsome one, my Tushar Kona, my star," the girl murmured.

"What did you call him?" I asked, feeling a little shy.

Mati looked up at me with steady caramel eyes. "Tushar Kona—snowflake."

"You didn't realize that was his name, my lady?" Lal asked. "I thought you must have heard that from us—and perhaps that was why you were calling him Snowy."

The white horse whinnied and I could have sworn he was grinning at me.

"No, I didn't know," I admitted. "But maybe Snowy told me himself."

I would never have thought such a thing possible back in New Jersey, but stranger things had happened to me since leaving home than in my entire life.

"He likes you," Mati said. I believed her. Mati knew a lot more than I did, it seemed. About a lot of things. I peeked at her from under my eyelashes, watching her clean bejeweled tack and brush glossy coats. Now she was laughing at something Lal said, shaking her head. What made her so comfortable with herself? Did she ever wonder how people saw her, what they thought of her? Did little kids laugh or point or whisper about her on the street like they did sometimes with me and my scars? Somehow, I got the feeling that she didn't care, even if they did.

Mati was over by Midnight now, and she took the comb with which Neel was attempting to untangle the horse's mane. "Here, give me that, Your Highness; Raat doesn't like it when you pull."

"Whatever you say, boss lady!" Neel said as Mati gave him a shove.

My skin got all hot and prickly. I felt completely alone. These three were each other's family, and I was a total outsider. I bet they wished they hadn't brought me along. I bet they wished I wasn't even here.

"And I suppose Raat was the one who told you his name meant night?" Lal asked.

I nodded, not trusting my voice. I felt a sudden and overwhelming urge to get out of the cozy stables, to do something—anything—productive toward finding my family.

"Should I go look for this minister guy?" I asked,

moving toward the stable doors. "Maybe you could just tell me where he is . . ."

"No, you won't be able to handle him alone. He's a bit of a birdbrain." Prince Neel fell into step with me and beckoned to his brother. "Come on, Bro."

Lal looked sheepish. "Um, you two go ahead, I'll catch up."

Neel stopped and turned around so abruptly I almost bumped into him. "I am *not* leaving you alone here."

"Wait." I was so surprised I actually snort-laughed. "Aren't you the same guy that wouldn't save his brother from the rakkhosh on my front lawn until it was almost too late?"

"That was different." Neel didn't even have the courtesy to look at me as he said this.

I didn't necessarily want to be alone with Neel, but I also didn't want to rob Lal of his precious time with his friend. Plus, it was fun to annoy the bossy older prince.

"So here's the thing—Lal's a big boy. I'm pretty sure he and Mati will be okay."

"You don't understand—" Neel began, but Lal cut him off.

"Just Kiran is right, Brother, I am not a child any longer. I will be fine here in the stables."

"Lal, you know we should stay together . . ."

"Neel, stop worrying! We'll stay inside the stables and we won't invite anyone in," Mati said in a calm voice. "You said it yourself, I'm tougher than I look."

Neel seemed about to argue, but he looked from his brother's face to Mati's and then just nodded. "Come on, Princess."

I shrugged and followed him. Boys were so weird.

CHAPTER 12

Tuntuni's Tale

I walked with Neel out of the stable, wondering what I would say to the king's minister. He was probably some important, busy guy with a lot of government stuff to do. How was I going to get him to help me?

I turned to Neel, to ask him what the minister was like, but the expression on his face made the words dry up in my mouth.

"They're totally BFFs, you know. Best friends since they were babies."

"Huh?" I asked in my not-so-eloquent way.

"My brother and Mati." Neel gestured over his shoulder to the still open doorway of the stable. As Mati came to close it, I could hear the prince chattering away to the stable hand, telling the girl all about his adventures in the far-off and exotic land of New Jersey.

"They have these things called Giant Gulpies and machines that serve fizzy drinks—with free refills all day!" Lal's voice became more muffled as the heavy doors closed off the cozy scene.

"Mati seems nice. She reminds me of my best friend from home."

"They can't spend as much time together anymore." Neel picked up a stick from the ground and cracked it angrily in two. "Not since . . . well, since our father gave Lal so many more responsibilities."

Not knowing what else to say, I just mumbled, "Oh?"

We were walking away from the stables on a pebble path through a manicured lawn. On either side of us were fragrant fruit trees and flowers. I could smell orange blossoms, hibiscus, some heady jasmine, and a dozen other perfumey scents I couldn't identify.

Neel kept talking, as if to himself. "Of course, in my father's eyes, a stable master's daughter isn't anywhere good enough to hang out with the precious crown prince."

That caught my attention. "Wait, didn't Chhaya Devi say *you* were the crown prince? Anyway, isn't Lal younger than you?"

"Yeah, well, that's a long, complicated story." Neel kicked at the ground, sending pebbles flying. "But it's totally for the best. There's no way I would want to be crown prince anyway."

Curiouser and curiouser. Did Neel really not want to be crown prince or did their father just not want his oldest son to inherit the throne? Why would that be? Had Neel done something really bad—or did their dad think he was just too arrogant to rule the kingdom?

"My poor brother. He can't stand disappointing our father, but he can't stand disappointing Mati either. He doesn't get that you can't please everyone all the time."

"I don't think it's such a bad thing to be a nice guy."

"That attitude's going to get him hurt some day," Neel snapped.

I tried a different tack. "Is your dad strict like that with you too?"

"You could say that." Neel laughed—a harsh, unhappy sound. "You could also say that as far as our father's concerned, I'm invisible."

"Oh, come on," I scoffed. "Not really?"

"Yeah, really. I might as well be a ghost." Neel pointed at a nearby coconut tree. "Like the one who lives in that tree trunk."

"Please, you're trying to tell me there's really a ghost that lives in that tree?"

"Usually. Unless she's out trying to impersonate a human woman and sneak into a real family again. Don't ghosts live in coconut trees in your dimension?"

"No!" I still wasn't sure whether to believe him, but quickened my pace just in case, to put more distance between myself and the tall brown trunk. "Are you just trying to scare me?"

"Maybe."

"Well, just lay off. I don't scare easily."

Neel snorted. "Good, 'cause I don't roll with scaredy-cats."

"Whatever. Could we go meet this minister guy now?"

Neel didn't say anything else, but loped off, leaving me to dash after him. To my surprise, he didn't head toward the palace, but toward the edge of the forest. I hurried to follow, and almost crashed right into him when he stopped. He stood under a guava tree whose branches were heavy with fruit.

"Tuni!" he called. "Oh, Tuni Bhai! Come on, Brother Tuni, show yourself!"

There was a twittering and a chirping from above our heads, and then something hard and fast pelted down at us.

"Ow." I rubbed my head. Something solid had hit me. Something solid that hurt!

Thunk. Neel rubbed his head too. "Stop it, Tuntuni!"

An adorable yellow bird with a bright red beak danced on the branch above our heads.

"Yeaaaaah, boy! I got you good!" The bird chewed on a piece of bamboo that bobbed up and down in his beak like a cartoon cigar.

"Come on, Tuni, chill out," Neel protested. "This is the princess—"

"From the other dimension!" the bird chirped. "You don't gotta tell me! I can smell the ordinariness on her from a kilometer away! Pee-yew!"

"Please don't tell me this rude bird is your father's minister." At this, the bird tossed a few more unripe guavas, which we managed to duck.

"Don't take the act too seriously," Neel muttered. "He likes to keep everybody thinking he's a few crackers short of a packet."

"Tuni doesn't want a cracker!" the bird rhymed, spitting seeds. "Especially from a royal slacker!"

"Tuni, sir . . . um, do you know where my parents are?" I asked as politely as I could.

"And why should I tell an unimaginative 2-D like you?"

"Come on, Tuni, strike us a deal—how can we convince you to tell us what we want?" Neel wheedled.

The bird considered the offer. "Okay, slacker, why don't you convince your royal father to arrest the barber?"

"I don't think the cuckoo thing is an act," I whispered.

"Nah, he's just a big poser," Neel said. Then louder, "Why should I do that?"

"When I had a thorn in my foot last week, that dratted barber wouldn't come—he made me wait and wait. Said he had *human* customers who came first." The bird spit more guava seeds. "The nerve!"

"I don't think my father would arrest the barber for that," Neel said.

"Well then, how about I ask the palace mouse to bite his royal potbelly?" Tuni suggested.

"Why would the mouse do that?"

"Well, what if I asked the castle cat to chase the mouse?"

This was getting silly. "Where are my parents?" I interrupted.

But Neel shushed me with a gesture. "And if the cat refused to chase the mouse?"

"Why then"—Tuni was gaining steam—"I'd ask the stick to beat the cat."

"And if the stick refused to beat the cat?"

"Why then, I'd ask the fire to burn the stick."

Neel was apparently enjoying the game. He picked up one of the hard guavas that the bird had thrown and began to toss it in the air. But I wondered if he was playacting too, because there was a muscle twitching suspiciously in the prince's cheek.

"And if the fire refused to burn the stick?" Neel asked the bird.

"Why then, I'd ask the sea to drown the fire!"

I was getting the hang of it. "Okay, so if the sea refused to put out the fire?" I asked. Neel gave me a glimmer of a grin, and I was startled by how nice it felt to be on the same team for once.

"Well then, I would ask the elephant to drink up the sea!"

"And if the elephant refused to drink the sea?" Neel and I asked in one voice.

"Why then, I would go to the smallest animal I could find."

"An ant?" I guessed.

"A gnat?" Neel supplied.

Suddenly, I felt a sharp bite on my arm. As I slapped the sting, something Neel had said in the market came to me.

"No, it's the mosquito, right?"

Tuni pecked at a guava. "Oh yes, I would ask the mosquito to bite the elephant."

"And if the mosquito refused—" Neel began to say, but now it was my turn to shush him. A light bulb went off in my head. Weren't all of Baba's animal stories about creatures fulfilling their destiny—their dharma? The moral always seemed to be that if you ever came across a tiger or a crocodile in the woods, you weren't supposed to trust it. Because no matter how much they promised they weren't going to eat you, they definitely would, because that was their nature. To eat people. Like a mosquito's was to bite people. I'd never thought there was much use for Baba's animal stories—I mean, it's not like I was bumping into tigers and crocodiles on a weekly basis in the Willowbrook Mall. But boy, was I glad for them now.

I called to Tuni, "The mosquito wouldn't refuse because that's what mosquitoes like to do—that's their nature—they bite, right?"

"Yessiree! The Princess Kiranmala will be performing nightly at seven and eleven in the royal forest tea salon!" the bird burbled into the stick, as if it were a microphone. "Catch the best puzzle-solving act this side of the transit corridor! And be sure not to miss our early-bird shrimp cutlets special!"

"So the mosquito—" I began, but Tuni interrupted me.

"Did you see what I did there?" He put his wing up to his mouth as if telling me a secret. "With the early-*bird* special? Early *bird*, get it?"

"Hilarious, I get it," I agreed. "The early bird catches the worm, the whole thing."

Tuntuni screeched in glee. "Early bird catches the worm! Good one! Going to have to remember that!"

Trying not to roll my eyes, I rushed on to solve the rest of Tuni's riddle.

"So the mosquito would threaten to bite the elephant, and then the elephant would threaten to drink the sea, the sea would threaten to douse the fire, the fire threaten to burn the stick, the stick threaten to beat the cat . . ." I stopped to take a breath.

"The cat threaten to catch the mouse, the mouse threaten to bite the belly," Neel supplied.

"And the king would then agree, after all, to arrest the barber," we concluded together.

"Which proves what, boys and girls?" Tuni twirled the stick of bamboo in his mouth like a baton.

"That cooperation is a good thing?" I guessed.

"That kings should invest in mousetraps?" said Neel wildly.

Tuntuni collapsed with a wing over his eyes. "Oh, the tragedy of stupidity. And I had such high hopes for you two."

I looked at the tiny bird, who had our fates in the palm of his yellow feathery hand. Er, wing. That's when it struck me.

"That the smallest creature can be the mightiest?"

Tuni sat bolt upright. "Is that your final answer?"

"Uh . . ." I glanced at Neel, who nodded. "Yes, yes, it's my final answer."

"You're sure you don't want to dial a prince?"

"No, she doesn't want to dial a prince," snapped Neel.

"I'm sorry, I'll need to hear it directly from the contestant," Tuni said in a fake game-show-announcer voice.

"No, I don't want to dial a prince."

"You're absolutely sure you want to lock it in?" the bird boomed into the bamboo stick/microphone. "This is for the whole kit and caboodle, you know."

"Yes, yes, I want to lock it in!"

"Oh, just get on with it!" Neel sniped.

"Well then . . ." The bird paused to flap around in a wobbly circle. "You are *right!*"

Absurdly, even though we hadn't actually won anything, Neel high-fived me and I jumped up and down, whooping.

"Okay, we've solved your riddle," Neel said. "Now will you tell us how to find Kiran's parents?"

The bird considered us, cocking his head this way and that. His bright eyes twinkled.

"If you can tell me why hummingbirds hum!"

"Oh, come on, Tuni . . ." Neel began, but I waved him quiet.

"Because they don't know the words!"

Neel gave me an impressed, raised-eyebrow look and I shrugged. "What can I say, I'm a girl of many talents."

Next time I saw him, I'd have to thank Niko for having such an endless collection of idiotic jokes.

"Enough of this. Just tell us where her parents are!" the prince demanded.

The bird looked offended, and so I quickly said, "Okay, how about I tell you a good one?"

"Egg-cellent!" the minister twittered. "Eggs-hilarating! Eggs-traordinary!"

I barely refrained from groaning and asked, "What kind of math do snowy owls like?"

"The prince has a brother that's an owl, you know," the bird chirped.

Neel rolled his eyes. "We don't have all day. If you don't know the answer, just say so!"

After a few minutes of twirling his stick-slash-cigar and mumbling "what kind of math," "snowy owls like," the bird gave up, and I supplied, "Owlgebra!"

Tuntuni and Neel looked at each other, perplexed. "I don't get it," Neel said flatly.

"Like algebra? Snowy owls like owl-gebra?"

"Must be a 2-D thing." Tuntuni shook his head sympathetically.

Neel gave a patronizing thumbs-up. "Good try, though."

I practically growled. "How can you guys not know what algebra is?"

"That's okay, Princess. Not everyone can have a good sense of humor like me." The bird tilted his little head. "But maybe you should stop wasting so much time. Your parents are missing, you know."

"You don't say?" My hands itched to strangle the bird. "You think you could tell us where they are?"

"Remember, I'm just the oracle for truth. I can't help you interpret it," the bird said rather mysteriously before he cleared his throat, puffed out his yellow chest, and began:

"Neelkamal and Kiranmala, heed my warning well
Your families will crumble, your life an empty shell
Unless you find the jewel in evil's hidden room
Cross ruby seas full of love beneath the dark red moon
In a monster's arms be cradled and cross the desert wide
In the Mountains of Illusions find a wise man by your side
On a diamond branch, a golden bird must sing a blessed song
Follow brother red and sister white, but not a moment too long
In your heart's fountain, set the pearly waters free
Let golden branch grow from the silver tree
Only then will you ever find beauty that is true
The magic bird's every song will shower bliss on you."

"But . . ." Neel asked. "What does all that mean—the family crumbling? The ruby sea?"

"I already told you. I'm just the vessel. Any interpretation is far beyond my pay grade."

"But you must be able to tell us something? Where to start looking for my family?" I begged.

Tuntuni relented, puffing out his chest again. "In the East of North of East, the Maya Pahar climbs. Stars are born in its clouds beyond the reach of time. Outside our understanding, the Maya Mountains hide. Bravery and wisdom can be your only guide."

Then, as abruptly as he had spoken, the bird rudely belched, flapped his wings, and started to fly off the branch.

"Wait a minute!" I called. "The East of North of East—where's that? How can I find these Maya Mountains?"

"What, d'ya want me to draw you a map?" the bird snapped, spitting a few more seeds before it flew away. "This ain't Joisey, Princess, *fuggedaboutit.*"

CHAPTER 13

A Costly Mistake

Just what I needed, a bird with a bad attitude!

"Now what?" I asked Neel.

"Well, first things first, we write down the poem." He pulled a half-ripped piece of paper out of his pocket. "After you've been around the Kingdom Beyond Seven Oceans and Thirteen Rivers awhile, you realize almost everything around here—even silly poems—have hidden meanings."

"Why can't he tell us what all that stuff means?" I complained. "That seems totally unfair. I mean, we solved his riddle. And the dumb joke."

"I don't get it either, but those poems just come to him— he doesn't know what they mean any more than we do," Neel said as he scribbled on the paper with a stubby pencil.

"People used to get so mad at him about it. That's why he developed that nasty personality to fend them off."

"Is that why you do it too? Have a nasty personality, I mean." The words were out of my mouth before I could stop them. I realized how mean they must sound, so to back-pedal, I laughed in a super-awkward, high-pitched way, then immediately wanted to bash myself in the head. Real smooth, Kiran. Real smooth.

"Yeah, sure. Whatever," Neel said as he folded and put the paper away. "Come on, let's go and see what my father has to say about Tuntuni's poem."

Still embarassed by my own words, I glanced down at myself and wondered what he saw. "Um, shouldn't I wash up and change before I present myself to a . . . king?"

"You're fine," Neel said without even looking at me. But he was wearing silks and jewels, and I was in dirty jeans, a smudged T-shirt, and muddy combat boots. I realized I hadn't even bathed since being covered in rakkhosh snot on my front lawn. For the first time in my life, I wished I wasn't always so worried about fading into the background.

"Seriously, Neel?" I put my hands on my hips and stopped walking. "Seriously?" There was a chunk of hair loose from my braid and it drifted right in front of my eyes. I blew it away with a gust of breath, but it settled back on my face.

He studied me, considering. "My father won't care what you look like. Now, my stepmothers, that's another story."

"Your stepmothers?"

"Yeah. Lal's mom, and the other queens, they're kind of sticklers for how people dress and junk like that."

"Wait a minute." TMI—this was definitely a case of too much information all at once. I remembered that in a lot of Baba's stories, the kings had more than one queen. ("Once, long ago, there was a king with three queens—Big Rani, Middle Rani, and Little Rani.") But it was one thing to think about stuff like that happening a long, long time ago, and something else entirely to think about a boy you knew having a family so totally different from your own.

"Your father has a lot of wives? And you guys are *half* brothers?"

"Is that a problem for you?" Neel crossed his arms over his chest.

I bit the inside of my cheek. "No, not at all." I definitely wasn't in New Jersey anymore.

"Good."

We walked in silence for a bit longer. I kept sneaking looks up to Neel's face to see if he was angry, but he was staring straight ahead. Although his expression was more thoughtful and sad than anything else.

"Um, Neel?" I said after a few minutes.

"Yeah?"

"So do you think I could, like, clean up a little before I meet your dad and stepmoms?"

"Oh, right." Neel raised that eyebrow. "You do look kind of a mess."

"Nice. Thanks a lot."

We entered a courtyard of the palace, with lots of doorways leading off of it. A few people—who must have been palace servants—scurried here and there with brooms and dust cloths and piles of clean and dirty laundry. Neel called over a young woman who was carrying bed linens over an arm.

"Hello, Danavi!"

The woman smiled and nodded. "Welcome home, Your Highness."

"This is the Princess Kiranmala." Neel gestured to me. "Will you please help her get cleaned up and changed?"

The woman bowed in my direction. I gave her a goofy half curtsy in return. She looked at me like I was as kooky as Tuntuni.

"Is my father in the audience chamber?" Neel asked.

"Yes, Your Highness."

"Please bring the princess there when she is ready."

Neel was scowling again. "I have a lot I want to discuss with the Raja."

"Yes, Your Highness."

I watched his departing back, wondering at my own hurt. He hadn't even said good-bye. Then, just as quickly, my feelings turned to annoyance. Neel was so predictably irritating.

Danavi gave me a curious glance. She didn't even try to hide the fact that she was studying the scar on my arm. Clearly, people here were a lot less worried about being caught staring.

My reaction, though, kind of startled even me. Rather than trying to hide the scar, I just stared back at her. It felt good not to hide.

Finally Danavi spoke. "So you are the princess who has been living in exile?"

"I guess so. I didn't even believe I really was a princess until yesterday."

The woman nodded. "Yes, this is the way it is, I have heard, for those living in the two-dimensional realm. It is safer that way."

With all the excitement, I hadn't had time to ask about the details of my "exile." Everyone kept talking about it.

"What do you know about why I was sent away?" I asked

as the woman led me to a beautifully decorated bedroom off the courtyard. The walls of the room were covered with creeping vines, and blossoms drooped fragrantly from the ceiling. It was like a magical indoor garden. I got a little dizzy from the heavy smell of the flowers, like I had in the marketplace.

"I don't know very much, only what people say." Danavi filled up a claw-foot tub in the middle of the room. She tossed in some rose petals and something that made pink foam in the water.

"Tell me what you know," I begged. I didn't even care that the water was pink, my least favorite color. As long as it was warm.

"Are you sure, my lady?" She put a folding screen around the tub, and waited on the other side as I took off my clothes and hopped into the sudsy water.

"Please."

I sank into the tub and blew some pink bubbles from my hands. It was heavenly.

"Well." The woman's disembodied voice came floating from the other side of the screen. "Long ago, when the moon maiden was once wandering the earth in human form, she fell in love with the handsome king of the underworld, and he with her. He convinced her to follow him below the surface of the water to his serpent kingdom, and marry him. And his love was so powerful, that she did this. But first, she made him swear to one condition. And her condition was that she be made to visit her husband's dark land only one night of every month. And on this night there is no moon in the sky."

"The night of the new moon," I murmured, stretching my aching limbs in the water. I wasn't bothered that the woman wasn't getting right to my life story. I was used to Baba's tales, which always started off in a meandering way too.

"Now, the moon maiden was wise to strike such a bargain, but none of us can be as wise as we think we are."

"Mmm," I answered, barely listening. I worked at scrubbing the nasty out of my hair. Some leaves, twigs, and . . . was that a rakkhosh tooth? *shudder*

On the other side of the screen, the story continued. "Unfortunately, the maiden forgot to include a clause in her agreement about her children."

I poured water over my head with a silver cup. The moon was casting a shimmery glow across the floor in front of the tub. Then there was a muffled bumping on the other side of the screen. I prompted, "Danavi?"

For a minute, the shadows in the room shifted.

Then the woman coughed, cleared her throat, and continued in a raspier voice. "The moon maiden grieved as her first seven children were turned into snakes by the underworld king—doomed to live forever in his dark kingdom under the earth."

"That's horrible!"

"Yes, my princess," she agreed. "And so, when the moon maiden's eighth child, a girl, took her first breath, she decided that she would save her daughter from the fate of her seven brothers. She put the baby in a clay pot and floated her down the River of Dreams."

I sputtered, wiping wet strands of hair off my face. Wait a minute, this part of the story sounded familiar.

"Who found the baby?" My skin broke out in goose bumps. The water felt suddenly cold.

"A kind farmer and his wife."

With trembling hands, I touched the crescent-shaped mark on my neck. A curved moon. "And then?"

"And then, my princess," the woman went on, "what you might imagine happened. The Serpent King decided to claim his daughter—to add another powerful snake to his court."

I jumped out of the bath, grabbed a towel Danavi had

left for me, and started drying off. My head was spinning. "And then?"

"Well, there was a terrible struggle. The baby was marked on the arm as the Serpent King tried to capture her."

I stopped drying. Marked on the arm? Oh no, could it be?

The woman continued, "The moon maiden did all that was in her power—she exiled the farmers and the child out of the Kingdom Beyond Seven Oceans and Thirteen Rivers to a smoggy place at the end of a dark tunnel, a place where wide tarred roads stretch on and on, and no one can ever take a left turn . . ."

"A place called New Jersey?" The pieces were all fitting together.

"Why yes," the woman agreed. "But the moon magic was only so powerful. The exile would last a mere dozen years, and on the child's twelfth birthday, the spell would begin to implode, forcing the two farmers back to this land of enchantment."

Water dripped off me onto the floor. I couldn't seem to stop my teeth from chattering. How could I have not known? Neel had said something about the people I thought were my parents, and back then I hadn't believed him. But some deep instinct told me the woman's tale was true. That my parents weren't my parents. That my biological father was a serpent king, and my mother a moon maiden. It felt like a nightmare—like I'd just stepped into one of Baba's stories. Yet, unlike those, I'd never heard this story before and had no idea how it was supposed to end.

"Are you ready, my princess? May I come in?" the woman asked.

I wrapped the towel around myself. My eyes were hot. *I will not cry. I will not cry. I will not cry.*

"One sec," I mumbled.

Ma and Baba—they probably hated me. I was some kind of royal burden to them, a baby they'd saved and then been saddled with because of a dumb enchantment. I thought about Baba's fear of snakes, his efforts to make sure one never got into our house. He was trying to protect me. And Ma's thing about having no curtains—she was trying to make sure the moon could shine on me.

No wonder they'd insisted I be a princess every Halloween. They were trying to tell me. I just wasn't willing to listen. My whole face stung. *I will not cry. I will not cry.*

"Your Highness?"

All I could think about was what kind of brat I'd been. And how much Ma and Baba had given up for me. Their whole world. Their yard. Curtains. They probably were glad to be rid of me. My throat felt woolly. I could barely breathe. *I will not cry.*

"May I come in?"

I was all alone. With no idea of who I really was. Who was I? Who was Princess Kiranmala? I couldn't begin to imagine.

"Do you invite me to enter?"

"Yeah," I managed to get out. "I invite you to enter."

In a flash, Danavi was around the screen. Maybe I hadn't paid so much attention before, but there was something different about her. I was so distracted thinking about my parents, though, that I couldn't put my finger on it. Instead I stayed lost in thought as the woman helped me into a delicate silk tunic and loose pants embroidered with a lotus pattern. I didn't even notice it wasn't black. Or that the scar on my arm was totally visible from under its tiny sleeves. I sat numbly in front of the mirror, my head full of moonbeams and serpents' tails.

"You are like a lotus, my princess." The woman combed my hair, braiding it and twisting it into an elaborate style. "You are a flower that has thrived even in the most dark and polluted waters."

"What?" I jerked away as Danavi yanked a little too hard.

"Well," she explained in a wheedling voice, "you are a beautiful blossom, despite being raised by simpletons who toil in the dirt." She pinned my hair up, away from my neck. I felt her fingers graze my hairline.

"Those are my parents you're talking about," I snapped, even as I felt a familiar embarrassment creep up on me. It was the same feeling I got when Jovi sneered at me for having parents who owned a Quickie Mart.

"They are *farmers*, my princess, no kind of parents for one of royal blood. No kind of parents for one with both the *moon-mark*"—she touched my neck again—"and *snake sign*." She touched my arm now, smiling toothily in the mirror.

The snake sign? Those U-shaped eyeglasses. Why hadn't I realized it before? Or had I just not let myself? The scar on my arm was the same as the markings on a cobra's head.

"They are no parents for the likes of you, my princess," Danavi cackled.

I whipped around to face her, my temper burning. "You have no idea what you're talking about!"

I felt something strong harden inside of me. Something I couldn't hide from. The truth. Had Ma and Baba ever treated me differently? Like I wasn't their own? Granted, they were seriously kooky. Ma was always stuffing me full of food. Baba was always stuffing me full of stories. But they didn't hate me; they adored me. And all I could think about was how much I wanted to be with them again.

I waved off the slippers the woman offered me and jammed my still damp feet into my trusty boots. My eyes were hot, but my voice was firm.

"My parents saved my life," I said, "and raised me. They may not be perfect, but they didn't ask to get dragged into this mess. Only now they have been, and I'm going to get them out of it."

"Oh, a thousand pardons. Of course you are, my princess. You and your companions are very brave. You will go now and rouse the good princes Lalkamal and Neelkamal from the palace . . ."

"No, just Neel's in the palace," I corrected before I could stop myself. "Lal's in the stables with Mati."

"In the stables?" The woman's eyes shone strangely in the mirror. "Without his brother's protection? Well, well, isn't that convenient . . ."

Wait a minute. A terrible feeling came over me.

I stood up and started to back away. "Who are you?"

Something was seriously not right here. Too late, I

remembered how Mati answered when Lal asked if he could come into the stables. She said no. What had Neel said? That it was a custom in their country? That you never granted someone permission to enter?

"I'm Danavi—don't you know what my name means?" The maid threw off her cloak, revealing an entirely different form. A beautiful, dark-haired woman with a bejeweled crown stood before me. All the hairs on my neck stood at some serious attention.

"What?" I squeaked.

The woman smiled, revealing two fangs that hung below her ruby lips. "Demoness!" she said. "But you can call me Demon Queen!"

Aw, bilious rakkhosh snot. Here we went again.

I tried to run, but the rakkhoshi ripped a handful of her own hair from her head and threw it at me. It might as well have been a handful of quick-drying cement. As soon as the magical hair hit me, I couldn't move at all. I realized with dread that the demoness's smile reminded me of someone I knew.

"Rakkhoshi! Be gone!" a voice commanded from the doorway. It was Neelkamal, his sword drawn. Beside him was the real Danavi.

"I felt a cold mist enter the room, and then all became dark!" exclaimed the maid.

No wonder the woman's voice changed mid-story. No wonder she seemed different—the demoness had switched places with the real Danavi!

"Leave Kiran alone!" Neel shouted.

It was only then that I realized the Demon Queen's sharp-nailed hands were at my throat.

"Ayiiii!" the rakkhoshi screeched, turning toward Neel. "There is nothing so upsetting to the digestion as an ungrateful child!"

I could kind of wiggle my fingers and toes again. Without her concentration, the demoness's spell lost its grip pretty quickly.

"You aren't welcome here anymore!" Neel approached the Rakkhoshi Queen with his sword raised. "What trick is this that brings you here?"

"Oh, that is where you are very wrong, you source of my acid reflux, you betrayer from my own womb!" the Queen cackled, growing into her full size. The poor maid shrieked and ran out the door.

The Demon Queen was still beautiful, but with pointed ears, jagged teeth, and enormous horns rising from behind her crown. She towered above us, her horns brushing the vines on the ceiling. With another toss of her hair, she froze Neel where he was standing. I could tell he was trying to move, but couldn't.

"Let me go, now!" he ordered. The Queen cackled, her inhuman voice echoing weirdly.

I ran for my bow and arrow, which I'd put on the floor next to the bath, but with a motion of her warty finger, the demoness flung them out of the way. Her eyes raged with fire, and puffs of smoke shot out of her nostrils.

She rubbed her chest with a clawlike hand. "All those years just hovering in the shadows, waiting for some newcomer fool who didn't know about the rules of my banishment; it gave me a terrible case of heartburn." The Queen turned her creepy smile to me. "But you can thank your little friend here for inviting me once again into the kingdom."

"No!" Neel protested.

"I didn't!" I yelled, even as I remembered how the "maid" had asked me if she could enter. It was true. I said yes, and by mistake, I had unleashed this terrible monster.

"For that favor, my slithery princess," the Queen crowed, "I will not kill you—at least not today." She licked her lips with a black tongue. "But I am afraid I cannot say the same for that tasty morsel Lalkamal!"

With a thunder-like clap, the demoness vanished into thin air. Neel struggled in place, still frozen. He howled in a voice transformed by fear and rage.

"Mother! Ma! No!"

CHAPTER 14

The Gold and Silver Spheres

*T*hat's your mother?" I shrieked.

"You should talk!" Neel could obviously move again, and threw my bow and arrows in my direction as he ran toward the door. I grabbed them midair. "At least my dad didn't force me into exile because he wanted to turn me into a snake!"

"You're half a rakkhosh, which means half a monster!" I yelled, threading an arrow from the quiver into my bow.

"And what do you think *you* are, Princess? Ever wonder where your nasty side comes from?" Neel snapped even as he was already running for the courtyard. "I don't have time for this! I have to warn my brother!"

I sprinted after him, feeling his words burning in my ears. If Neel was half a monster, then so was I. I thought about the last time I saw my parents and how cruel I'd been to them. Was it because, as they would say in the movies, I had bad blood?

Being half serpent certainly wasn't helping my running stamina, and I was getting winded trying to keep up with rakkhosh-powered Neel.

"Your mom wouldn't hurt Lal, would she?" I shouted to his sprinting back. But the rate at which he was moving told me all I needed to know.

Obviously, Neel's mom had a serious case of the wicked stepmothers. Wanting to eat your stepchildren definitely ranked up there with all-time evildoer moves. I felt sick. It was my fault she was after Lal.

Prince Neelkamal ran like the wind. I guess I hadn't noticed before how fast he could move. Or how strong he was. Or how tall. Or how broad. It had been so easy for him to defeat the rakkhosh on my front lawn. And yet, he hadn't wanted to kill it. Was it all because of his half-demon heritage?

We approached the royal stables, which were glowing in the evening darkness with an unearthly light. Somewhere, a crow shrieked and a fox howled. A chill ran through my body. The demoness had already gotten here!

There was terrified whinnying as Midnight and Snowy galloped away from the stables toward the woods.

I ran in the direction from where they came, but when I stumbled into the building, I faced a terrible sight. The Rakkhoshi Queen stood on the hay in the middle of an empty stall, a nauseated expression on her face.

"Where is Lal?" Neel thrust his sword at his own mother. "What have you done with him?"

"Oof! That too-proud boy!" She belched. "That willful girl!"

"Ma—tell me that you haven't eaten my brother and Mati!"

"Eaten them? Of course I've eaten them! What do you think I have been waiting for, eh, all these years?" The rakkhoshi turned her red eyes at her son. "Only *you* were always by your brother's side, my son, you traitor who nursed at my breast, you were forever protecting him!" She shifted her piercing gaze to me. "But so lucky I am, isn't it, that this girl finally distracted you away from him. If not for her, this pretty-pretty moon-brat, you would never have left Lalkamal alone!"

The walls of the stable felt like they were closing in. What had I done?

Neel fell to his knees, letting out a demonic yell. "You won't get away with this, Mother!"

"Vah, such big, big talk!" the rakkhoshi cackled. "My son wants to kill me—what a proud maternal moment! But no, for that you'll have to find and kill my soul—which is hidden away somewhere even you will never find, my little matricidal maniac!"

Rage boiled in my body. Neel was still on the ground in front of his mother. The demoness might destroy him at any moment. Like everything else, this was my fault. I had to protect him.

I aimed the arrow that was still in my bow. The rakkhoshi was distracted, and I had a clear shot. I closed one eye, and imagined I was shooting a target behind the gym at school. The arrow flew straight and true, hitting the Queen in the middle of the chest.

"Ay-yo!" the demoness exclaimed.

Unfortunately, the next thing she did was to pluck the arrow out as if it were nothing more than a splinter. "Not a bad shot for a skinny moon-chickie!" She used the sharpened end to pick at her teeth.

Uh-oh. *That* wasn't good.

But I'd given Neel time to collect himself, and now he ran at his mother, his sword raised. The Queen stopped the weapon with her hand. With a terrible glint in her eye, she brought the sword to her mouth and licked it. The shining steel now dripped with gloppy black saliva. Neel grimaced, throwing it to the ground.

"You think you can kill me with your mortal weapons, you snotty-nosed smarty-pants?" The demoness's expression was pained. "Really, I *cannot* believe you young people these days! Just the other day I was telling my interdimensional poison-brewing club what a disappointment my child was to the demonic race. You never listen, do you? The only way to kill me is to find the exact location of my soul!"

"Ma—how could you?" I was startled to see that there were tears falling freely from Neel's eyes. His face was a mask of pain. "My brother—Mati—what did they ever do to deserve this?"

"Deserve?" the Queen screeched, thumping herself on

the chest with her words. "How can you talk to me of who deserves what? *I* was the king's senior wife; *you* are his oldest son. It's *you* who deserves to be the next king, not that puny-shuny human brother of yours. *You* should be king, you disrespectful fruit of my loins, not Lalkamal!"

"I don't want to be king!" Neel yelled. "Do you think the people would accept a king who is a half demon? A king with a mother like *you*?"

The Rakkhoshi Queen clutched her stomach. "Aiii! Aii!" she cried. She shook a long taloned finger at me. "May you have children this ungrateful, my little Luna Bar, so you know the intestinal agony that only your progeny can give you."

The demoness turned a shade of clover green. "That ridiculous, show-offy boy! That Little Prince Fauntleroy!" she moaned, belching clouds of acidic red smoke. "That prissy-shissy girl! So noble in her poverty! So sickeningly honorable!"

Ew. What was going on?

The rakkhoshi began to make disgusting, retching sounds. "I knew I should *not* have swallowed without chewing," she moaned. "Oh, the gaseous indigestibility of youth! Oh, the digestive agony of their sugary friendship!"

She was going to lose her lunch. I raised my hands to my

face. This was going to be gross. Way grosser than the corn-dog-vomiting incident.

But then the Queen did something that topped the bizarre-o-meter. As if her mere existence wasn't bizarre enough. She stretched her mouth so wide that me, Neel, and the whole stable could have fit into it. And what I saw in that eternal blackness, I don't think I can ever forget.

Because there, in the Demon Queen's open mouth, were spinning—could it be?—suns, planets, moons: a whole series of solar systems.

No. Barometric. Way.

This was heavy stuff.

Something Shady Sadie the Science Lady once said on TV came rushing into my head. It was about a brand-new discovery that some astronomers had made: a monster at the center of the galaxy. It wasn't really a monster, she'd explained, but some kind of super-huge black hole they discovered with powerful telescopes. Apparently, it was so hungry it gobbled up planets, stars, anything in its way. But the monster was greedy, and it couldn't digest everything it took in. Instead, like a fire hose being aimed at a soda can, half the stuff it tried to inhale came shooting back out of it. It proved, Sadie explained, that black holes didn't just consume and destroy energy, they created it as well.

Which is why I wasn't as surprised as I could have been when the Demon Queen vomited out two enormous spheres—like little planets, really. One was deep gold and the other a glowing silver.

"Drat! Dread! Demonic doo-doo!" the rakkhoshi shrieked.

Whoa. Holy public television station. Was Neel's mom the monster at the center of the Milky Way? What was it Lal said about rakkhosh being black holes—spells that had gone beyond their expiration dates?

The demoness was still clutching her stomach when she vanished again in a flash of blinding light. "This isn't over, you good-for-nothings, you lazy loafers. You can count on it!"

Her voice and the smell of her belches lingered, but she was gone.

"What the . . . ?" Neel stared at the gold and silver balls, and let out a big sniff.

I walked up to the objects. They weren't really little planets, I guess, more about the size of bowling balls. Had I imagined what I saw in her mouth? Had it been some kind of a psychedelic dream?

There was a faint red light emanating from the golden sphere, and the silver one smelled like—what was it? Fresh cotton and honey.

"It's them!" I realized. "It's Lal and Mati!"

At the sound of their names, the spheres began to vibrate and hum. The gold one even rolled a little, bumping against Neel's foot.

"Serves us right for relying on *Nosferatu*," Neel muttered, swiping at his eye.

"Huh?"

"The original *Dracula*," he explained, almost to himself. "Lal and I love that movie. Not like that idiotic teenage vampire—sparkling skin! Not drinking human blood! How ridiculous!"

He was talking about one of my favorite books-turned-movies, but I decided to let the comment go without protest. Neel was upset, after all.

"It's going to be okay," I said in my most soothing, come-down-from-the-ledge-you-nutter voice. His brother had just been turned into a bowling ball, and he was debating the relative merits of different vampire movies?

"No, I'm serious," Neel insisted. "Vampires. Like—'I vant to suck your blood'?"

"Yes, I'm familiar with 'I vant to suck your blood.'"

"That's where we got the idea of an enchantment that would banish my mother's physical form from our kingdom unless someone specifically invited her in."

Oh, *that* was what all that permission getting was about. In those old movies, vampires couldn't enter someone's house unless they had an invitation. Something I myself had given the rakkhoshi.

To quote the demoness herself: Drat. Dread. Demonic doo-doo.

But something still didn't make sense. "How did she get inside in the first place, to change identities with Danavi?"

"She must have ridden in on the mist or in the vapor of a storm cloud." Neel rubbed his eyes. "But she couldn't take on her physical form until you gave her permission."

It *was* all my fault.

"Neel, I'm so sorry . . ."

"I should have known better." He shook his head. "I shouldn't have listened to you."

"About what?" I felt so bad for inviting the rakkhoshi into the kingdom, I didn't even realize that Neel blamed me for something else.

"You're the one who insisted we leave Lal alone." Neel kicked at the ground in frustration. "Why did I listen to you? A stranger! Someone who has no idea what she's talking about! Someone so selfish she never thinks about other people's feelings!"

"It's not all my fault!" I shouted, my shame and horror making me defensive. "What about you? You didn't think you should tell me you were a half demon and your mom was out to snack on Lal? Or that you two had come up with some horror-movie spell to keep her out of the kingdom?"

Neel lifted the two spheres onto his shoulders without another word. But his jaw was working like he was chewing and swallowing down bitter emotions.

"Look, Neel, I'm sorry," I said, blinking back tears. "I'm so sorry. For your brother, for Mati, your mother, for everything."

Still, the prince said nothing.

"Do you hear me? I'm sorry! I'm going to help make this right—I promise!"

"Don't you get it?" Neel's eyes were shining with water, but he ground his words out with a fury that startled me. "You can't do anything to make this right! Nothing will ever be right again!"

CHAPTER 15

Stepmothers

The silence was painful as we walked back to the main part of the palace. Neel set a fast pace even though he carried both the golden and silver spheres, and didn't look over at me once. My emotions slingshotted between rage and guilt. *How dare he blame me?* I thought one minute. *How could he not?* I thought the next.

We walked down a marble hallway decorated with shields and curved swords. The ceiling sparkled with gems set in patterns to look like stars, moons, and swirling galaxies. There were lacy cutouts in the walls that let the breeze waft through, and I could see one after another fountain-filled courtyard stretching off in either direction. At the end of this hall was the throne room, and in front of the throne room stood a pair of moustachioed guards in tunics and baggy pants. The swords in their belts glittered. But they didn't stop us, instead just bowed to the prince and let us through.

Before the royal audience chamber was a reception area separated from the throne room by a curtain. There were a bunch of people crowded there—merchants and customers arguing about who cheated who, nervous villagers waiting to complain about their landlords, courtiers in silk saris and tunics just milling around for no apparent reason. The glittering curtain parted and a gray-haired man in regal clothes, gold earrings, and miles of gold necklaces came out. He bowed to Neel, adding a kind of unnecessary set of hand waves.

"Your Royal Highness, welcome home."

Neel inclined his head. "Lord Bulbul."

"I am the Royal Minister of Sweets," the elderly man said to me with a flourish, before he caught full sight of me. Then I saw his expression change into disgust. Man, what was this dude's problem?

In the meantime, the guard parted the entrance curtain and Neel walked through, leaving me behind with Lord Bulbul. As I watched the prince's retreating back, the hollow feeling in my stomach grew. To make matters worse, I noticed the minister guy was still staring at me. Following his gaze, I realized there was a gloppy mess on my beautiful tunic that looked as if I'd been playing with tar. To top it off, there was a bunch of long rakkhoshi hairs stuck in it.

"Eww." I tried—pretty ineffectively—to clean myself off with the cloth that the guard supplied me. Unfortunately, I just smeared the stain even more over the silk top.

It was only then I realized that Lord Bulbul wasn't bothered by my clothes, he was grimacing at the cobra mark on my arm.

"A bad omen," he hissed, spitting in my direction. "An evil eye has touched you." The minister backed away. He looked like he wished he had a bunch of garlic to ward me off.

This would have been a good time for my half-monster side to kick in, I thought, so I could smite this guy to death with an evil glare or something. But instead, I just stood there feeling small, and not particularly smite-y. Or snaky. Neel's mom had called me a moon-chickie. Maybe I took more after my biological mom? I could only hope. Although what a moon maiden was like I had no idea. And I'd never heard of anyone moonbeaming someone else to death.

Finally, the guard just pushed me along. There was nothing else to be done but to follow Neel into the throne room.

I kept my hand over my scar, held my breath, and prayed no one would notice me. I didn't feel any more regal now that I'd found out about my biological parents. In fact, I felt like an ordinary sixth grader from New Jersey masquerading in pretty clothes (that I'd already ruined).

In front of me was a long, carpeted aisle lined on both sides with all sorts of jabbering lords and ladies of the kingdom. Everyone was decked out in blinding color combinations—magenta and kelly green, turquoise and orange, violet and hot pink. The men were in turbans, chains, and earrings; the women in saris embroidered with gold thread and real pieces of glass, their dark hair threaded with heavy jewels. They were flirting, arguing, eating, laughing. Everyone, even the pretty ladies, seemed to be talking with their mouths full. No one seemed particularly interested in what anyone else had to say, but really interested in hearing their own voices. I shouldn't have been nervous about anyone noticing me. A woman in a chartreuse sari and magenta blouse belched delicately, but no one gave me a second glance as I walked toward the royal dais.

Neel stood in front of his father's throne. Its back was a golden peacock's open feathers, and its armrests each a roaring lion's head.

As I approached, I realized Neel was mid-story.

". . . and then she vomited these out," he explained. "I'm pretty sure they are the Prince Lalkamal and the stable master's daughter, Mati." The golden and silver spheres vibrated and rolled around in front of the throne.

The Raja was weeping fat, embarassing tears. He looked a lot like Lal, but older and softer. Precious gems sparkled from his ears and the rings decorating every single one of his fingers. And on his shoulder, like yet another ornament, was the golden bird, Tuntuni.

"Our son and heir!" the Raja groaned. "How could you do this? Your only job was to protect your brother and future sovereign—with your life if necessary! What have you done? What have you done?"

Neel's face grew stony, his dark brows knitting together. "Father, I swear I will do everything in my power to bring my brother back."

"Not everything!" the Raja shrieked, jumping up and almost dislodging Tuni from his shoulder. "You promised to control that part of yourself!"

"You know that's not what I meant!" Neel practically growled, and the Raja flinched, sitting quickly back down in his seat.

I might have flinched a little too. Neel appeared scarier than I'd ever seen him look. He was even shaking a little, as if desperately trying to control his temper. It was like watching someone put a lid on a volcano.

"I don't know anything about you anymore, boy." The Raja's words were angry but his voice was trembling. He looked like he was going to say something else, but was interrupted by a number of women bursting into the throne room.

"This is all of your causing!" A stunning woman in a buttercup-yellow sari and diamond jewelry knocked over a bunch of courtiers to rush toward the throne. When she got to the golden ball, she collapsed, pounding her fists on the marble floor. A gaggle of similarly dressed women—in necklaces and bangles, diamond nose rings and tiaras—followed buttercup lady into the room, and, after a minute of watching her cry, began to wail too.

"To see our queens so distraught is terribly vexing to us." The Raja blew his nose into a large, lacy handkerchief.

Neel's face lost a little of that thunderous expression, and he rolled his eyes in annoyance.

Ah, this must be Lal's mother and the other stepmothers.

The head queen's long-lashed eyes flashed at Neel as she screeched, "This is *your* fault. You are no prince of this realm, demon-born spawn!"

Whoa. Lal's mom was giving the Rakkhoshi Queen a run for her status as wickedest stepmother of the year.

Instead of exploding in rage, Neel's voice took on an icy, sarcastic civility. "How pleasant to see you too, my royal stepmother," he mocked, bowing low.

The buttercup queen then turned her venom on me. "It is *you* who has brought this evil wind into our kingdom again, you moon rock, you viper child, you serpent in girl's clothing!"

"My darling lady," the Raja cooed, "this is the Princess Kiranmala, exiled these many years to the land of"—he shuddered—"two dimensions. What will she think of us if we behave so? Come, my dear, you must not distress your-self. We do not desire you to become ill!"

"Royal husband." Now the queen's tone was cloying. "You will exile them, won't you? You will banish them from the kingdom for what they have done to my son, your heir, the future Raja of this kingdom?"

I wanted to hate her, but she was right. I *had* done this to her son, twice over. Once by separating him from Neel, and then again by inviting the Rakkhoshi Queen into the kingdom. I felt smaller than a cockroach and only half as loved.

"My royal stepmother," Neel said, his voice tight, "Princess Kiranmala didn't do this to Lal. It was my fault entirely. No one else's."

Neel's words confused me. Why was he taking all the blame?

"Do not address me, boy!" the woman shrieked at Neel. "And do not tell me about this"—she indicated me—"snake in the grass, this asp, this cobra dropping!"

Neel kept his eyes fixed straight ahead, but I could see that muscle twitching at his jaw that told me how angry he really was. The volcano, it seemed, was bubbling again.

One of the other queens was staring at my clothes. "You do realize that you have, like, demon snot on your shirt?" she twitted through pink lips. "I mean, seriously grody!"

"Yes, and it's demon spit, thanks," I muttered.

"My queens, we observe your sister-queen is a bit distressed." The Raja waved his handkerchief in the direction of Lal's mother. "Perhaps you can remove her from the throne room and allow her to get some well-deserved rest."

"I refuse to leave without my son! I will not leave without the golden ball!" Lal's mother shouted, but at the Raja's slight shake of the head, several queens grabbed each of her arms and legs and began forcing her out of the room.

"It's all of your faults! You all did this to my precious boy!" the queen yelled as she was bustled away. "Not to mention all the time he spent with that horse-girl, that stable wench! No good can come from mixing with the poor, I tell you! No good can come from letting the son of a rakkhoshi and the daughter of a snake loose in the kingdom!"

The entire throne room stayed quiet as the queen's rants became less and less audible. Then everyone started jabbering again as if nothing had happened. I was surprised the Raja didn't even seem embarrassed. He was probably used to the drama. He actually looked pretty chipper as he picked up some sweets from a silver platter. I remembered that Neel had said Lord Bulbul's title was Minister of Sweets. Now I understood how important that position would be in this kingdom. The Raja scarfed down a number of desserts all at the same time.

"This one has real silver sliced on top," he said as he popped a diamond-shaped sandesh into his already full mouth. Some of the ministers seated to his left clapped, as if impressed by their Raja's dessert-eating abilities. For his part, the Raja looked ridiculously pleased by their approval.

"Now where were we?" the Raja mused when he was done smirking for his court. "What was it we were talking about?" He had disgusting globs of molasses hanging from his moustache hairs.

I stole a glance at Neel, whose brown skin was turning seriously ruddy. I worried the lava of his rage was about to bubble up and out.

"We were talking about your *younger* son, Your Majesty." My voice was thin and nervous. "He got turned into a golden sphere?"

"Oh, yes." The Raja swallowed, then whipped out his handkerchief to dab his lips and eyes. "We are so very dismayed at this unexpected turn of events." Of course, his dismay didn't stop him from shoving some more sandesh in his mouth.

"I'm sure you are, sire," I said quickly.

"We are even more distressed," mumbled the Raja through his stuffed mouth, "that our son was with that inappropriate friend of his. The daughter of a stable master! Really!"

"Father." Neel spoke through clenched teeth. "I said I would do whatever it takes to bring the Prince Lalkamal back, and I will."

"And Mati," I added.

"Indeed," the Raja said to his son, "you will bring your brother home, or you will not come home at all."

"Without my brother, I have no home here." Neel bit off the words like they were poison.

I felt horrible. If not for me, Lal and Mati would be with us right now. If I'd just believed their stories, maybe my parents would be safe at home too. I straightened my shoulders, feeling that unfamiliar warrior spirit in my stomach. Even if he hated me, even if he was more rakkhosh than human, I would help Neel get his brother back. And I would get my parents back too. There was no other option. This was my destiny.

I turned to the yellow bird, who was perched on the arm of the Raja's throne. "Minister Tuni, what do we do? How can we get them back in their old form?"

"In the East of North of East, the Maya Pahar climbs—" Tuntuni squawked, pecking crumbs out of the Raja's open palm.

"Yeah, yeah, we heard you the first time," I interrupted. "So we have to go the Maya Pahar to save Lal and Mati—the same place my parents are?"

"All your solutions," the bird agreed, "lie in the Mountains of Illusions."

"Okay, great, let's go!"

"Wait." The Raja stopped me with an upturned hand. "Do you know how to get there?"

I was surprised. "It's like the bird—"

A squawk of protest.

". . . Minister Tuni said. In the East of North of East. I mean, wherever that is. Right?"

"Stop being such a ruler, Kiran," Neel snapped. "Here, north isn't always north. East isn't always east . . ."

"Oh, right." I sagged in defeat and scowled at the bird, who was hopping from one of the Raja's armrests to the other. I was no closer to finding Ma and Baba. No closer to helping Lal and Mati back into their human forms. Maybe Neel was right. Maybe I couldn't do anything right.

Unexpectedly, it was Tuntuni who seemed to notice my plummeting mood. "Say, Princess, what do you call a sad bird?" he squawked.

"This is really not the time . . ." Neel began, but I blurted out the answer.

"Easy. A bluebird."

"Eggs-ceptional," Tuni chirped, flying onto my shoulder. For whatever reason, that made me feel a little better.

"In a place where nothing—not even countries—stay put, it's useful to have a moving map. Why don't you use yours?"

Both the Raja and Neel snapped around to look at me. "You have a moving map?" father and son asked at the same time.

"Jinx." It popped out of my mouth before I even thought about it.

"What is this jinx?" the Raja asked. "We are not familiar with this custom."

"Well, if you say something at the same time, then one person can say 'jinx' and the other person can't talk until the first person, or somebody else, says the other person's name . . ."

"Oh, bullock's biscuits, there's no time for that now," Neel yelled. "You have a *moving map* and you didn't tell me this whole time?"

"I . . . I . . . uh, I didn't think it was important. What's a moving map anyway?"

"You didn't think it was important!" Neel shouted, while his father explained, "A moving map is what you need if you're going to a place that doesn't stay still. It's a map that knows how to keep up and tell you where somewhere is at any particular time. They're very rare and most difficult to find."

Neel was still ranting, his voice getting louder, "If I'd

known you had a moving map, I wouldn't have even come home to talk to Tuni, and if we hadn't come here . . ."

He didn't have to say it. I finished the thought for him. "If we hadn't come here, then Lal and Mati would still be okay."

Bullock's biscuits was right. Here was yet another way that I was directly responsible for everything going wrong.

I felt worse than ever.

CHAPTER 16

The Moving Map

What is this thing?"

We were back in the bathing room with the hanging vines, where I'd left my backpack. The mood between Neel and me was still tense, but at least he was talking to me. Together, we examined Ma's map, which looked just the same as the first time I'd seen it. As opposed to being covered with images of roads, mountains, lakes, or rivers, the entire page was smudgy and blank.

I reread the birthday card, the last message I had from my parents to me. "It says right here it's a moving map."

Neel stared at the blank paper with a serious expression, as if commanding the map to appear.

We were both quiet for a minute. Then Neel held the paper up to his face and sniffed it.

"What are you doing?"

"Just what I suspected," Neel replied. "It smells fishy."

"Very punny."

"I'm serious." Neel's grim face reminded me that he was only tolerating me out of some sense of princely duty. "There's a map here; it's just invisible. It's probably coated with Tangra fish juice."

"Some kind of invisible ink?"

Neel nodded.

Why not? A map that keeps up with moving land masses drawn with invisible fish juice. It certainly wasn't the strangest thing I had heard about so far. Of course, it wasn't exactly the kind of atlas we sold in our convenience store—the most exotic things on those were, like, the Garden State Parkway and the New Jersey Turnpike. (Though I used to think the Holland Tunnel sounded super exotic, like it was in Europe or something, but it's actually in Jersey City, New Jersey, which, in case you haven't been, isn't really that exotic at all.)

I squinted at the paper. "How do we decode it? With secret spy rings?"

"Let me look it up." Neel fished a battered little book out of his pocket. The cover read:

The Adventurer's Guide to Rakkhosh, Khokkosh, Bhoot, Petni, Doito, Danav, Daini, and Secret Code
Khogen Prasad Das

"Rakkhosh I know, decoding I get," I said. "But what are all those other words?"

"Oh, different kinds of demons, ghosts, witches, goblins, that sort of thing. K. P. Das is a senior demonologist of the highest caliber. He's one of Lal's and my tutors."

Neel's voice was carefully neutral, and I could practically feel the distance between us. I took a big breath.

"Um . . . Neel?"

"Yeah?"

"I just wanted to say I'm sorry. I'm really . . ."

Neel lifted his face from his book and looked, for the first time in what felt like forever, straight at me. I couldn't tell if he was upset or angry or . . . hungry. I realized how alone we were and felt a spasm of fear.

But his words weren't as much scary as they were just sad. "I'm . . . I'm just going to need some time, okay? I just . . . I'm going to need some time before I can forgive you."

I felt like crying, but I just jammed my nails into my fist. "No, I get it, that's cool."

"So let's just get on with what we've got to do, all right?"

"No, fine." I felt like I wasn't getting enough air. "Good idea. Lots of people to rescue."

"Lal would have just remembered how to decode Tangra fish juice." Neel sighed. "Decoding's my worst subject."

"What's your best?" I asked in as normal a voice as I could manage while still trying to stuff down tears.

Neel flipped to the glossary and began scanning the *T*s. "Talons, Tambourines . . . Here it is, Tangra," he read. "My best subject is demon slaying of course. Even though I believe more in demonic violence prevention and restorative justice than actual demon slaying."

"Oh."

It couldn't be easy, I guessed, for Neel to be half demon himself and have to hear all the time about how much people hated rakkhosh. He knew—maybe even better than me—what it was like to feel different.

"Well, Professor Das says here that there are only three ways to decode something written with Tangra fish juice."

"All right, shoot."

"One." Neel counted on his fingers. "Blow a powder made from ground-up rakkhosh bones on it."

"That doesn't sound too bad."

"You see any dead rakkhosh lying around here? And no, a half rakkhosh doesn't count. Even if it did, I'm not sacrificing my bones for your map."

"Fine." My face was as serious as I could keep it.

Neel looked huffy. Then he realized I was joking. "Very clever. You're such a comedian." He concentrated again on the book. "Two, dip the map in the waters from the River Jogai."

"Much easier than killing a rakkhosh," I said, "so let's go; where is this river?"

"Dried up years ago."

"Better and better." I sighed. "Okay, and what's the third?"

"You're not going to like it."

"Just tell me," I insisted.

Neel read from the book. "Well, the third way to decode something written in Tangra fish juice is to look at it through the prism of a python jewel."

I had a bad feeling. "A what?"

"The jewel from a powerful python's head. And of course, the place to get that is the underworld Kingdom of Serpents." He waited a beat. "Your father's kingdom."

"My birth father," I corrected. I'd made up my mind: I wasn't going to buy into that movie-of-the-week sap—like I was supposed to run into the arms of some dude who'd tried to kill me when I was a baby. Just because he'd donated his genes to my existence didn't make him Daddy Dearest. I mean, the Rakkhoshi Queen was Neel's mom and had actually raised him, but you didn't see him making any "I Heart My Demonic Mama" clay spitoons for her in art class.

"It's our only choice. Luckily, I have a working map to the serpent kingdom. And there are no other ways to decode something written in Tangra fish juice. At least that exist in this world."

"What—there's another way?" I jumped on his hesitation.

Neel nodded. "Lal and I discovered it by mistake when

we were trying to get to your house. We didn't realize the New Jersey map we had was encoded—probably written with Bhetki fish scales—until it was too late. We didn't think we'd ever make it to Parsippany in time to save you when Lal knocked his Giant Gulpie over on the paper."

I remembered Lal's love of soda fountains and fizzy drinks. And what was it that they had been arguing about when I opened the door? *If it wasn't for that Giant Gulpie, we wouldn't have found her at all?*

"So he spilled soda on the map, and the hidden ink showed itself?"

"Yup. I don't suppose you brought some with you?"

I shook my head, and was about to say something, when Neel went on. "Wait a minute, what's this writing on the other side of the map?"

"What?" Maybe Ma hadn't kept everything encoded.

But the opposite side of the map just held a note, written in Ma's handwriting:

You might get thirsty on your travels. Why not take some pek-pek with you?

Blast. That didn't help. It was also a code, just a lot simpler than the one in Tangra juice. No one but me and my parents would know that as a kid, I pronounced the word for a brand of soda like *peksi* and that, over the years, the word had become *pek-pek* in our family.

I explained that to Neel, who wasn't that amused by my childhood anecdote. "Your Ma wanted to make sure no one else could follow the map to Maya Pahar," he growled, "and she gave you this clue to figure out how to decode the map. She went to all this trouble and you couldn't bother to bring a can of soda with you?"

"Uh, if you'll remember, Your Imperial Oh-So-Super Royal Highness, I was a little occupied right when we left New Jersey. I was saving Lal's butt from that rakkhosh on my lawn, while you, his big, strong half-demon older brother, sat around and did nothing."

"I would have gotten around to saving him," Neel countered. "I saved you, didn't I? Not that you seem particularly grateful."

"Grateful?" I snorted. "Since I've met you, my house has been destroyed, my parents have disappeared, I've almost been eaten by a tantruming transit officer, then practically got arrested for stealing someone's *moustache*"— I took a breath—"I got beaned with guava seeds by a delusional bird, and pretty near got devoured by your demon mother."

"And you've loved every minute of it," Neel drawled, finally smiling for the first time in what felt like forever.

The thing was, I kind of had.

CHAPTER 17

Flying Fangirls

Neel and I left almost right away to find a python jewel in the Kingdom of Serpents. Without one, we couldn't read the moving map and had no hope of finding Maya Pahar.

The journey started off fine enough. The night sky was clear with perfect visibility. But it wasn't long after we started, Neel on Midnight and me on Snowy, that I knew something was wrong. At first, it was just a feeling in the cold night air that made goose bumps come up on my arms. Then it was the faint flapping sound that I could hear off-time from either Midnight or Snowy's wing motions. Finally, it was the smell: the sort of scent that filled up our convenience store van once when Baba forgot to close the vents and we were driving right behind a giant garbage truck.

Neel and Midnight slowed down, until they were flying next to Snowy and me.

"I think there's someone following us," I said, gesturing behind us into the night.

"Rakkhosh," Neel said flatly. "I smelled them almost as soon as we left."

"We're being followed by demons? What do we do?"

Sensing my tension, Snowy bucked and snorted. "Whoa, boy, take it easy." I patted his soft neck.

"We ride faster and try to lose them. If we're lucky, it's

just a coincidence, and they're heading somewhere else and won't follow." With that, Neel whispered something into first Midnight's ear and then Snowy's, and the pakkhiraj horses took off like shots. I almost couldn't catch my breath, we were riding so fast, but as soon as I got used to our new speed, I realized the sound of chasing wings had also grown faster. And louder. Not to mention how intense the smell of garbage was getting.

"We're going to have to outrun them," Neel called from Midnight. "Rakkhosh are afraid of snakes. They'll never follow us all the way to the Kingdom of Serpents."

I really hoped he was right. Midnight swooped to the left in a complex and unexpected zigzag and Snowy followed. I couldn't help letting out a choked scream.

As we regained altitude, though, something else made me want to scream even more.

"Neel is dreamy! Neel is sweet!" a cackling voice called from somewhere behind me. "Prince Neel's toes are a great treat!"

That was all the incentive I needed to urge Snowy to go faster. The rakkhoshi knew who we were. This was no coincidence. They *were* after us. They were going to catch up to us soon. They were already telling us how they were going to eat us, starting with Neel's feet. I remembered what Baba had said about rakkhosh using the bones of their victims as toothpicks, and felt like I was going to die for sure.

But when I looked over at Neel, I realized he didn't look as scared as he did just a minute ago. In fact, he kept looking over his shoulder with a confused expression, like—could it be?—he recognized the rakkhoshi's voice?

I took the risk of looking back at the demons now close behind us. Though it was dark, they were lit up with an inner green glow. They were a group of young rakkhoshis in saris and earrings, their unbound dark hair flying, wings flapping, and fangs glinting in the unnatural green light. They were flying in a bunch, their clawed hands outstretched in our direction, with kind of goofy expressions on their faces. Could I be imagining it, or did they look more like lovesick demonic cheerleaders than marauding murderers?

"Don't be frightened, don't be blue! Don't run, dear prince, for we love you!"

And then chanting rhythmically: "Princie! Princie! He's so fly! We'll eat his friend if she's nearby!"

They said this with a tittering that sounded, for all the world, the way that Jovi and her gang sounded when they were talking about their favorite TV stars and pop singers.

I urged Snowy forward, drawing even with Midnight. "You have demon groupies?"

"It's, uh, nothing," Neel said. But I noticed he kept his gaze straight ahead. "Just some rakkhoshis who sometimes send fan mail and care packages of nasty baked goods from Demon Land—usually without enough postage." Neel pulled at Midnight's reigns and made a sharp right, and Snowy followed.

"Then how did you recognize their voices?"

"Oh, right." Neel sounded uncomfortable. "They also sometimes leave voice messages, and, like, send me mixtapes of their favorite songs—but really, that's it!"

"Really? That's it? They don't send you selfies of them biting the heads off tarantulas or anything?" I screamed as I tried to hold on to my horse's reigns with almost numb fingers.

"Okay, maybe a couple times," Neel shouted over to me. "You probably shouldn't risk getting anywhere near them. The Neelkamalas have been known to get a little, erm, jealous."

"They call themselves the Neelkamalas?"

What the heck! *Neel* was the word for blue, and *kamala* was the name for an orange—so these idiot rakkhoshis had dubbed themselves *the blue oranges*? Being eaten by a rakkhosh was bad enough. I really didn't want to be killed by some demonic fangirls with no taste in names.

Snowy flapped his wings in rhythm with Midnight's as the horses continued in their headlong gallop away from the rakkhoshis.

"What's the matter? What's up? If that's your girlfriend, we'll chew her up!" yelled the Neelkamalas.

"Get lost, freaks!" I shouted over my shoulder. "You picked a terrible group name and your rhymes stink!"

In hindsight, I'll admit, insulting lovesick demoness fangirls probably wasn't the smartest decision I've ever made. The rakkhoshis seemed to redouble their efforts to reach us.

"Princess stew! Such a treat! Your girlfriend's gonna be good to eat!"

"Neel! Do something! Your groupies are going to kill me!" I screamed as the closest rakkhoshi, in a checkered sari with clashing colors, reached her dirty nails toward my horse. She caught a bit of Snowy's tail, but lost it when the animal bucked and increased his speed.

"Almost there!" Neel pointed down to the green land below us. "You better head home, ladies! Unless you want to join us in the Kingdom of Serpents!"

"Snakies bite! Snakies stink!" The Neelkamalas gnashed their teeth in my direction. "We'd like the princess's blood to drink!"

But they were already slowing down, and the distance between the rakkhoshi girl gang and our horses was increasing.

"Better luck next time!" I called to the now retreating demonesses. "And by the way, I'm not his girlfriend! He's all yours!"

"You don't know how to leave a good thing alone, do you?" Neel griped.

The horses began to descend. The sun was just rising when we landed next to a glassy hilltop lake surrounded by a thick forest of trees.

After we landed and dismounted, Neel turned to face me. "You okay?"

"You almost got me killed just there!" I pushed him with all my might. My hands were freezing cold, but he was like a furnace—probably another annoying perk of his rakkhosh blood. "What is wrong with you? You couldn't warn me that you were some kind of rakkhoshi heartthrob?"

"Hey, watch it." Neel grinned, looking stupidly proud of himself. "It's not my fault that I have an interspecies sort of charm."

"Who told you that?" I scoffed. "Those selfie-sending cannibals?"

The rising sun reflected like crazy off the mirrored surface of the lake, so that we were bathed in this shimmering, golden light. The ancient trees rustled all around us. The air was crisp and cool. The beauty of the surroundings did nothing to diminish the irritation I was feeling. The Neelkamalas girl gang had almost snacked on my limbs back there!

I shivered, rubbing at my goose-bumpy arms.

"Sorry." Neel pulled out a coat from his saddlebag and threw it around my shoulders. "I should have remembered you weren't too warmly dressed."

"Don't think this makes up for almost getting me killed," I snapped even as I cuddled into his warm coat. It smelled like him.

"Nah, I'd never think that." Neel smiled in a way that made me feel all confused.

"I'm serious," I said, my face heating up and voice rising. "I mean, how do I know you're not a secret double agent or something? Really working for the demons? Maybe you wanted me to invite your mother into the kingdom! Maybe you wanted me to blame myself! Maybe you actually wanted your mother to . . ." I let my voice trail off. What was I saying?

"Eat Lal and Mati?" Neel asked. "Is that what you were

going to say? That I *wanted* my mother to transform my brother and friend into this?" He indicated the gold and silver spheres resting on one side of his saddlebags.

I felt the shame rise like steam from within me, and wished I could stuff my stupid words back in my mouth. "No, I didn't mean . . ."

"Yeah, I think you did." Neel ran his hand harshly through his hair. "I have every reason to hate you, you know? Every reason. But I'm still here, helping you find your parents, helping you not get killed. And what do you do? Insult me at every opportunity!"

"Hate me?" My stomach went all wibbly-wobbly at his awful words, and I could feel myself almost shaking. "Hate me? What about all the reasons I have to hate you?"

"Right, because I'm a 'secret double agent,' as you put it," Neel snapped. "You're totally wacked, you know that? I don't know why I even try with you!"

"You know, I don't know either," I shouted. "And maybe you shouldn't anymore; what do you think about that?"

CHAPTER 18

The Kingdom of Serpents

I pelted off, half expecting Neel to chase behind me. When he didn't, I let out a sob but still couldn't let myself cry. I wasn't about to start doing dumb cliché things like crying over boys.

I bit back my tears, pushing branches and leaves aside as I ran into the beautiful wilderness, away from the shining lake. The moss was soft under my feet and the trees all thick with greenery. There was a gentle breeze, making it seem like the leaves were dancing all around me.

I was well out of sight of the lake's shores when I heard something more than freaky. It came from my right: a rustling in the trees, a cracking of branches. Oh gods, it was probably one of rakkhoshi girls, braving the Kingdom of Serpents to come and get me! Why had I been so moronic and told them "better luck next time"? As Baba always said, only a fool poked a sleeping tiger. I don't know what he would say about someone who poked a flying rakkhosh.

I reached for my new bow, only to realize that I'd left it and my quiver hooked on Snowy's saddle. Stupid, Kiran, stupid, stupid, stupid! I looked around for a fallen branch I could use as a club, but there was nothing big enough. I'd have to take her with my hands. I took a big breath, raised my fists as I'd seen Lal do back in Parsippany, and clenched them hard. I channeled all the anger I'd felt toward Neel now into thinking about how I'd defeat a rakkhosh with my bare fists. I had to believe I could do it. Failure was not an option. Not only Ma and Baba, but now Lal and Mati were counting on me too. If I could just keep the element of surprise.

The rustling was louder now, and I heard some raspy breathing and coughing. The sounds were all coming from behind a large clump of bushes. Fists raised to protect my face, I rounded the foliage with careful steps and then jumped.

"Got you!" My mind whirling with self-preservation and not much else, I launched myself at the intruder, tackling the creature to the ground. Somehow, the target was smaller than I thought it would be. And squishier than I thought a rakkhosh should be. Then I realized there were a bunch of yellow feathers shooting into the air from my arms.

Wait a minute, this wasn't a demon.

"Why in the world are you strangling Tuntuni?" It was Neel, having followed me through the woods. "I know he's a pain, but I really think you're overreacting."

The bird was a disaster. Bleary-eyed, missing feathers, and with some leaves stuck in one wing.

"Oh no! I'm so sorry! Are you okay?" I disentangled my hands from around the bird's neck and tried to smooth some of his ruffled feathers. "How did you get here?"

"What . . . do . . . you . . . call . . . a . . . bird . . . who's . . . out . . . of . . . breath?" Tuntuni panted.

I petted and cooed at the obviously shell-shocked bird, but Neel asked, "What?"

"A . . . puffin!"

"Shhh . . ." I soothed the little yellow bird I'd just almost killed. "No more bad jokes now. Save your breath."

"Have . . . you . . . ever . . . tried . . . to . . . keep . . . up . . . with . . . a . . . flying . . . horse?" he wheezed. "I've been fly-ing all night!"

"Why were you following us?" Neel demanded.

"Only . . . because . . . the Raja . . . insisted." Tuni coughed. "Doesn't trust you to finish the job, Princie . . . thinks you're as much of a slacker as I do."

"You're here to spy on us?"

"I'm here to make sure you ding-dongs do the job right!" Tuntuni squawked. "But I didn't think I'd have to chase a pakkhiraj, hide from those boy-crazy rakkhoshis, and then get attacked by you, Princess! The Raja is going to have to give me a serious pay raise after this—I mean, benefits, stock options, hardship pay, the works!"

"All right, all right," Neel said. "Don't get your tail feathers in a bunch."

Tuni pointed a yellow wing over my shoulder. "Hey, dummies, what's *that*?"

"Where?"

Neel and I both turned to where the bird was pointing. I didn't understand what I was looking at. The ground looked like it was moving.

"That doesn't seem right," I said.

Without a word, Neel grabbed my hand. Not romantic or anything. Just hard. Really hard.

"Ouch!" I tried to pull away, but Neel ignored me.

"Move!" he ordered, yanking me back toward the horses. He ran almost full-out, pulling me along, until we reached a grove of trees to the side of the lake, with Tuntuni squawking beside us.

Snowy and Midnight lifted their heads to greet us, but then whinnied—shrill and fierce. The noise shot a ripple of fear down my spine. I just had a chance to grab my weapons from Snowy's saddle when, with flapping wings, the horses took off into the distant sky, the golden and silver spheres still tucked in Midnight's saddlebags.

"Wait, the horses . . ."

I stumbled after Neel, my legs tripping over themselves. He wasn't letting go of my wrist and I couldn't seem to get my balance. We finally stopped beside an old gnarled tree with a lot of knobbly branches, and I looked at him, confused.

"Kiran, hurry!" Neel shoved me up the rough trunk of the tree. "Grab that branch!"

He was starting to really freak me out.

"What is going on?" After I managed to pull myself up to the lowest branch, Neel clambered up behind me. Then, with a panicky glance toward the ground, he dragged me to a branch even higher than the first. When he finally let me sit, I turned on him.

"What the—" I stopped short as a shaking Tuntuni crash-landed on the branch next to me. Some more of his tail feathers were missing.

"Look down, Kiran," Neel said. "Look!"

I squinted to see what he was pointing at. At first, I thought that my eyes were playing tricks on me. I could swear the grass was moving. Then it seemed like the very ground itself was slithering. With a queasy start, I realized what I was seeing.

"Holy moly, there are thousands of snakes down there!" I met Neel's own wide-eyed stare with my own.

"Maybe hundreds of thousands."

Tuntuni shuddered. "Oh, I hate snakes!"

From my perch on the tree, I could scan the area all the way around the lake. And what I saw made my skin crawl. From every direction, scores of snakes were slithering their way toward the lake. They occupied every square inch of land. Cobras, pythons, boa constrictors, asps, rattlesnakes, and a lot of kinds of snakes I'd never seen before and couldn't identify. And didn't want to identify. Big ones, small ones, fat ones, thin ones. There were so many snakes that the aggressive ones crawled over the slower ones. Some of those who got crawled over didn't get up again. It was like a snake stampede.

"They're nocturnal," Tuntuni chirped. "They hunt at night and go to sleep in the daytime. It's morning, so they're all coming home."

The bird was right. The sun had risen even higher in the sky, and as its rays reached across the entire surface of the lake, the water itself became almost transparent. And then an elaborate, arched doorway opened on the water itself, and the snakes streamed down through the passage.

"There's the entrance to the Kingdom of Serpents."

"We're going to have to go down there, right, to get the python jewel?"

Neel nodded, our past argument apparently forgotten in the face of our certain deaths.

"We can't; we'll get poisoned by all those snakes," Tuni protested.

"Pythons and boas don't have poison, they just squeeze you to death," Neel corrected, chewing on a fingernail.

"Details!" Tuni squawked. "All I know is we're going to die, I tell you! We're going to die!"

I tried to calm the bird down by telling him a joke.

"Hey, Tuni, do you know what they call a bird who can open doors?"

"A para-keet?" Neel suggested distractedly.

"No, a kiwi!" I said, but poor Tuntuni just kept burbling, "We're going to die, we're going to die," at regular, demoralizing intervals.

CHAPTER 19

The Python Jewel

It took more than an hour for the snakes to all slither down through the open doorway in the lake. The sun was fully in the sky before we made our way down to solid ground again. In fact, there were still a few snakes slithering their way toward the lake when we came down, but we had to risk it. Neel figured that the doorway might close up again after all the snakes had gone within.

He was right. No sooner had we followed—at a little distance—the last few snakes down the secret entrance than the doorway of water closed behind us.

It was dark as midnight below the surface of the lake. I held on to the back of Neel's shirt as I basically stumbled through the archway and down the long flight of stairs. As unpredictable as it made him, I was grateful for his warm rakkhosh constitution. His back was like a little heater on my hand, a relief in the cold and clammy cavern under the lake.

"You know, I was ten when I found out what my mother was," Neel whispered as we stumbled along, one stair at a time. "I always knew the other queens didn't like her, but I thought they were just jealous because she was the senior rani and her son would be king."

"Um . . . maybe we could exchange life stories later . . ." I hissed back. Neel was exhibiting a less-than-ideal sense of timing. We were climbing down a magical under-a-lake staircase into a kingdom filled with killer snakes. This really wasn't the time for a heart-to-heart chat about our childhoods.

But Neel just kept rambling. "When it came out that she was a rakkhoshi in disguise, they wanted to exile both of us, or maybe kill us."

The dank underwater air, not to mention my own overwhelming sense of doom, was making me shiver, and I wondered if all this gabbing was Neel's way of dealing with his own nervousness.

"Okay," I hissed as we kept climbing down. "I'll bite. I'm guessing, since you're here now and we all know your mom's alive and kicking, that your father stopped people from killing you?"

"Yeah, but he threw her out of the palace and made Lal crown prince instead of me."

Ah, so that's how it happened, I thought, my eyes just barely adjusting to the darkness. The Raja had unfairly discriminated against Neel because of who his mother was. I felt a new sense of sympathy for the half-demon prince. His family life was a lot more complicated than I knew.

"So I guess after that, your mom got angry and ate everything in sight?"

"Basically." We were nearing the bottom of the stairs. "The thing was, she'd promised herself she would live a human life when she fell in love with my father."

"And she felt betrayed, after all that sacrifice."

"I had to banish her from our lives, otherwise my father would have found a way to kill her for sure."

When you got right down to it, the Rakkhoshi Queen hadn't been treated very fairly. Not that it was an excuse for eating people, but it was an explanation.

As we got to the bottom of the stairs, the darkness grew steadily lighter—from black to gray and then ash. There was a light coming from somewhere ahead of us. As we went down the last step onto the muddy floor of the cavern, the light grew even brighter.

"There it is!" Neel whispered.

I looked where he was pointing. Wow. The light in the cavern was coming from a huge jewel in the middle of the otherwise empty room.

"It must be the python jewel." I stepped forward. "It's beautiful."

"Just grab it, Princess, and let's get out of here," Tuntuni said, his claws digging painfully into my shoulder.

"Why is nobody guarding it?" Neel pulled me back behind him into the shadows. "Wait, something's not right."

We stood a couple of minutes in a dim corner below the staircase. Neel was directly in front of me, so I didn't see what he did, but I did hear his intake of breath.

"What?"

"Well," Neel whispered back, "there's good news and bad news."

"Good first."

"Good news is—that probably is a python jewel, so it'll work to read the map."

"And the bad?"

"Bad news—it's being guarded by the most humongous python I've ever seen."

I peeked from behind his broad back and had to stifle a yelp. Tuntuni dug his nails in harder. I couldn't blame him.

Just as Neel had said, a gargantuan python was prowling

the room, slithering in broad circles around the stone. It was so big, it made that rakkhosh from my front lawn look like an overgrown garden gnome.

My fingers and feet felt like ice. The cold of the cave had seeped into my bones, making me shiver from the inside out. Saving my parents, Lal, and Mati depended on us getting to the Mountains of Illusions. And us getting to the Mountains of Illusions depended on us being able to read the moving map. And us being able to read the moving map

depended on us getting that stupid python jewel—and somehow getting by that huge snake. But there was no way we could possibly do that and still be alive.

My stomach clenched and my teeth started to rattle so much I was afraid the snake might hear them. I was having trouble getting in enough air and started seeing black spots in front of my eyes.

"Breathe, Kiran." Neel turned around, placing a warm hand on my shoulder. "You've got to keep it together. We need that jewel. Our families are counting on us."

His words melted a bit of the brain freeze that was paralyzing me.

"How are we going to get it without that thing noticing?" It seemed impossible.

"It's impossible!" The talking bird was totally histrionic. "Impossible, I tell you!"

"We'll let the python notice, that's how we get the jewel." Bringing his lips to my ear, Neel whispered his completely insane idea. I realized that it just might work. Problem was, if it didn't, we'd all be snake chow.

"Are you sure?" I asked again, trying to keep my teeth from rattling.

"It's the only way I can think of," Neel muttered. "Believe me, if I could think of a better plan, I would have suggested it."

"We're all going to die, we're all going to die," Tuntuni mumbled, a yellow wing over his eye.

"Shut up, Tuni. Just stick to the plan." Neel grabbed the bird and plunked him on his shoulder.

With a crooked smile he said, "Just don't screw up, okay, Kiran?" And then Neel stepped into the light of the python jewel.

It took the serpent a minute to notice him. "Hey, snaky!" Neel waved his arms, distracting the snake away from me, and away from the jewel as well.

Then Tuntuni, who was now flying around in high circles near the ceiling, started singing a childish snake-charming song:

"Baburam Sapure
Where do you go, Bapure?
Come on, Baba, come and see
Snakes for you and snakes for me."

As Neel had planned, the python hissed and turned away from the treasure it was protecting. It slithered rapidly toward Neel. I crept out of my hiding place and toward the jewel. I was supposed to grab it while Neel distracted the serpent. The problem was, Neel hadn't calculated how much faster the snake would be able to travel over the muddy ground than I was. As I tried to run toward the jewel, my feet got more stuck in the cloying silt. No matter how hard I tried to urge myself forward, the ground didn't seem to want to let me. Oh, this was bad. Very bad.

"Come on, snaky, is that the best you can do?" Neel taunted, even as the python gained ground toward him. "You need a little snake charmer to teach you a lesson?"

Tuntuni sang:

"These snakes are alive
In your basket they thrive
Bring me one or two
And I'll beat them black and blue."

So far, Operation Distract and Annoy was working, but at this rate, there was no way that I would make it to the jewel before the snake reached Neel. In fact, it was on him now, and even though he fought its parries with his sword, he couldn't seem to injure it. Tuntuni carried on singing near the ceiling but seemed too afraid to help in the fight.

With a hiss, the snake almost knocked Neel over. I struggled to hurry, but the cavern floor's muddy surface was like walking through molasses. My thighs burned from the strain of fighting to move faster and faster. But I hadn't progressed anywhere near where I needed to go. At this point, I was still closer to Neel and the serpent than the jewel.

Then the snake grabbed a hold of Neel, wrapped itself around him, and began to squeeze. It was obvious how much stronger the animal was than the half-demon prince. Neel was struggling. He had kept a grip on his sword and tried to injure the python with its slashes, but the snake's skin was unbelievably tough. The sword barely made a dent. Tuntuni, to his credit, made a few haphazard dives down from the roof, flapping his wings in the snake's eyes, but he couldn't break the python's concentration now that it had its prey. Neel's face got redder as the snake squeezed.

"Princess, do something, the slacker's gonna die!" Tuntuni shrieked.

CHAPTER 20

A Change of Plans

Save him!" Tuni yelled. "How am I gonna break it to the Raja if the prince croaks?"

Neel's plan was based on the fact that pythons aren't poisonous; they squeeze their prey to death. And he'd figured, as a half demon, he should be able to withstand a little squeezing until I nabbed the jewel. Problem was, neither of us calculated the silt floor.

I struggled to move, but every step was such an effort. Neel was still wrestling with the enormous serpent. Muscles of steel or not, how much longer could he stand this monstrous snake? There was no way I was going to reach the jewel in time.

Okay, that was a really dumb plan. Time for a new one.

In the struggle, the python's tail flailed around the room. It landed with a thump right next to the spot where I was struggling with the cloying ground. I made a split-second decision. It was now or never.

I jumped with both feet on the python's tail. Feeling my weight, the snake lifted up the back of its body, trying to dislodge me. But I just lay down, and slid down the snake's body as if it was a huge Slip'N Slide. It was rough, slimy, and scaly on my skin but *much* easier than running through the muddy quicksand of the cavern floor. I landed with a thump about midway up the giant serpent's body, and, trying to imagine I was doing nothing scarier than riding Snowy, I hung on for dear life with my thigh muscles. I reached back to my quiver and chose one of the "special" arrows Neel had made me prepare before we left his kingdom. He'd shown me how to attach a long, thin rope made out of a super-strong Thirteen Rivers material to some of my arrows. At the time, I couldn't figure what I'd need them for. But now I was glad for his forethought.

My fingers were slippery with sweat and I fumbled with the bow a little. The snake was bucking and writhing underneath me, and it wasn't that easy to concentrate.

"Take your time, there, Prin-cess," Neel gasped from

somewhere within the python's coils. He was turning an unbecoming shade of purple.

"Hold on to your pants, cowboy!"

I finally managed to nock the arrow onto my bow. My stomach churned as I rode the thrashing snake, and I could only pray there wouldn't be a repeat of the famous corn-dog incident. Neel's life was depending on my archery skills. No pressure or anything.

My hand shaking, I shot the arrow straight up above the snake's head, into the cavern ceiling. Would the arrowhead be strong enough to pierce the hard stone? Bingo! It went in, leaving the rope dangling behind it like a comet's tail. I didn't even have time to test it to see if it would hold my weight. I just used it like mountain climbing gear to clamber up the rest of the snake's slippery body to the top of its head.

"Show-off!" Neel choked out. Even with me climbing all over its body, the snake hadn't stopped squeezing.

"Go Princess, go Princess, go-go-go Princess," Tuntuni chanted.

"Remind me to thank you for the arrows after I save you!" I shouted to Neel.

I was straddling the snake's head now, trying to stab it. But just as its skin had been too tough for Neel's sword, my arrows couldn't make a dent. I grabbed the dangling rope from the arrow still stuck in the ceiling and made a quick noose, which I slipped over the snake's neck. It held! The snake hissed and thrashed around. In the process, it actually dropped Neel. He fell with a thump on the soft earth.

"Go!" I shouted at Neel.

I didn't even bother to see if he was all right. How long would one magical rope hold this massive, super-strong snake? I shot an arrow into another part of the ceiling, making another noose out of the dangling rope and looping it over the snake's head. I kept going like that: shooting an arrow into the ceiling, grabbing the rope, threading it under the snake's chin, and then starting all over again. In this way, I tied the snake with a halo of ropes each attached by a different arrow to the stone ceiling.

One huge bonus of all the ropes was that the snake couldn't move its head as much. Which was a relief, because I was still sitting astride its neck and could feel my breakfast in my throat.

Of course, the respite wasn't for too long. The snake's muscular body bunched and swayed as it tried to free itself, or at least ditch me onto the floor.

"Snaky's in a terrible mess!" Tuntuni sang. "Sewn up by a royal seamstress!"

It was like being on a bucking bronco ride at a cheesy Western-themed restaurant. The snake bumped up and down, left to right, trying to shake off the ropes that pinned it to the cavern ceiling. As it fought, the ropes actually started to give way.

Oh no.

Pop.

The snake managed to yank one of my arrows from the ceiling. The weapon dangled, harmless, from the rope still around the serpent's neck.

"Hurry, Neel!" I yelled. "I don't know how long these things are gonna hold it!"

Pop. Another arrow gone.

Neel struggled through the mud over to the python jewel. Being Mr. Demonic Dude, it was a lot easier for him than it had been for me. But even still, would he make it in time? The python had just yanked out two of my special arrows from the ceiling. I felt back to my quiver. I only had one roped arrow left. Did I want to use it? Would it make a difference? I threaded it into my bow, aiming at the ceiling.

Pop. Pop. Pop. The snake was almost entirely free of the confining ropes now.

In the meantime, Neel reached the jewel. Rather than just picking it up and running, as had been our original plan, he kicked mud from the cavern floor over the jewel's shining surface. As he kept doing that, the room darkened. My heart started to speed up. I'd found the courage from who knows where to ride an enchanted snake like it was some kind of horse, but there was no way I could face doing that in the dark. If I'd had the energy, I would have yelled at Neel to stop, but it was all I could do at this point just to hang on to the thrashing serpent.

In the graying light, I saw Neel bury the hilt of his sword deep into the mud in front of the jewel, its point facing up.

He shouted, "On my count, do a Tarzan!"

A Tarzan?

"One . . . two . . ."

Right, a Tarzan. Underneath me, the python tore the last remaining rope out of the ceiling. The ropes and arrows hung from its neck like some kind of weird necklace, but they certainly weren't doing anything more to slow it down.

I shot my last special arrow into the ceiling and hoisted

myself up the rope and off the snake. It took all my remaining strength. I hung there, thirty feet off the ground, my muscles trembling.

"Three . . ." And with that, Neel kicked a clump of mud over the remaining part of the jewel, dousing its emanating light.

The cavern was an inky black. The darkness was filled with the rancid smell of snake—or it might have been the smell of my own fear. I started to panic, squeezing my eyes shut so hard I saw stars. But at least it was a familiar darkness, as opposed to the blackness outside them. Holy serpent poop. My hands were so sweaty, I was slipping down the rope. For the zillionth time in the last few days, I was going to plummet to my death. It seemed like a recurring theme at this point.

Then I heard Neel's familiar voice cut through the darkness like a lifeline. "Hey, slimeball, where's your precious python jewel?"

The serpent hissed and slithered away from me. I heard it move down to the other end of the underwater cave.

My grip was slipping, but I desperately hung on. I didn't want to die. I wanted to see my parents again. I wanted to hang out with Zuzu again. I even wanted to argue with Neel again.

Then the cavern was filled with a wailing as the snake, searching for its jewel, found instead the point of Neel's sword. The cries were horrible—high-pitched and almost human. There was a thrashing sound like a giant drum being beaten on the ground. But in a few minutes, all was silent.

As quickly as there had been darkness, there was light. Neel cleaned some of the dirt from the jewel's surface, allowing it to shine once more like an unnatural, underground sun. I'd never been so happy to see.

The python's giant body lay still, oozing dark blood on the cavern floor. Trying to reach its jewel, it had instead split itself in two on Neel's sword. Neither of us had been strong enough to harm it, but it was strong enough to kill itself.

I breathed a very long sigh of relief, and slid down my rope. Unfortunately, it stopped what felt like a bazillion miles too short of the ground.

"Oh, for Pete's sake."

Neel, now holding the muddy python jewel, was standing under where I hung.

"Let go," he said.

I shook my head, unable to move.

"Come on," Neel coaxed. "You've got to trust me. Like it or not, we're in this together."

Did I trust Neel? It was hard to say. One moment I felt like strangling him, the next, one of us was saving the other's life. At the very least, until we rescued our families, we were partners. And I guess that deserved some trust.

"I suppose we half monsters have got to stick together."

We had a lot in common, Neel and I, even if I didn't like to admit it.

I let go. It wasn't like one of those scenes in a movie, where the princess floats lightly into the waiting hero's arms. I was more like an anvil that comes plummeting down on a cartoon character's head. I fell, like a graceful barbell, right on top of Neel.

Squelch. We both sank even farther into the mud.

"You did ask for it." I swiped some silt from my face.

"Yeah." Neel grinned through the dirt. "I guess I did."

Unfortunately, the muddy moment was shattered by the sound of a terrible hissing that sent shivers up my spine far worse than any darkness.

"Welcome home," seven voices hissed, "Sssissster."

CHAPTER 21

The Serpent King

The seven-headed cobra towered above us, bobbing and swaying. His scaly green skin shimmered in the light of the python jewel, which was now knotted into its muscular tail. Dimmer lights shone from each of seven smaller jewels sitting on each of its seven heads. As it danced its twisting dance, I saw reflected, seven times over, the same U-shaped marking on my upper arm. Like two cruel eyes that had been staring at me my whole life.

It was terrifying and horrible and a bit fascinating all at the same time.

When I heard the story of the moon maiden's seven stolen sons from "Danavi," somehow I assumed that my seven brothers were turned into seven snakes. Now I realized they were each of seven heads attached to one powerful serpent body.

The magic snake hissed as I moved right. It flicked out its seven forked tongues as Neel moved left. With a hissing and a bumping, it forced us both to walk straight ahead. And in this way, my brothers escorted us, none too politely, out of the cavern and into the Serpent King's throne room.

"A plan," Neel muttered as we shuffled side by side, shoved along by the seven-headed snake. "We need a getaway plan. Like right now."

"What do we do?"

"I'm thinking. I'm thinking." Neel's voice was desperate. "I don't suppose you have any good ideas?"

"If I did, would I be asking you?"

Tuntuni, for once, was unable to speak. He shook like a—well—like a feather in my arms.

Not that he didn't have good reasons. After the emptiness of the jewel cavern, the throne room was a shock. It positively writhed with snakes. Snakes carpeted the floors, hung from the ceilings, wrapped around the pillars, and decorated the light fixtures. Even the enormous throne at the end of the room was made of writhing, hissing, green, black, yellow, and brown serpent bodies.

And among all those slithering snakes, hundreds of jewels of all shapes and sizes. Each serpent seemed to be protecting one. None were as big as the python jewel that the seven-headed cobra had taken from us, but the serpents were hoarding untold riches down here in their underwater kingdom.

Almost in unison, they all bared their fangs as we entered the room.

"Frightened, Sssisssster?" the cobra's seven heads hissed as one. "You shhhould be!"

I'd just come face-to-face for the first time with my brothers—well, what used to be my brothers anyway. I hadn't thought much about them, but assumed that when I saw them, I would feel some sort of sibling connection. Instead, all I felt was revulsion. And fear. The cobra didn't seem to hold too much brotherly love for me either. With a hiss, it pushed us again toward the throne.

"Father, ssseee what I have brought you!" I could clearly hear the eagerness to impress the king in all seven of those voices.

We had no choice but to move forward. My seven-headed band of brothers were baring their fangs right behind us.

But so too were the serpents in front of us. They slithered forward, hissing, winding themselves around our arms and legs, hanging over our heads from the ceiling. It was like a horrible nightmare. At first I tried not to scream as I felt their cold skin slip across mine—but soon I couldn't control myself. Slip—a snake was climbing up my shin. Squeeze—another wrapped itself across my chest like a purse strap. I couldn't even see Neel anymore—my vision was entirely blocked by writhing serpents. I thought of Baba and how he had tried to protect me from this. I shut my eyes, trying to imagine myself a little girl again, safe and secure in my father's arms.

A familiar voice screamed and screamed. It took me a couple of moments to realize it was my own.

After what seemed like hours but must have been minutes, a voice commanded from the end of the room, "Serpents begone! Make a path, and bring them to me!"

The snakes unwound themselves from our bodies. Even the ones in front of us wiggled away, making a clear path from where we stood to the throne.

My skin felt slimy and clammy. I felt shaken and bruised. I shuddered as the seven-headed snake pushed me forward again.

"I'm so sorry," I mumbled brokenly to Neel. He reached out and held my damp hand in his own. The warmth of his skin took a small edge off my fear.

"For what?" he breathed.

We walked forward as slowly as we could toward the snake throne.

"He's my dad. We wouldn't be in this mess if it wasn't for me."

"Not true. We needed to find that python jewel."

"Well, I'm sorry anyway."

"It's not your fault," Neel muttered. "He's your dark matter."

"My what?" I asked, but we were in front of the throne by then and the Serpent King's green eyes flashed.

"Silence!" he bellowed. I dropped Neel's hand. Tuni cowered on my shoulder somewhere near my ear.

"I see you have met my son Naga," the Serpent King hissed. "I am Sesha, King of the Serpents, guardian of the primordial ocean of divine nectar, keeper of time."

My skin broke out in goose bumps. My mouth felt dry. This was my biological father, at last. The Serpent King had a human form: dark hair tinged with gray, shimmering green clothes, a crown made of serpent's teeth, a handsome but cruel face. Was there any similarity there to mine? I searched but couldn't see it.

"Welcome to the Palace of Desires," the Serpent King hissed. Beside his writhing throne of snakes were urns of rubies, emeralds, and diamonds. He ran his hands through these as he talked, letting the jewels fall back through his fingers. "Do you see anything that pleases you?"

His green eyes glowed in my direction, and I could feel their almost physical pull. Here he was, not five feet away. My father. And he wanted me back; he wanted me to join him. What was wrong with that? That was only natural, wasn't it? I had a swimming, goofy sensation, like I was filled with the golden honey that Mati had been feeding the pakkhiraj horses. I felt the nectar swimming through my blood. My father wanted me back. And I would go.

I swayed, my eyes half hooded, as if in a trance.

Until I felt a sharp peck on my neck, that is.

"Princess, don't look directly at him. Still your mind. Don't believe the sweet lies he's feeding you," Tuntuni squawked.

"Silence!" the Serpent King snarled, waking me out of my trancelike state. I stared at the floor, my mind racing. I could still feel my father's pull, though. Was it magic, something about his personality, or just our shared history? I couldn't tell but I couldn't trust myself to resist him either.

"If she is the one, it is fate that has brought her back to me." I could feel more than see the Serpent King's green eyes were boring into me. "She will be a valuable weapon in the coming war."

"Yesss, Father," Naga agreed in his multiple voices.

My heart was a mess of contradictions. I was afraid. I didn't want to be turned into a snake, or a weapon, or to stay in this underground reptile zoo for a minute longer. On the other hand, it was hard not to feel the power of finding my birth father. Then, like a wave, the guilt washed over me. How could I be thinking of this monster as my father when my own dear Baba was still missing?

"She has my mark on her arm," the Serpent King hissed, "but what makes you so sure she is the one?"

"Shhhe bearsss this mark alssso, Father!" The seven-headed serpent pushed me to my knees.

"Hey!" Neel protested.

The cobra's tail pushed my head down, revealing the moon-shaped scar on the back of my neck. The Serpent King's laugh boomed through the cavern.

"So, it's true. You are the brat my queen hid away. And now you've come back—to steal from your *poor old* father?" His voice was mocking. I was pretty sure Sesha didn't think he was either poor or old.

Neel helped me to my feet. My legs were like jelly.

"I am Kiranmala." I held my head up, hoping the trembling in my lips wasn't too obvious.

For a second, I thought the Serpent King smiled. But his expression remained cruel.

"And who are you, young rakkhosh?" he asked. "What do you want with my"—he paused—"filthy little offspring?"

"I'm, er, friends with your, erm, daughter. Uh, sir," Neel stammered, sounding more like he was addressing a friend's dad at after-school carpool than a mortal enemy. Maybe he was feeling the Serpent King's strange power too.

"Silence!" Sesha shouted. "*This* puny imp is my blood? I can hardly believe it." He sneered, his upper lip curling in an ugly way.

I was rooted to the spot. This was way more awful than I thought it would be. How could I ever have thought I might have anything in common with such a horrible father?

"Just like your mother," he continued, "so soft and weak and *moony.*"

My throat constricted, but I pushed down the tears. Part of me refused to blubber in front of this monster. But truth be told, another part of me didn't want to disappoint my father.

"You will thank me." The Serpent King raised his arms above his head. "You will thank me for sparing you from a life of drudgery and giving birth to your inner glory!"

I hid my eyes. I could feel his green gaze boring into me again, and that pull, like some kind of a magical rope between us. Like he had shot me with an invisible arrow attached to a string and all he had to do was reel me in.

"Join me!" the King thundered, a blinding green light building between his hands.

"No!" Neel shouted, as if forcing himself to resist Sesha's magic. "I kind of like her the way she is." He pulled out his sword, which flashed in the light of the Serpent King's glowing energy.

But Naga pushed Neel to the ground, looming and hissing above him.

"Stop!" I cried, reaching for my bow.

None of us noticed that Tuntuni had flown out of my arms while the King talked. Now he flew up, flapped his wings in Sesha's face, and then snatched something out of Neel's shirt pocket.

It was the shadow seller's purple vial with the cork top.

"Tuntuni, wait . . ." Neel began. But with one swift gesture, the bird smashed the vial to bits at the feet of the Snake

King. There was a tinkling of broken glass, but beyond that, nothing happened.

We all stared at the broken bottle like participants in a strange wax-museum tableau. The king, the bird, the prodigal daughter, the looming serpent, and his princely prey.

Sesha was the first to break out of the expectant trance.

"Ha!" The Serpent King's moustache twitched as he laughed. "I haven't been that amused in a long time!"

But then a thick gray smoke swirled out of the shattered glass. It wrapped itself like a never-ending sari around the throne room, circling the pillars, weaving through the furniture, threading its wispy form above and below the throne. It wrapped us, the snakes, everything in its expanding folds.

"Hang on, y'all, here it comes!" Tuntuni chirped.

"Here *what* comes?" I eyed the growing mist.

"Just don't let go!" Neel grabbed me with one hand, the bird with his other.

An earthquake-like rumbling shook the teeth in my head. The snakes hissed and slithered around in panic. Then enormous roots shot out of every nook and cranny of the throne room, breaking right through the snake pillars and snake chandeliers, the snake tables and snake throne chair. From the roots, a sturdy trunk exploded like a rocket toward the sky.

"Father! The sssky isss falling!" Naga shrieked.

And it was. The banyan tree shadow, which had been trapped inside the purple bottle, was reconstituting itself now that it was free—like a dry sponge exposed to water. The mighty branches shot up and out, crashing through any obstacle before them. Pieces of stone ceiling plummeted down like giant pieces of hail, crushing snakes.

"This isn't the last time you'll see me!" The Serpent King waved his arms, and in a flash of green, he transformed himself into a hideous serpent with a hundred heads. His endlessly coiled tail vibrated with a primordial power. Already, the banyan tree was destroying the room. Now, with every rattle of his mystical tail, the entire cavern shook and spun. Cracks shot along the walls and floors. A huge one beneath the throne opened up, and the Serpent King and Naga disappeared through it.

Neel pulled at my arm. "Wait!" I shouted, breaking free of his grasp.

In the chaos, the seven-headed serpent had left the python jewel. I grabbed it, tucking it inside Neel's jacket, which I was still wearing.

Neel took my hand again in his steely grip and pulled me toward his body. "Hold on!" he ordered, and I wrapped one arm around his shoulder, holding Tuntuni with the other. Neel lunged, grabbing one of the branches that shot its way toward the sky.

"Wait a minute!" We were flying straight toward the stone ceiling, chaos and destruction all around us. Oh, I had a bad feeling about this. "Aren't we right under the . . ."

"When I say so, you both take a big breath!" Neel commanded. "One . . . two . . ."

But he didn't even have a chance to count to three, because the tree trunk charged a huge hole in the ceiling of the underground cavern, and lake water poured into the room, drowning the snakes. And, oh yeah, us.

We were underwater. I panicked in the swirling tempest and tried to kick away from Neel with my legs, toward what I guessed was the surface of the lake. But Neel held on to me. I fought him, panicking. I couldn't breathe. I couldn't even see which way was up. My lungs were going to explode.

Air.

Oh, I needed air.

CHAPTER 22

A Princess's Tears

I shook my head. The pressure on my lungs was too much. I was going to drown. I didn't want to die like this. I had to get air . . . had . . . to . . . get . . .

With a burst, the tree branch Neel was hanging on to cleared the surface of the water. I gasped big breaths into my lungs.

I breathed.

I breathed.

I breathed.

The air tasted so sweet. I would never take the simple act of breathing for granted again.

The tree deposited us on the shore, its branch acting like an enormous hand. As soon as we tumbled off, the branches kept shooting upward and outward. The banyan's roots stretched and grew until the entire surface of the lake was gone. And with it, the underworld kingdom was buried without a doorway to the upper realm. Where the lake had been, with its magic door, was now a majestic banyan tree.

Neel and I lay side by side near the tree's roots, panting.

"We're alive!" Neel's eyes glowed in a way that made me feel a little dizzy.

"You don't need to sound so surprised." I groaned, trying to sit up. My entire body ached like I'd been through some giant car wash. Except without a car. I felt all vomit-y again.

"Dark energy!" Neel stretched his arms, cracked his neck, and then began wringing out his shirt. "Dang, that's some powerful stuff in Chhaya Devi's shadows."

"Dark what?" My breath was still jagged and hurt my raw throat. My hair was plastered to me, but I couldn't find the strength to brush it from my eyes.

I couldn't help but resent Neel, who looked almost chipper now. There was something really annoying about a boy who never seemed tired, even after fighting a passel of poisonous snakes, then getting half drowned.

"Dark energy. It's the energy that helps the universe keep expanding. You might call it a part of the universal life force."

That sounded vaguely familiar.

"My Baba always tells me we're all connected by energy—trees, wind, animals, people, everything." I tried to get my ragged breathing under control. "He says that life energy is a kind of river flowing through the universe."

"And that our souls are just a bit of that river water held inside the clay pitcher of our bodies?" Neel smiled at my surprise. "Yeah, I know that story too. They say that when our bodies give out, that's just the pitcher breaking, pouring what's inside back into the original stream of universal souls."

"So no one's soul is ever really gone," I finished, repeating the words that Baba had said to me so often.

"Yup." Neel nodded. "It's the same idea that governs Chhaya Devi's shadows. When unleashed, there's nothing more powerful than the desire of nature to reunite with the universal soul."

I was about to ask Neel to explain some more, when I noticed the still, yellow body a couple of feet away.

"Tuntuni!"

The little bird wasn't moving at all. His wings were dark with water, and his head and beak were at a funny angle. Panic sent energy shooting through my cramped muscles. I half crawled, half scrambled over to where his tiny form lay on the ground.

I shook him, calling his name. The poor thing just flopped in my hands. I tried looking for a pulse (did birds have pulses?) but couldn't find one. My own heart fluttered alarmingly in panic. Where was a phone to dial 911 when I needed it! I started to do CPR, pumping his little yellow chest with two fingers. Problem was, the only CPR I'd ever learned was from a hospital TV show.

"He might be gone, Kiran," Neel murmured. He touched the bird's feathery head. "Returned to the universal stream of souls."

"I won't let him die! He saved our lives!" I wailed, but then I noticed Tuni's chest was moving—although very slightly—on its own. I didn't know what else to do except to cradle him in my lap, stroking his feathery head. His breathing was uneven, now rapid, now stopped entirely. He made a strange choking sound, and then the movement in his chest slowed down even further.

"Kiran," Neel said, but I ignored him, rocking and cooing to the bird in my arms.

Within a few seconds, I realized that Tuntuni's breathing had stopped altogether.

No, no, no.

"Kiran," Neel said again. This time he put a gentle hand on my shoulder.

"He can't die!" I cried. "He can't!"

Everything crashed in on me. Being away from home. Inviting Neel's mom into the kingdom. Fighting that awful snake in the dark. Coming face-to-face with my über-awful birth brothers and father. The ticking clock on my real parents' lives. My chest burned until I thought I would explode. And then it happened.

I started to cry. Not just cry, but sob, complete with pathetic bleating noises. My eyes stung, my throat caught. And that doorway in my chest that I'd kept tightly shut for so long burst open, releasing everything that I'd stuffed inside. Salty tears poured down my face, mingling with the lake water on the bird's body.

But Neel didn't laugh or point or even say useless platitudes about how the bird had lived a full life. How everything would be okay. He just sat there in my presence, letting me be sad. He just was.

And then the most remarkable thing happened. The stone-still bird took a shuddering breath. He stirred, and grew warm in my arms. I watched, stunned, as Tuntuni opened his eyes.

"What should you buy a bird?" he chirped weakly.

"He's alive!"

"Looks like it." Neel looked at me with a curious expression. "He's alive."

Tuni coughed and sputtered, shaking his soaked wings dry. "Something cheep!"

I laughed in relief. If Tuni was telling bad jokes, he was going to be okay. I hugged the bird to me until he started to protest, and I put him down.

"Let's get out of here, numskulls!" Tuni croaked weakly. "Before those snakes figure out how to come back!"

"We can't." I looked around wildly. "I don't know where the horses are!"

"You still have the python jewel, right?" Neel asked.

It took me a couple moments because my fingers were still numb. Neel helped me struggle out of his sopping jacket, and finally we pulled out the python jewel from the pocket. The light from the magic stone illuminated the dark forest.

I heard the flapping of large wings. Like some kind of a beacon, the jewel had called the horses from wherever they'd been hiding. Snowy and Midnight trod their way through the banyan tree roots, neighing and tossing their manes.

"You couldn't just have told me to take out the jewel sooner?" I said as Snowy snarfled my ear with a wet nose. "There's fresh clothes in the saddlebags!"

"I'm sorry; I was a bit preoccupied watching you heal Tuntuni."

"I didn't heal him!" Where did Neel get *that* idea? "He just got better on his own."

"If you say so."

"I do." I scuttled off, shaking with wet and cold, to go change behind a distant tree.

After I was in dry clothes, I felt almost myself again. I pulled out Ma's map. In the light of the python jewel, we had no trouble reading it. The decoding trick was actually easy. You just had to shine the jewel at the paper, then put your eye up to the back of it, so you were viewing the map through the prisms of the python jewel's surface. Just like that, the blank sheet was covered with the recognizable symbols on a map.

"Look, some kind of body of water—a sea—separates us from the Maya Mountains."

I stared at the paper. The writing on it was actually *moving*. Where, just a second ago, had been the lake entrance to the underworld kingdom was now the drawing of a huge tree. And, if I wasn't mistaken, there were also two little human figures and a bird next to two creatures that looked like winged horses.

Neel was unfazed. "*You are here*," he said, pointing at the shorter of the two human figures. "And the sea we have to cross is"—he dragged his finger not a long distance on the map—"here."

"And then over the sea to the Maya Mountains, easy!" I slung my quiver on my back.

"As long as the mountains don't move again before we can get there," Tuntuni mumbled. "Or if we don't get eaten by sea monsters. Or catch our deaths of pneumonia . . ."

"Your secret's out, Tuni." I picked up the bird and put him on my shoulder. "You're not as much of a grump as you pretend to be."

"Oh, yes, I am!" squawked the bird. But he puffed out his feathers in pleasure.

Neel rolled his eyes at the both of us as he tugged on Midnight's reins. "Come on, boy, let's go!"

CHAPTER 23

The Ruby Red Sea

We were on our way to the Ruby Red Sea, when something else Neel said in the Serpent King's throne room came back to me. We rode side by side, but I still had to shout a little to make myself heard over the wind.

"Hey, Neel, what was that other thing you said about my . . . I mean, the Serpent King? You said he was my dark matter? Is that the same thing as dark energy?"

"Nah, dark matter's a whole other mysterious force." Neel clicked his tongue at Midnight, who kept straining at the bit, trying to gallop faster. "In your dimension, dark matter's the invisible presence that surrounds galaxies. Your scientists can't see it, except sometimes like a halo around star systems."

"And that relates to the Serpent King how?"

"Dark matter has this incredible gravitational pull," Neel explained. "It wants to incorporate everything into itself. Think about how badly the Serpent King wanted to draw everything into himself. Your brother-snakes. You."

"There is no light without the darkness," Tuntuni chirped from my shoulder. "No darkness without the light."

It was the same thing the merchant of shadows had said to Neel. She'd also said that Neel had to face his shadow self but not get pulled into the darkness. I guessed the same was true for me. My biological parents had been invisible my whole life—but hovering around me like a dark halo even as Ma and Baba filled my life with light. And now that dark pull had brought me back to this place, threatening to extinguish my parents' light forever.

I couldn't ask anything else because we had already gotten to the edge of the sea. As we landed and dismounted the horses, I noticed there was a long line of colorful barges on the shore of the lapping water, carved and painted to look like peacocks. Neel pulled the barge closest to us in more securely onto the land.

"Can't the horses just fly us over?"

Neel shook his head, pointing to a sign that read:

PFDBMHNFZ

Then in smaller letters under it:

Pakkhiraj, Flying Demons, Bird Man, and Helicocroc No-Fly Zone

"Another no-fly zone, huh?" I remembered the Mandhara Mountain.

Neel nodded. "Any land mass that tends to move is a no-fly zone. There've been cases of flying horses getting trapped in the space between here and there if they're flying when the land under them decides to shift around."

"And I guess I don't really want to know what a Helicocroc is, huh?"

Tuntuni shuddered. "Just be glad, Princess, they can't fly here."

Neel heaved the golden and silver spheres out of Midnight's saddlebags and into the barge, while I packed what food and supplies we had left into my backpack. As we worked, I picked up the conversation from before.

"I don't get it, Neel. Is the Kingdom Beyond Seven Oceans and Thirteen Rivers some kind of version of outer space? Back in the stables, I think I saw something really weird in your mother's mouth . . ."

"Like planets and moons and stuff?" His smile was twisted and didn't really reach his eyes. "Like I said before, it's all really complicated to explain. That's why we call people from your dimension 2-Ds. Most people from there can't imagine that there are a lot of realities that exist at the same time. That one thing can have multiple forms. That the difference between inner space and outer space might just be an illusion."

I remembered a Shady Sadie the Science Lady show about how our reality might just be one of many, and that these parallel dimensions might be like a bunch of vibrating strings in a row—each dimension clueless about the existence of the others. But even though I'd heard about it before, it was still really hard to imagine. Just trying to think about it hurt my brain.

But then something else struck me. "So if we don't get to my parents in time"—I gulped—"they really will get swallowed into a black hole?"

"You could say that. Every time a spell collapses, it gives birth to a new rakkhosh from a well of dark energy. The amount of time that takes varies—usually rakkhosh are born the night of a new moon. And when they're born . . ." Neel trailed off. "Well, let's just say, they're hungry."

"So what are we waiting for? Let's go!"

Before I got into the peacock barge, I hugged Snowy's muzzle.

"I'll miss you, Tushar Kona," I murmured, using his real name.

And then, as clearly as if the horse were speaking to me, I heard his voice in my mind.

Don't get killed, Princess. I really like you.

"Okay, I'll try not to get killed," I whispered, tickling Snowy's ears.

"Are you talking to your horse?" Tuntuni made a cuckoo gesture with his wing, drawing circles at the side of his head. "Isn't that a little wacka wacka?"

"Look who's talkin'," muttered Neel.

And with that, we pushed offshore in our peacock barge, waving good-bye to our loyal horses.

The full, red moon hung high in the sky, beaming down on us with an eerie light. The tides were on our side, propelling the little boat forward on the water. We didn't have to row, but Neel steered us straight with the wooden rudder. To balance out the long barge, I sat at the far front end, with the golden and silver spheres in the middle. Tuntuni plunked himself in my lap and fell asleep.

As we floated along, something strange began to happen. Just like I could hear Snowy's thoughts in my mind, I felt a buzzing all around me, as if something—the sky, the sea, the very air—were speaking to me.

No, it's the moon.

"Did you say something, Neel?"

"Hmm?" he called from the back of the boat.

Look at the water to see my reflection, Daughter.

The dark red moon was enormous in the mirrorlike surface of the sea.

"Mother?" I whispered, barely believing it.

I have been a poor mother to you, my little piece of the moon . . .

The voice sounded so sad. Did she know what we'd just been through?

"The underworld kingdom," I started. "We buried the lake . . ."

He will rise again, I fear, the moon replied. *Until then, Daughter, you have freed me of my obligation. And this month on the night of no moon, when I come down to Earth in my human form, I can visit you.*

My birth mother could come down to Earth on the night of the new moon! It couldn't be a coincidence that was the same amount of time I had to find my parents before they became baby-demon food.

The sea wind whipped my hair and the salt water stung my cheeks. I looked back at Neel, who was staring ahead, steering the boat into the dark water. My eyes fell on the surface of the sea, and I started. Was I seeing what I thought I was seeing?

The moon shone even more brightly than before, making the surface of the water shimmer as if made of bobbing red rubies. Tentatively, I ran my fingers in the sea. Then I scooped my hand back into the boat.

Clunk, clink, thunk.

I didn't leave your father's kingdom entirely empty-handed, Daughter. These are your birthright.

I scooped my hand along the sea again.

"What was that?" Neel called.

I didn't know what to say. At my feet glimmered dozens of bloodred rubies I'd just plucked from the water's surface. Wordlessly, I held up one of the stones. The night was dark, but in the glow of the python jewel, the ruby shimmered.

"Where did you get that?"

I pointed at the sea. With a grin, Neel started scooping in fistfuls of rubies himself.

At the sound of all the clunking, Tuni woke up.

"Cross ruby seas full of love beneath the dark red moon," he recited.

I slid the smooth jewels through my fingers. "Thank you," I whispered, "Mother."

You're welcome, Daughter. I'm afraid you'll need them in the terrible place you're going.

"We're not going straight to Maya Pahar?" I felt a pit of dread growing in my stomach.

Check the map, the moon said before disappearing behind a gray cloud.

In the back of the boat, Neel whooped as he scooped up more and more rubies.

"Watch it," I called. The boat sunk pretty close to the surface of the water. "We're heavy enough as it is."

I took Ma's map from my pocket, and peered at it in the python jewel's light.

"Oh no . . . the thing's shape-shifting again."

"Look, we're approaching shore!" Neel pointed to a vague gray line on the horizon.

"Neel," I warned, "according to the map, that's not the Maya Mountains anymore."

The lines on the paper finally stopped moving. The little bird peeked over my shoulder. "Okay, now the Maya Mountains are on the other side of . . ." Tuni stopped. He made a choking noise, and discharged several yellow tail feathers.

"What?" Neel asked.

"That shoreline in front of us is definitely not the Maya Mountains." My stomach was in knots.

"What is it, then?"

I turned around to face him, my eyes wide. "It's Demon Land!"

CHAPTER 24

The Land of Demons

We pulled the boat onshore as quietly as we could, hiding it beneath some dried palm fronds. Neel made a sort of sling with the silk scarf around his waist, and tucked the golden and silver spheres into it. If the whole situation weren't so dire, I would have made a joke about his bowling ball babies. Instead, I slung my backpack, bow, and quiver onto my shoulders in silence. We both stuffed our pockets and packs full of the rubies we'd gathered from the sea. We didn't speak once, except in looks and gestures. This was bad. Really, really bad.

I tucked the python jewel inside Neel's jacket, which I was still wearing, so there was only the light from the stars to guide our way. The moon seemed to have disappeared permanently behind the clouds. I couldn't blame her. She probably didn't want to watch her daughter get eaten by a horde of hungry rakkhosh.

The thin strip of beach was empty, except for piles of rotting animal carcasses. I wondered if some of those skeletal remains might actually be human. Beyond the beach, there was evidence of wanton destruction everywhere. Trees pulled out by their roots, burned remains of wood and paper, candy wrappers, gigantic balls of chewed gum, empty soda cans—many of them half-eaten with teeth marks all over them. The trees hung heavy with goopy body fluids—snot or spit or boogers, I couldn't tell, but their rancid odor made my eyes water.

"Hygiene is clearly not a priority here!" Tuntuni sputtered.

We crept as quickly as we could through the woods at the edge of the shore. There was the long-dead corpse of a vulture hanging from one of the trees. I shuddered, swatting away a sticky string hanging from a branch.

I saw the remains of a lawn mower that someone had tried to snack on. And what was that other thing behind the rock? A front-loading washing machine with a gigantic bite out of its side?

"Some gourmet tastes your relatives have," I said before I could stop myself. Nice going, Kiran.

Neel didn't answer, but even in the darkness I could

tell he was scowling. "Look, they'll all eat me as easily as they'll eat you."

"Except for your fangirls, of course." I tried for a lighter tone, but Neel didn't look like he was in the mood to laugh.

To our left, something was crashing through the forest. We all froze. A raucous, bawdy, and yet horrifying singing filled the bitter air.

"Hob, gum, goom, geer! Pass the blood! Pass the beer!
Hob, goom, gum, geet! We want to feast on human
meat!"

The noise came from a little too nearby—just beyond a clump of palm trees.

"Run!" Neel yanked me behind him as he dashed through the trees. I kept up as much as I could. My arms got scratched by hanging branches, and my feet bruised by roots sticking out of the ground, but I ran like my life depended on it. Which, basically, it did.

"Princess, help!" Tuntuni called from behind me.

I ran back. The bird had flown straight into a net of demon goo as thick as a spider's web. I tried to untangle his wings, but couldn't.

"Neel!" I screamed.

The prince came running, and together we struggled to pluck the little bird out of the gloppy mess.

"We don't have time for this!" Neel drew his sword.

"What are you doing?" For a second, I panicked. He wouldn't hurt the bird, would he?

"Getting us out of here!" Neel cried. He sliced Tuni out of the goo and thrust the tangled bird into my arms. "Let's go!"

"Oh, my beautiful feathers! Oh, the horror! The stench!" the sticky bird wailed in my arms. But I kept running. The band of drunken demons was getting ever closer. And they had a serious case of the munchies.

"Gob gaam! Khom khoo!
We want some human stew!"

"There!" I pointed.

We'd entered a clearing. An old deserted cabin stood in its center. The door of the cabin was kind of rickety, but the walls seemed strong enough.

We dashed into the dark building just in time. With a thrashing of bush and tree, the demons came into the clearing themselves.

"Thakata-thakata-dang-dang-dort!
We love hunting meaty sport!"

I helped Neel prop the cabin's broken table, chairs, and a cabinet against the front door. Unfortunately, there was still a small opening in the frame where the hinge had come off.

"We're in luck." He peeked through the opening into the moonlit clearing. "They're khokkosh."

"What's that?" As my eyes adjusted to the darkness, I tried to shake the remaining strands of demon goop off of poor Tuntuni, who still looked shell-shocked.

"You remember how bright the rakkhosh we met in New Jersey was?"

"He was an idiot. He tried to eat my toaster."

"Yeah, well, these khokkosh make that guy look like Albert Einstein." Neel's face was grim. "One of the few 2-D geniuses who recognized the multiplicity of dimensions."

Okay, what? But there wasn't time now to ask Neel about that. I watched as he ran around the small cabin, grabbing the oil lamps that were littered here and there.

"If they're so dumb, then why do you still look so worried?"

"They may be stupid," he muttered as he lit each lamp, "but they're strong. And obviously, hungry."

I took a peek through the door opening myself. Yipes. The clearing was thick with the ferocious khokkosh. They were smaller than rakkhosh, and more animal-like. They had yellow skin, crooked teeth, and pointy ears that made them look like a cross between giant rabbits and enormous bats. Their claws seemed plenty sharp, and their long, skinny arms were twisted with stringy muscles.

"Don't say anything," Neel whispered. "Just do what I do."

I nodded.

Tuni let out a low, soap-opera-style wail. "Oh, the humanity! The humanity, I say! We're all going to die, we're all going to die," the yellow bird cried, falling to the floor with a wing perched dramatically over his head.

Neel and I stood still, our every muscle tensed. My straining ears could even make out the snuffling and shuffling as someone, or something, walked toward the house.

It was all I could do not to jump when a horrible, nasal voice called from just outside the door. "Hub, hum, hai, hower! Who's awake at this dark hour?"

"We are hungry rakkhosh!" Neel growled.

At that the khokkosh retreated from the door. We could hear them whispering to one another from a few feet away.

"Huum-humm hoam! Let's plunder and roam!" said one group.

"Gumm-guum gaam! Let's go home!" said another.

But they didn't leave. The khokkosh gathered away from the door to engage in some more whispering and negotiating. One, who I assumed was their spokes-demon, a stupid-looking guy with a scar over his eye and a half-chewed-off ear, walked up to the cabin again.

"Goom-goom, doom-dite! If you're really rakkhosh, turn off the light!"

"No we won't!" Neel held the lamps high even closer to the door and gestured to me to do the same.

At my raised eyebrows, he hissed, "Everyone knows khokkosh can't see in the light!"

"I'm sooo sorry!" I whisper-yelled. "I must have missed that lecture in demonology class!"

There was some more murmuring from outside as the demons consulted one another to figure out their next move.

"Shoom-shaam, hoom-hails! If you're really rakkhosh, show us your nails!"

Neel put down the lamps and picked up a bunch of arrows from my quiver. He shoved the points through the opening. Tuntuni handed me a few arrows with his beak, and when I stuck them through the hole, I was gratified to hear the spokes-demon yelp.

"Oh, my mother's sainted fart! This demon's nails really smart!"

There was more mumbling from outside, and even the sound of a fistfight. Someone seemed to be biting someone else. The spokes-demon approached the cabin again, this time with an even stupider-looking fellow with a wart the size of a watermelon growing out of his forehead.

"Dum-doom, ding-dung! If you're really rakkhosh, show us your tongue!"

With only a second of hesitation, Neel thrust the blade of his sword through the opening, making both the spokes-demon and his assistant screech.

"Oh, my uncle's rotten guts! That rakkhosh's tongue really cuts!"

This time, a whole troop came up to the doorway. "Gob-goob, flim-flit! If you're really rakkhosh, let's see your spit!" They chanted in one voice.

"What do we do now?" I moaned.

Neel looked desperately around, mumbling, "Spit, spit."

The khokkosh outside the door began shrieking and howling. "Let's see your spit! Let's see your spit!"

A few of the bolder ones began banging and scratching on the door. A few more seconds and they just might realize we were lying, and decide to bash the door down.

"Anytime now, Neel!" I'm not ashamed to say I was kinda freaking out.

The noise outside was getting louder and louder, and the wood of the door was starting to splinter from the force of the demons' blows. What were we going to do? Neel was still dashing around the hut, looking for some-thing that could substitute for rakkhosh spit. I looked desperately around too, and then my eyes alighted on the oil lamps.

"Neel!" I pointed. As he figured out what I meant, he started to grin.

I mouthed the words, "On three," and he nodded. On my count, we picked up the lamps and spattered all the hot oil through the opening. The khokkosh howled, dousing the spots where the oil had burned them with their tails.

"Oh, my grandpa's nose rings! That rakkhosh spit really stings!"

This seemed to be the last straw for the khokkosh, who didn't even consult one another before running out of the clearing.

"Gob-gum! Dum-dack! There's rakkhosh here, let's go back!"

As the monsters ran pell-mell out of the clearing, we all sank to the floor of the hut. We were safe, for the moment at least.

It took a couple minutes for everyone's breathing to go back to normal. Neel was the first to recover. He glanced around the shack. "This is as good a place as any to hide out for the night. In the morning, we'll have to find my grandmother, to see if she can get us to the border safely."

"Your *grandmother*?" I asked. "Wait a minute, I thought all demons came from some faucet of evil or something."

"Well, not all, obviously." Neel pointed at his own chest. "But yeah, most full rakkhosh are born from wells of dark energy."

"So how is she your grandmother?"

"Come on, your mom doesn't have to be the one who gave birth to you, but the one who raised you. I'd think you of all people would understand that. My Ai-Ma is the one who raised my mother."

It was hard to imagine the Rakkhoshi Queen once being a baby demon in someone's warty arms.

"Some nanas knit or cook; his eats flesh!" Tuntuni quipped.

"Don't start," Neel snapped, "unless you want me to give you to her for lunch." He turned to me. "Listen, you get some rest. I'll take the first watch."

CHAPTER 25

To Grandmother's House

It was the gray morning when I at last opened my eyes. I realized that Neel hadn't woken me up to take over the watch.

"You looked tired," he explained, yawning himself.

Neel hadn't slept all night but was still pretty energetic as he gathered our things, including the golden and silver spheres, cradled like twin babies in his makeshift sling. This morning they were buzzing and humming, letting off a red glow and the warm smell of cotton and honey.

"They're happy to be together," I said.

"Make new orbs, but keep the old; one is silver and the other gold," Tuni sang.

"Tuni," I warned, "maybe it's a little too soon."

"You are so spherical, so round and spherical, you make me hap-py when rakkhosh stay," the bird continued, ignoring me.

"Hmm . . . wonder if my grandma would fancy some Tuni-bird stew," Neel snapped. Immediately, the bird stopped singing.

"Come on, let's go."

It was a long walk over a rubbish-filled stretch of land—broken yo-yos, half-eaten peanut butter sandwiches, a few scary-looking skulls, and more than a few smelly old socks, none of them with a proper partner. As we walked, we saw no one.

"They're mostly nocturnal," Neel said.

"Like the snakes," I offered. Neel gave me a half smile. He seemed to get what I was saying. That my biological relatives were just as terrible as his.

We were heading for a giant gorge between two steep mountains on either side. When we got closer, gooseflesh broke out on my arms. I wasn't sure if it was coming from the gorge itself, but the air was filled with an almost-deafening rumbling sound. It sounded disturbingly like some very large creature snoring.

"We're almost there." Neel stopped walking to look critically at me. "You're wearing my jacket, so that's good."

Neel picked up Tuntuni and, to my surprise, sat him right on my head.

"Hey, what's the big idea?" I asked as the bird squawked his surprise too.

"As much as I don't mind if my Ai-Ma makes chicken stew out of the bird, I think I'd better try to get him home in one piece. And he'll be safer out of sight." Neel pulled out a long cloth from his pocket and wound it around both Tuntuni and my hair, making a big, only slightly lumpy turban.

There were muffled sounds of Tuni squawking nervously. "How do chickens get strong?" Without waiting for an answer, the bird yelled out from inside the turban, "Eggs-ersize!"

"Chill, Tuni. We'll be all right." I patted my head. "Just try not to dig your claws in, okay?"

"How do crows stick together in a flock?" came the muffled question. And again, without waiting for an answer, the bird squawked, "Velcrow!"

"How did the dead chicken cross the road?" Neel snapped. "It didn't, because it was dead!"

That shut the bird up rather quickly.

Neel made a few more adjustments to my outfit, then stepped back, obviously satisfied with the results. "You'll pass."

I wasn't sure what I was passing *for*—a bird-containing turban certainly wasn't going to fool anyone into thinking I was a demon—but I was too exhausted to protest. Just like Tuntuni, if I wanted to make it out of Demon Land alive, I was going to have to trust Neel.

He reached into the food pouch at his waist and brought out a handful of dark seeds. "Keep these just in case she asks you to chew on anything," he said.

Chew on something? I wanted to ask but the prince kept walking. "Come on, we better get there before any of the other rakkhosh wake up."

We entered the gorge, and I realized that the awful snoring had been coming from here after all. Those horrible rumbling, shrieking, trilling noises were coming from the nose of an elderly rakkhoshi who was fast asleep in the riverbed.

"Ai-Ma! Ai-Ma!" Neel called, gesturing to me to stay behind him. "It's your grandson, Neelkamal!"

The old crone sat up mid-snore, and then came flying at us. Her knobby arms and legs were flapping, her gray hair was streaming behind her, and her near toothless mouth was fixed in a wide grin.

"Oh, my sugar plum yum-yum, my lollipop dum-dum, my molasses-sweet grandbaby, oh me, oh my, oh, come and give your old Ai-Ma a kiss!"

"She can't see very well, and she can't hear very well," Neel hissed as the old woman approached. "And she can't remember very well." I felt my heart lighten, then fall again as Neel added, "But unfortunately she can still smell really well."

The old rakkhoshi crone bent far down, and standing high on his toes, Neel gave her a gingerly kiss on her hairy cheek. Then Ai-Ma began to sniff the air like a crazed hunting dog catching the whiff of a fox.

"Grandbaby, my sweet boo-boo, have you brought a pet? A human being to play with? A gift for your poor Ai-Ma?"

My turban shuddered. Neel slapped it. I didn't love the thought that Tuni or I might be considered a delicious gift, like a box of cookies, for Neel's grandmother.

"Ai-Ma!" Neel exclaimed. "What are you saying? This is my brother, Lalkamal, and he's your grandson too!"

The crone reached for me, but, feeling my turban first, withdrew her hand.

"The brother of my gum-gum must be my grandbaby too," the old crone mused. "But why does he smell so much like a human pup?"

Neel's grandmother drew herself up to her full height, and then, randomly, snorted out some iron pellets from her left nostril.

"If you are my family true, here's some iron pellets for you to chew," she sang, handing the booger-covered iron pieces to me.

I had no choice but to take the revolting things. I slipped the pellets into my jacket pocket, and substituted the seeds Neel had given me. I chewed them as loud as I could. Ma would be horrified at my table manners, but Ma would be even more horrified if I was this old biddy's main course for dinner.

Ai-Ma smiled, but kept sniffing the air. "Is old Ai-Ma's nose fooling her? Why do I smell human flesh? And mixed in with a nice roasted chicken?"

My turban muttered and wobbled again, but I gave it a good punch.

"How can my grandbaby be so small? Let me see your eyeball!" Neel's grandmother demanded.

I looked in shock at Neel, who handed me the golden ball from his sling. I held it out to the crone, who felt the bowling-ball-sized object, and smiled.

"Oh, boys, what has become of your Ai-Ma? Why do I still smell delectable meats?" The old crone's mouth was watering, and giant drops of spittle rained down from her mouth like a fountain. She slurped loud and long.

"If of my flesh you are a part, why, let me see your beating heart!"

"Ai-Ma!" Neel protested.

But I had an idea. I grabbed the biggest ruby from my pocket. It was the size of a small lunch box, and gritty with sea salt and sand. I rubbed it off the best I could and shoved it toward the old rakkhoshi.

"Anything for you, Ai-Ma!" I said in a low voice.

The crone held the ruby up to her eyes, and murmured, "So hard and large and red, and still I want my grandbaby's head? Oh, what have I done, what did I do? You must be my grandson true!"

Returning the ruby to me, Ai-Ma grabbed us each in one of her gangly arms and drew us up to her chest, crooning, "Oh, my darling pom-poms, my shriveled beanpoles, my scrawny-crow grandbabies!" Ai-Ma rocked and sang. "I am Ai-Ma, mother of mother, for Lalu and Neelu, there is no other!"

I held my breath as the crone cooed at us. It was more than a little disturbing. Finally, she put us down.

"Come, my honey-drenched num-nums, my caramel boo-boos. It is time for Grammy to finish her nap. Neelu, you rub old Ai-Ma's feet, and, Lalu, you pull out her gray hairs."

Ew. Really? I grimaced, but Neel gave me a warning glance. It was obviously too dangerous to do otherwise. The prince took a big bottle of mustard oil and began rubbing the crone's warty feet, while I sat by her head, massaging her greasy scalp and pulling out long gray hairs one by one. They were hard, the texture of steel guitar strings, plus they were slippery, so it wasn't easy. A few times, I had to use both hands, with my foot on her head for leverage. Ai-Ma didn't seem to notice, but smiled blissfully and kept her eyes shut, like we were giving her some kind of five-star spa treatment.

Her snores shook the gorge for about half an hour, but then, with a mighty shake, she was awake again. Ai-Ma snorted and hacked, then asked, "What can I do for my grandbabies who have traveled so long to visit me?"

"Oh, we couldn't ask for anything, Ai-Ma," Neel protested, still rubbing the noxious stuff into her feet. He stared at me with big eyes.

"Oh, no, how could we, Ai-Ma?" I added in my fake princely voice. My arms were aching from massaging the crone's head, and I had more than one cut on my hands from pulling her awful gray hairs.

Without warning, Ai-Ma sat up. Neel and I both tumbled off her.

"Oh, shame shame, puppy shame, all the donkeys know your name!" she protested. "How can this be? My grandbabies must have a gift from their Ai-Ma—I have prepared no food, I have no new clothes or toys to give you. Please, please do not embarrass an old woman. What can Ai-Ma give you?"

"Well, Ai-Ma," Neel suggested, "you could take us as far as the border of Demon Land."

"Done!" Ai-Ma promised, scooping us both into her giant arms.

The rakkhoshi walked us through the desert of Demon Land for seven days and eleven long nights. Her arms were large enough to be warty hammocks, and Neel and I each rested in the crook of an elbow. As comfortable as a warty hammock may sound, let me assure you it was hard traveling. The only trees on our path grew thorns or poisonous-looking pods. There was little water, even less food, and no respite. Ai-Ma grew tired once or twice, but I was so nervous of what would happen if she stopped, that I kept telling her stories from back home. Appropriately adapted for a demon, of course. In most of them, Jovi was a greedy khokkosh.

As we left the desert, I was shocked to see such wanton waste, filth, and destruction everywhere the rakkhosh had been. There were piles of Styrofoam cups, mountains of single-use drink bottles, and plastic cola six-pack holders that no one had bothered to cut through.

"Demon Land needs a better recycling program!" I protested. "Look at those plastic rings; if ducks get caught on them, they might choke and die, Ai-Ma!"

"Well, I certainly hope so," the old woman responded, her eyes a little glassy. Her long tongue was drooling like a dripping faucet on my turban, "Oh, grandbaby, forgive me, this nose of mine keeps making me think of roasted goose, partridge pie, chickadee stew!"

The turban almost jumped off my head in fright, but I held it on tightly.

After seeing almost no one on our long walk, we now approached a group of marauding rakkhosh, who were marching as they sang:

"Good flesh, warm flesh,
Toasted nice and sweet!
We'll suck their marrow, chew their bones,
And curry up their feet!"

"Old woman, what tasty morsels are these you carry?" the head rakkhosh asked, peering at us with all three of his bulging eyeballs.

Neel gulped audibly, and my own heart beat in time to Tuntuni's shudders on my head. Ai-Ma may have been half-deranged, besides being sweet on us in a twisted sort of a way, but these rakkhosh weren't. They weren't going to mistake me for a demon prince with an oversized, live turban. If Ai-Ma decided to hand us over, or got overpowered, we were goners.

Luckily, as Baba would say, Granny still had some chutz-pah left in her.

"Be gone, you fart-faces!" Ai-Ma shrieked, waving a knobby arm. "These are my darling grandbabies, and if you so much as break wind in their direction, my daughter the Rakkhoshi Queen will have your entrails stuffed with gold and made into necklaces!"

The other rakkhosh responded immediately.

"Oh, terribly sorry, ma'am," the head rakkhosh apolo-gized, bowing low as he backed away.

"Entirely our misunderstanding, madam," said the one with extra arms growing out of his chest.

"Unforgiveable, wretched thing to suggest," said a third demon, who had what looked like teeth for hair.

"Scram! Scat! Hato! Shoo!" Ai-Ma yelled, and they ran off in the other direction.

"Your mother's name sure packs a punch," I said under my breath to Neel.

He said nothing, but pointed ahead of him. We were finally approaching the border. We knew this because of the sign that read:

Thanks for Visiting Demon Land!
"The Bloodthirsty State"

State Symbol: The Razor Blade
State Flower: The Thorn
State Bird: The Vulture
State Song: "Meat, Glorious Meat"
100 million victims eaten daily

Be sure to visit again soon!
(Please drop by our gift shop for
a complimentary toothpick!)

With tears, hugs, and more than a few slobbery kisses, Ai-Ma let us down.

"Good-bye, my licorice toadstools, farewell, my candied beetle dungs, come back to visit your poor Ai-Ma soon!"

CHAPTER 26

The Maya Mountains

"I guess we're in the Mountains of Illusions."

It was hard to miss the drastic change of scenery. Instead of the carcass-filled, rubbish-strewn desert, we were now walking through rolling hills, the kind I'd never seen before. The colors were mesmerizing—shimmering blues, violets, yellows, magentas, and greens swirled all around us. In fact, it was hard to tell where the ground ended and the low-lying clouds began.

As soon as we were out of view from Demon Land, we stopped to rest. We drank our fill from a sweet turquoise-colored stream, and Neel helped me free Tuntuni from under my turban. The poor bird was half-comatose from fright and heat exhaustion, and crumpled next to me. It was great to feel my head again. The mist was cool and the air rushing down from the hills whistled through my hair.

"Now what?" I pulled out Ma's moving map and studied it through the python jewel. I was leaning against some pink grass that felt like cotton candy on my skin. Well, cotton candy minus the stickiness.

"I'm not sure." Neel peered at the map over my shoulder. "What was the next part of Tuni's stupid poem?"

I looked around to ask the bird, but he wasn't there. "Tuni?" The violet-colored trees had some kind of fluffy fruit hanging from them, and there were bushes with polka-dot magenta-and-orange leaves. But no bird.

Where was he? Our diminutive yellow companion was nowhere to be seen.

Neel and I walked down a steep hill, all the while calling Tuntuni's name. The swirling mist was thick around our feet. To my surprise, it also sparkled and made squeaking noises.

From a distance, we heard an odd little song,

"Ev-ry-thing
Is connected to
Ev-ry-thing,
But how?"

We followed Tuntuni's voice until we came upon sort of a valley, with folds of multicolored mist all around it. We floated, more than walked, through the silky atmosphere. There were shimmering lights everywhere—silver, yellow, hot red, intense blue. My body felt light and airy, like I had turned into cotton candy myself.

Then Tuni came into view, hanging from the branch of a nearby tree.

"What in blessed bison jewels is he going on about?" Neel muttered. Then he paused. "Are you seeing what I'm seeing?"

I caught my breath. The yellow bird was sitting on a sparkly branch that looked like it was covered in—could it be?—diamonds.

"On a diamond branch the golden bird must sing a blessed tune," I quoted.

"Actually, I don't think those are diamonds on that branch." Neel's wide, dark eyes turned to mine. "I think they're stars!"

Say what?

I took in the scenery around me—the swirling mist, the colors, the sparkling lights. I had a sudden flash to a video that Shady Sadie had shown on her science program about the Andromeda Nebula.

"Where *are* we?" I whispered.

A different voice, not Tuntuni's, but a man's, answered from very nearby.

"Why, it's a star nursery of course, young lady. Ze birth-place of baby stars."

Who said that? I saw no one. Then I looked up and realized Tuntuni wasn't alone after all. An old man with a turban and a white moustache sat cross-legged on a branch just above the bird's head. Or to be more accurate, the man levitated off the branch above Tuni's head.

"Your Brilliance!" Neel bowed. "It's an honor to finally meet you."

"The famous half-demon prince," said the man. "And this must be Princess Kiranmala!"

Tuntuni chirped in agreement. "Yes, Smartie-ji. This is them!"

I stared at Tuntuni, then at Neel. They knew this guy? And somehow, this floating stranger knew us?

The mist swirled around him, obscuring his features, but I couldn't shake the feeling that there was something really familiar about him. What was he, like, a yogi with ESP? A wise man, at least, from the way that Neel and Tuni were addressing him.

Not wanting to seem rude, I dropped an ungraceful curtsy. "Uh, hello, sir-ji."

"Can you help us, Your Brilliance? We need to find Kiran's parents and rescue my brother and friend"—here he indicated the gold and silver spheres hanging from his sling—"who are trapped by a curse."

But the wise man just smiled, adding even more crinkles to his already wrinkly face. "You arrived just in time for my next class. Find a seat! Find a seat! Quick now!" He clapped his hands gleefully, like our presence was the best treat he could receive.

From who knows where, there appeared a number of little colorful chairs attatched to desks, like the contents of a kindergarten classroom. From somewhere in the distance, a bell rang, and suddenly almost all of the seats filled up with sparkling orbs of light: little giggling, wiggling star-babies.

"Good morning, mein *star* pupils!" The wise man's singsong European accent made him seem familiar, but I couldn't place where I knew him from.

"Good mowning, pwofessor," the infant stars chorused back as Neel and I found the only two empty seats, near the back of the floating classroom. The chairs were ridiculously small, and the two of us barely squeezed ourselves into them, our knees all splayed out in awkward ways.

"Now let us say our morning pledge together," said the mysterious professor from his position on the branch. All the glowing star-children seemed to place their little hands over their unidentified middles. Even Tuntuni placed a yellow wing over his chest.

"We pledge allegiance to the element hydrogen, and also its partner, helium," chanted the little star-lings.

Neel and I giggled from the back row like we were the classroom delinquents. Luckily, no one seemed to hear us, and the stars kept pledging allegiance.

"And to the principle of nuclear fusion. Luminous light, born from dust, nebula to stars, red giants to supernova, white dwarf, neutron star, or black hole!"

"Very good, students! Gold stars for everyone!" The floating wise man clapped his hands again. The force of his pleasure turned him upside down, so that now he hung suspended, folded legs above, moustache and turban below.

From this awkward position, the teacher pulled down a rolling chart from the middle of the air. It showed a diagram illustrating the pupils' pledge—the life cycle of a star. He cleared his throat and waggled his bushy white eyebrows in my direction.

"Your parents, Princess, will soon be in danger of being swallowed forever by what you know as a black hole." The upside-down professor pointed with a yardstick at the end of the diagram.

"How do I save them?" I begged.

"Shall we tell her, pupils?" the professor singsonged as he spun himself right side up once again.

The baby stars laughed and shimmered. Pushing their chairs aside, they joined what I supposed were their hands and began dancing in a circle. Like a game of intersteller Ring Around the Rosie. Then they started singing:

"Red, red, red are all my clothes
Red, red, red, is all that I have
Why do I love all that is red?
Because my brother is a red giant."

The teacher waved his fingers in the air like he was conducting the music. "A nursery rhyme from my own youth!" he said.

"Lal?" Neel's voice rose suddenly in alarm, and I noticed, just as he did, that the golden sphere—Lal's sphere—was beginning to glow. It now looked far more red than golden. Red like his name. Red like the red giant a star becomes when it is in the process of dying.

"Your Brilliance," I began, but the wise man just shook his head, indicating that the stars were about to start singing again. They whirled in the other direction, faster than before, their bodies a dizzying display of light and energy against the multicolor backdrop of the nebula.

"White, white, white are all my clothes
White, white, white is all that I have
Why do I love all that is white?
Because my sister is a white dwarf."

"Mati!" And sure enough, the silver sphere in Neel's makeshift sling was now glowing with a bright white light. Both spheres were also pulsing strangely, the red-gold one looking like it was growing and the silver one like it was shrinking.

"What's happening, Genius-ji?" Neel shouted out, but Tuntuni pecked him on the head and squawked, "Raise your hand, raise your hand."

I felt like slapping the bird, but Neel obediently did as he was told, wiggling his hand in the air with impatience. Yet the old man ignored him, despite Neel's repeatedly calling out, "Sir, I have a question! Sir, I have a question!"

As the star pupils began their last verse, I felt my stomach do a double back handspring into a round-off layout, and not stick the landing.

"Black, black, black are all my clothes
Black, black, black is all that I have
Why do I love all that is black?
Because my parents got swallowed by a really evil
*   rakkhosh and then got lost forever and*
*   ever in a black ho-o-le!"*

"How do I stop that from happening?" I asked, but as it seemed to be recess in the star nursery now, the wise man couldn't hear me over his pupils' racket.

The star students were all tumbling about, tossing balls of poofy pink clouds, playing double-Dutch jump rope and what looked like hopscotch. One of the stars was asking another one riddles: "What's red, then white, then black all over?" it asked. The other pupil shouted out, "A dying star!"

In the meantime, the wise man sang out Tuni's meaningless song again, clapping in beat to the syllables.

"Ev-ry-thing
Is connected to
Ev-ry-thing,
But how?"

"But what should we do? We need your help here!" I blurted out in frustration. "Enough riddles, enough poems, enough songs with ominous meanings. I need some answers that make sense!"

"None of us can hide from who we really are," the professor said unhelpfully. He batted one of the round pink ball-clouds in our direction, making Neel's entire head invisible for a moment.

"What does that mean?"

"You must see yourself in the birthplace of darkness. You must travel through the darkness to find your inner light." The wise man picked up a few sparkling crystals from the branch and started juggling some stars who were even smaller than his pupils. They giggled and squealed in glee as he tossed them in the air. "Darkness and light must always be kept in a fine balance."

I shot to my feet. "What darkness? The spell holding my parents?"

The old man opened his palm to show me one perfect shimmering orb. "Stars are not only spells, but a deeper magic still: the wishes and dreams nurtured in the deepest places of our souls."

He blew the star out of his hand like it was a bit of dandelion fluff, and watched it float to another cluster of playing stars a few feet away, who gathered up the baby star in their game. The man spun in the air so that now he was levitating again with his crossed legs up, and his twinkling blue eyes down.

"Kiran!" Neel warned. He showed me the sling. Lal's sphere was now entirely red and vibrating ferociously. I could also swear it was double its original size. Mati's sphere, in the meantime, was glowing bright white but was now about the size of a large grapefruit.

"What's happening to them?" I demanded of the professor.

"The prince and the stable maiden—they wanted to be together, however that was possible, yes?"

I considered that. Lal and Mati, they did want to be together. But not like this, surely?

"And your parents, Princess, they wanted you to discover who you are, to be proud of where you came from, yes?"

He was right on the money there. That's the only thing my parents ever wanted. But had they imagined they would have to risk their lives for it to happen?

"These wishes cannot happen without consequences. Darkness is the night side of light. The forgotten brother. The exiled self."

Now that hit a little close to home. Was he talking about Neel—the forgotten brother—and me—the exiled self? Were we the dark matter to Lal and Mati's friendship, to my parents' deepest wishes?

The old guy kept spinning, so that now he was lounging sideways in the air, his fingers twirling his white moustache.

"It is the separations between darkness and light that are the illusion, my dear." He waggled his bushy brows. "Illusion like the ring you see when light tries to travel around the dark matter in its path. Remember this, my dear, remember my ring and you will find what you are looking for."

"I don't understand," I began.

But he was singing again, "Ev-ry-thing is connected to ev-ry-thing."

"But how?" I asked.

"Eggs-actly! Perfectly put!" He pulled off his turban, and made an old-fashioned bow in my direction. "Chase the giant, cradle the dwarf, and find the well of dark energy before it folds in on itself and those you love are lost forever. But hurry!"

Then, just like that, he disappeared.

CHAPTER 27

A Well of Darkness

Why was the wise man so familiar? That crazy hair going in all different directions, that accent, that moustache. Oh my gosh!

"Was that who I think it was?"

Tuntuni squawked and nodded his yellow head. "The one and only Einstein-ji."

"The physicist from your world whose name is practically synonymous with intelligence," Neel added.

I swallowed my spit the wrong way and choked. Tuni had to swat me on the back with his wing for me to regain my breath. "Albert Einstein?" I finally managed. "Albert Einstein is our golden bird on a diamond branch?"

"He was one of the few scientists from your dimension

to understand the seven parallel worlds, the thirteen simul-
taneous universes."

"But isn't he, like . . ." I paused. "Dead?"

"Well, technically, yes. At least, in the way we understand death. Remember, this is a guy who unlocked the
secrets of space, time, and a bunch of other things I don't
even know about. It's he who first predicted dark matter to
begin with."

But I didn't have time to process this mind-blowing
piece of information, because the red and white spheres
were making noises, groaning and squeaking. The red one
hopped out of Neel's sling on its own, and began rolling up
the hill and out of the star nursery.

"Wait, Lal, stop!" Neel yelled, chasing after him.

I had no option but to run after Neel, and what I was
soon realizing was Lal manifesting into a red giant star. As
Neel ran after his brother the red giant, the white sphere,
which had shrunk now to the size of a nectarine, slipped
out of his sling and began rolling down the hill toward me.

"Mati!" Neel yelled, but I dived for the rolling star-
sphere, catching it and holding it in my palm like it was one
of those crazy predict-your-future Magic 8 Balls.

"Got her!"

We ran after the red giant, who now looked less like Lal,

or even a sphere, as opposed to a huge mass of pulsating solar energy. Although no less scary, this was no fee-fi-fo-fum kind of giant, but something else entirely. It was as if a huge forest inferno suddenly grew some legs and began running across the landscape.

In fact, as the red giant ran, he wreaked havoc all around him. The fuzzy purple trees of the nebula caught on fire, exploding in cracking cascades of flames.

"Lal! Stop!" Neel called, but the red giant didn't hear him. This wasn't Lal anymore but something beyond human. He was a solar phenomenon.

We ran through walls of flames exploding over the formerly azure plains. Branches cracked and fell too near my head for comfort. Where was the red giant going? How would we survive chasing a monster essentially made out of fire?

The white dwarf in my hands buzzed, as if with worry for Lal too. I shook it desperately.

"Mati," I called. "If there's something of you left in there, help us. I need to save my parents before they get swallowed by the spell turning into a black hole. But I don't know where they are, and I don't know how long they have."

Tick, tick, tick . . .

Amazingly, some part of Mati must have heard me. The ticktocking noise was coming from the white dwarf. Its face resembled something like a clock now. But the labels on the clock's face were like nothing like I'd ever seen before. They were the phases of a star cycle—nebula, star, red giant, white dwarf, supernova, and black hole. And the clock's single hand was pointing right at the third position, the red giant.

"Where is he going?" Neel called out desperately. "Lal! Bro! Stop! It's me! Dude, it's me!"

But the red giant kept running, setting everything in its path on fire. Neel and I were running side by side, a charred-looking Tuntuni on his shoulder, and the white-dwarf-slash-clock in my hand. The mist was getting thicker, and the ground looked more orange than blue now, because the entire nebula was on fire. The heat was getting unbearable, and poor Tuntuni squawked as he lost one feather after another.

"Lal!" I tried. "I know some part of you can hear us! Tell us where we're going before you burn us to cinders!"

Tick, tick, tick . . .

Mati's timepiece was now pointing at the space in between the red giant and white dwarf. Which meant it was creeping even closer to the black hole. Which was essentially my parents' death.

"We've got to hurry, Neel!" I showed him the clock,

indicating the all too rapidly moving arm. "My parents don't have much more time!"

As if in answer to the danger my parents faced, the landscape itself seemed to change. Instead of the pastel colors and glowing atmosphere, there were spiky bushes and black trees with thorn-covered branches. In front of us, the red giant ran through a hastily put up cardboard archway. It was a little crooked, and decorated to look like a demon's open mouth, complete with fangs hanging down toward us. On the garishly painted signboard, near the top, was the word:

DENGAR

As the red giant ran through it, it set the flimsy sign on fire. Neel and I both stopped short, avoiding the falling embers and pieces of burning cardboard.

"Dengar?" I shouted, to make myself heard above the noise of the burning sign. "Really?"

"English is not everyone's first language," Neel explained defensively, raising his arm to protect Tuntuni from a floating piece of flaming cardboard.

I realized there were a few other signboards here and there around the burning archway with crazy slogans painted on them too. Before they started to catch fire and burn, I saw that most of them were warnings for people setting out to fight rakkhosh:

AFTER WHISKY, FIGHTING DEMONS RISKY

and

IF YOU SLEEP, YOUR FAMILY WILL WEEP

in addition to

RAKKHOSH BABIES DON'T SAY MAYBE!

and the ever popular

FIGHT DEMONIC FOOLS AND FORM BLOOD POOLS!

"The well of demonic energy must be nearby, right?"

Neel didn't have a chance to reply, because, just then, Mati's clock hand started ticktocking even louder than before.

"Oh no! Neel! Look!"

We watched as the clock hand now swept right past the

white dwarf to hover somewhere right before the black hole mark. As it did so, the glowing white shape in my arms began transforming once again into the silver sphere I knew and loved.

"Neel! I'm running out of time!"

But Neel had run ahead of me through the almost burned-out "Dengar" archway and was picking up the other sphere. It had magically transformed back into the golden bowling ball that we were used to, its red giant manifestation complete. And while that brought some strange degree of comfort—to see Mati and Lal back to their magical sphere forms—it also reminded me that the spell we were dealing with was almost at an end. As was the time I had left to find my parents.

"What do I do?" I cried.

"Look for the ring! Look for the ring!" squawked Tuntuni from Neel's shoulder. The bird was pointing at what looked like a simple pile of boulders in front of us. Now that it had stopped raining fiery cardboard from the sky, I could approach it.

"What *is* this?"

I wasn't sure if I actually had tears in my eyes, or if it was the swirling mist, because, all of a sudden, the rock formation began to glow.

"Dr. Einstein said to look for a ring of light . . ." I remembered aloud.

"Einstein's ring! Of course!" Neel was tucking the golden and silver spheres back into his makeshift sling. "Einstein predicted that dark matter must exist in the universe because he noticed that light from distant stars sometimes looks like circles of light instead of pinpoints."

"Oh, right, I heard about this on a science program," I added. "He realized there must be something in the way—so that the light had to travel all around the object before making it to Earth. Hence, Einstein's ring."

At Neel's surprised expression, I shrugged defensively. "I never said I wasn't good at science."

Neel nodded, squinting at the glowing rocks. I followed his gaze.

In between the gaps in the boulders, I could make out something glimmering with a strange, magical force. Without a second thought, I began to climb up the slippery stones.

"What are you doing?" Neel took my arm.

I glared at him, and he dropped his hand. "There's something in the middle there, and I'm going to find out what it is!"

CHAPTER 28

The Thirsty Crow

I scrambled up the rocks, but when Neel tried to follow me, I waved him off.

"You might have to come rescue me!" I cautioned. "My Baba always says, two men should not go into a jackal's den."

"Your Baba has a lot of really, uh, fascinating sayings," said Neel as I began to climb, carefully placing my foot in one crevice and then another. My hands gripped and slipped and got cut on the sharp stones, but I kept on climbing. I had no choice. My parents' lives depended on me.

Finally, after a slightly harrowing few minutes, I was at the top of the stones. Even though I hadn't been able to see it from the ground, I realized the boulders were surrounding a central hollow—a crater-like hole at the top. I perched on the edge of the open space, peering down, not understanding what I was seeing.

"What is it?" Neel called.

When I didn't answer right away, Tuntuni flew up to land on my shoulder. As the bird and I peered into the hole together, I finally understood.

"I don't think this is just any old pile of boulders," I called down to Neel. "I think it's a well!"

As I saw my own face and Tuntuni's birdy visage reflected back to me from the well's water, I realized it must be true.

"A well of dark energy!" Neel exclaimed. "Your parents must be there!"

"I know, but how do I find them? How do I get them out?" My voice echoed weirdly off the stone sides.

"We don't have much time!" Neel cautioned.

"It's the night of the new moon," Tuntuni said, looking at the sky. "When the dark moon rises is the time that marks when a rakkhosh is born."

The mist was getting darker now, swirling around in grays and blacks rather than vivid colors. Soon it would be time for the moon to rise. Or, rather, it would be the night of the new moon. And my parents' time would be up.

I blinked hard, trying to keep my cool. "Dark matter scatters light . . ." I repeated to myself.

I peered at the wobbly reflection of my own determined face in the well's dark fluid, its surface a bit thicker and more oily than water. But still, I saw myself in the darkness. Our golden bird was right.

"Ma? Baba?" I called tentatively. There was no answer.

"We found it," I mumbled to myself. "But now what?"

Neel said there were lots of wells of dark energy; how did I know this was the right one? Could I even be sure that my parents were in here? And if they were, how the heck was I going to fish them out of this magic, invisible goo?

I didn't have a lot of time. The mists were getting even darker. I had to find out if my parents were below the surface of that water. And there was only one way to do it. I yanked off my jacket and shoes, getting ready to dive into the well.

Stop! Ma's voice yelled.

What are you, a few mangoes short of a bushel? Baba echoed.

I stopped. As clear as if they were standing next to me, I heard my parents' voices.

"Stop, Kiran, you can't dive into a well. You'll kill your-self," Neel shouted from below.

"Yeah, that's what my parents just said." I put my shoes back on.

"Okay, let's just think this through," Neel continued. "Every step, we've known we're on the right track because we had evidence. The moving map led us over the sea, where we found the red rubies from Tuntuni's poem."

"Right," I shouted back. The jewels were still heavy in my pockets.

"Then the map led us through Demon Land to here—and we knew it was Maya Pahar because another one of the poem's lines came true—'on a diamond branch a golden bird must sing a blessed song.'"

"Yeah, yeah," I sputtered impatiently. Ma and Baba's time was running out while Neel was pontificating. "Let's move it along, haven't got all night here. On a bit of a pre-apocalyptic deadline."

"So let's think about the next part of the poem. It's gotten us this far."

"'Neelkamal and Kiranmala, heed my warning well,'" I muttered, "'Your families will crumble, your life an empty shell.'" My arms were covered in goose bumps. I wasn't going to let that happen. No way! "'Unless you find the jewel in evil's hidden room, cross ruby seas full of love beneath the dark red moon.'"

"'In a monster's arms be cradled and cross the desert wide, in the Mountains of Illusions find a wise man by your side,'" Neel said. "And then comes that line about Einstein-ji—on a diamond branch, a golden bird must sing a blessed song."

"And then those lines about Lal and Mati—follow brother red and sister white not a moment too long."

"What's the next line?" Neel asked, fishing around in his pockets. He pulled out some gum, a broken pencil, and some of the sea rubies, but not the paper he'd written the poem on. "I know I wrote it down here somewhere."

"Something about golden and silver balls?" I asked nervously, my mind a racing blank. I didn't have time to be discussing poetry stanzas, I had to get my parents!

"'In your heart's fountain, set the pearly waters free,'" said Tuntuni. "I can't believe you numskulls don't remember. Really, it is so hard to find people who appreciate good lyric verse these days."

"'In your heart's fountain, set the pearly waters free,'" I repeated, looking into the dark well. What did that remind me of? When had I heard about pearls and water? Waters and pearls? I snapped my fingers. The transit officer. What had that riddle been? The ocean's pearl, a grain of sand, more precious than all the gold in the land . . .

"Neel!" I called. "I think I know what we have to do!"

I reached into my pocket and ran my hand over some of the smaller rubies I had stashed in there. My hand came out gritty and sticky, full of salt from the sea. "Set the pearly waters free," I repeated.

"What are you talking about?" Neel yelled.

I raised my voice a couple notches. "Listen, when I had to answer the transit officer's riddle, the puzzle was something about the ocean's pearl, a grain of sand—something without which life would be bland. It turned out the answer was salt."

"Something white like a pearl, from the ocean, small like a grain of sand," said Neel. "Life would certainly be bland without salt."

"Neel, what if the word 'pearl' in Tuntuni's poem refers to salt too? What if we have to set the *salty* waters of the fountain free?" I started to empty the red jewels from my pockets into the shadowy well, and was gratified to hear a *plunk* with every stone.

"You think we have to get rid of all our rubies?" Neel shouted.

"Unless you have a saltshaker on you. The rubies are

coated in sea salt!" I dug out the jewels and threw them into the water. *Plink. Plunk.* I had them stashed all over: my pants, shirt, backpack.

"Baba used to tell me this story about a thirsty crow who found a well during a drought," I explained as I threw more jewels into the deep. "The well water was so low the crow couldn't reach it. Now a different animal may have dived in, to his death . . ."

"Isn't that what you were just about to do?" Neel was emptying all the rubies from his pockets, and Tuntuni was flying them up to me a few at a time in his beak. I tossed them all into the well of dark energy.

"But the crow was clever, and instead of jumping in, began to gather all the stones he could, and throw them into the well."

Plink, plunk, plink. The noise was getting louder now, as if the water level was rising. I cautiously leaned over. Sure enough, my wobbly reflection was several feet closer now than it had been before.

"Finally, the water rose high enough, and the crow could reach his beak in and quench his thirst."

I was getting down to our last rubies. *Plink. Plunk.* The dark water was now almost to the top of the well. My reflection was so close I could reach out and touch it.

"It's a good theory, Kiran," Neel called. "Except that I'm all outa rubies, and the waters still aren't flowing free."

He was right. My reflection was just teetering on the edge of the boulders. My heart sunk.

"Wait a minute, there's one more stone." With a deep breath, I pulled out the python jewel from my jacket pocket.

"Princess, stop!" squawked Tuntuni.

"No, Kiran, we have no way of reading the map without it!" Neel shouted. "How are we going to get home?"

"I have no home without my family," I explained, remembering that Neel had said almost the same thing about Lal to their father. "I'm sorry, I can't leave without them."

PLUNK.

And with that, the salty waters of the dark well overflowed. Maybe *overflowed* is the wrong word. More like exploded in a geyser-like fountain of intergalactic dark energy. The force of the stuff made me fly off the stones and onto the ground, landing with a crash—yet again—on Neel. I hardly had time to catch my breath, because then we were both being bombarded by boulders from the exploding well. Neel took the brunt of it, shielding me from the stones with his own body. We both ducked, trying to protect our heads from the falling liquid and debris. Okay, maybe the

python jewel was a little more *umph* than entirely necessary for this procedure.

But then there they were. A little wet, but none the worse for having been trapped under the surface of a magic well. My parents. Those horrible landscapers. Those overenthusiastic dessert-makers. Those total nuts.

"Ma! Baba!" I wrapped my arms around them. "I'm so happy to see you!"

"Darling moonbeam garland! Let me look at you!" Ma gushed, pulling away and taking my chin in two fingers.

"Such dark circles! Ki holo? Not been sleeping well without your bear?"

"Ma! You know I haven't slept with Binkie Bear for years!" I turned my face away from her prying eyes only to be accosted by Baba.

"Have you been getting enough fiber, darling? No problems with constipation, na?"

"Oof!" Ma joined in. "I remember that one time you had such terrible problems with your bowels . . ."

OMG! Forget a rakkhosh, my parents were going to kill me with embarrassment.

Luckily, they had no time to make any more inappropriate observations, because the misty ground started to rumble under our feet.

Wordlessly, Neel pointed at the dark sky, his face ashen. I saw nothing. No sliver of a moon, no trace of an outline. The heavens were entirely dark. But I knew. The new moon had risen.

"Run!" Tuntuni squawked. "A baby demon's about to be born!"

CHAPTER 29

The Baby Demon

As we ran, my parents yelled endearments, luckily minus any more unnecessary comments about my fiber intake.

"I never believed I would see you again," Baba sobbed as he vaulted over a misty boulder. "My sweet girl! Do you forgive us for not telling you about the spell?"

His belly bounced a little as he ran, and the end of Ma's sari flapped crazily behind her, not to mention how totally messy and off-center her bouffant was.

"Oh, I knew you would find us, my darling. I, for one"—and here, Ma gave Baba a superior look—"had faith in you. You are, after all, a real Indian princess! As I have told you all along!"

There was a horrible groaning behind us as the rakkhosh

baby woke up. Its time was up, and I was pretty sure, from its screeches, it was hungry.

Let me tell you, none of us needed a motivational motion device. Apparently, hanging out in all that primordial goop was like some kind of triple-wheatgrass shot for old folks, because my parents were hauling butt right along with Neel and me. In fact, Tuntuni was hitching a ride on Baba's shoulder. If we weren't running for our lives, we could have collected some of that well fluid and started a fabulous new line of vitamins: *Demonic Silver*—dark energy–filled vitamins for the senior set.

As it was, we had more important things to worry about. Like surviving the hunger pangs of a very persistent newborn rakkhosh. I snuck a glance over my shoulder. It wasn't in a diaper or anything, but something about its eyes was really—well, maybe *innocent* isn't the right word—but young, anyway. It was short for a rakkhosh, maybe only seven or eight feet tall. It had putrid, moldy skin, open boils, and about six horns coming every which way out of his head—maybe some kind of homage to Einstein-ji, I wasn't sure. Of course, it also had the requisite fangs through which a more-than-requisite amount of drool was flowing. Its mouth was open like a gigantic vacuum, and I saw a few infant stars, some space dust, and some trees get sucked in.

"Stop! Din-ner! No run! Bogli hungry!" the baby demon yelled. It screwed up its ugly face in a wail. "Go in my belly now!"

"'Bogli' doesn't rhyme?" I shouted at Neel.

"He hasn't been to demon school yet," he explained, helping Ma leap over some orange-colored bushes.

"If he wasn't trying to cannibalize us, I might actually feel sorry for him."

"Are you kidding?" he yelled back. "He'll chew us up and use our bones for rattles!"

The demon spawn was gaining on us.

"Kiran, try to slow him down with some arrows!" Neel yelled as he helped Baba regain his balance over a tough patch of magenta stones.

I shot a couple of well-aimed arrows to the demon's nose, eye, and belly—soft spots—which didn't seem to slow the rakkhosh down at all. In fact, the demon baby's eyes grew red with fury.

"Oo, you mean!" he shrieked. "Bogli eat *you* first! And make it hurt!"

Dang. I probably tasted better than vinegar and chili chips. I kept booking.

"Where are we going?"

It was dark, but the Maya Pahar mist had a luminous

quality, so I could see the outlines of shapes as we ran along. In fact, some of those fuzzy purple trees were looking a little too familiar.

When we passed a blinking neon sign, I knew my suspicions were right:

THANKS FOR VISITING THE MOUNTAINS OF ILLUSIONS

HOME OF THE ANDROMEDA STAR NURSERY!

BE SURE TO VISIT THE WELL OF DARK ENERGY (IF YOU CAN FIND IT)!

TAKE A TOUR OF THE WORLD'S OLDEST HALLUCINATION AND STAR FACTORY!

MAYA PAHAR: OUR ILLUSIONS ARE YOUR DELUSIONS.

COME BACK SOON!

"'Our illusions are your delusions'?" Baba panted as we ran past the sign. "A terrible slogan! I was just reading in the

New Jersey small business owners' newsletter how the right branding is very important to customer loyalty . . ."

"Never mind that now!" I yelled. "If we keep going in this direction, we're going to go back to . . ."

I didn't have to finish my sentence, because right in front of us was a familiar shoreline.

"Oh, rotting tail feathers!" Tuntuni squawked. "It's Demon Land again!"

It was. I'd recognize that carcass-riddled coast anywhere. Only, the moving land masses apparently decided it was a good time to start shifting. We stumbled as the ground beneath our feet started moving in a smooth semicircle. It was what I imagine it might be like to watch tectonic plates shift—like when Africa broke away from Europe—just in superfast time-lapse photography.

Demon Land's shoreline shifted one way, and Maya Pahar's another. To the left, the Ruby Red Sea came into view, with some of its peacock barges lined up close to the shore. It was a strange sight—three different land masses each rotating away from the other. And we were at the point of the bizarre triangle.

Tuntuni flew off Baba's shoulders to scout the moving ledge. "It's not too far—you'll have to jump for the barges!"

"You must be illusional and delusional!" cried Baba.

But Bogli the demon was gaining on us quickly. The ground trembled and the air was filled with his spoiled-eggy breath.

"Bogli eat you *now*!"

"It's the only way," Neel said apologetically to Ma and Baba. "I'll go last to help you all make it."

I looked at my parents, who nodded. Demonic wheat-grass shots, check. Ridiculous level of faith in Neel, check. No other choices, check.

I decided to jump first. If it wasn't possible to hit the boat from here, I wanted it to be me who found that out.

"I'll go to make sure—" I started saying, when a shrieking voice cut me off.

"In my belly!"

"Go!" I felt Neel's hand push me, and I was in the air. I fell for a ridiculously long time, but somehow, miraculously, made it. I landed with a thunk on the floor of a peacock barge. "Come on!"

Baba and Tuni came next. Well, Baba came next but the bird flew alongside him as he fell, shouting encouragement. He actually ended up hitting the water, but it was a short swim into the boat. As I dragged him in, I yelled up to Ma and Neel, "Let's go!"

They didn't have a lot of time. The demon was gaining on them. I was sweating bullets. Would they make it?

"Bweakfast! Lunch! Din-din! Snack!" The demon's claw was right over their heads.

"Jump!"

Neel and Ma leaped, hand in hand. But at the last minute, one of the demon's talons caught on Ma's sari. She lost hold of Neel's hand.

"No!" he yelled, trying to reach her. In mid-fall, he threw her his sword. Which—and this is the real testimony to how much horsepower must've been in that dark energy goo—Ma actually caught.

"Me eat the mommy! Me eat the mommy!" the demon brat howled.

"Hya!" And that's when my mother—my sweet-making, inventory-taking, ever practical, ever optimistic mother—did the bravest thing I have ever seen her do. Just as I had sliced through Lal's scarf to free him from the demon on our front lawn, Ma sliced through the loose end of her sari, leaving the demon rug rat bereft and meal-less.

Unfortunately, it also left Ma without anything to hang on to, nowhere near the peacock barge. She fell like a rock—right over Demon Land.

CHAPTER 30

The Demon's Mouth

"Ma!" I screamed. I couldn't watch, I couldn't watch, I couldn't watch!

Baba and I grabbed each other and held on.

My eyes were closed, but I opened them when Tuntuni exhaled. "She's okay!"

Unfortunately, what I saw made me scream again. Ma was alive, yes, but she wasn't exactly safe. When Ma cut herself free, she fell in the direction of Demon Land. And on that awful shore was a very familiar figure.

"Ai-Ma!" Neel shouted.

"Ma!" I yelled at the same time.

The drooling old crone held my mother in the palm of her ginormous, warty hand. Ma was looking right at her,

her hands in a "namaskar." I couldn't hear what Ma was saying, but she seemed to be pleading for her life.

"Bogli hungwy!" the demon brat wailed from the border of Maya Pahar, but we all ignored him. The border had shifted even farther away from us now, and the baby demon didn't seem to know how to get to us.

I focused on what was going on in Demon Land. I aimed my bow and arrow, not caring that it was Neel's grandma I was aiming at.

"Let her go, Ai-Ma!" My voice shook with fury. I didn't come this far to see my mother get eaten.

"Kiran, please!" Neel begged.

But I didn't let him distract me from my target. My arrow was pointed right at the old rakkhoshi's chest. "Put her down!"

And that's when Ai-Ma shocked the heck out of all of us. She reached her knobbly hand in Ma's direction, and, very gently, patted her on the head.

"Ai-Ma isn't so old she can't recognize a girl from a boy, or a prince from a pup," the crone cackled. As she guffawed, her hairy cheeks puffed out in pleasure. "You have a very brave—and yummy-smelling—daughter," she told Ma, her rough voice carrying over the distance.

Ai-Ma's lips were covered with drool and her tongue waggled a little, but she walked straight toward the shore of the Ruby Red Sea. No sign of even nibbling a little on her captive. The arm bearing my mother reached out farther and farther from the old rakkhoshi's shoulder, until, like some extendable fire hose, it reached our peacock barge.

"I give you back to your little coconut beanpole." Ai-Ma—or rather, Ai-Ma's extended hand—gently deposited Ma in the barge. "Your nub-nub was good company to old Ai-Ma, and old Ai-Ma always remembers a favor."

Before it retracted, Ai-Ma's warty hand chucked me under the chin. I know she was trying to be gentle, but she made my teeth seriously rattle.

"Be good, sweet beetle-dung toadstools," she cooed from the distant shore.

I threw down my bow and arrow in the bottom of the barge and held my mother tight.

"Thank you, Ai-Ma, thank you!" I yelled as Neel and Baba pushed the barge farther and farther away from the shore of both Demon Land and Maya Pahar.

"Head straight across the sea and you will make it home!" Ai-Ma waved to us, a three-toothed grin on her face. "I make it a rule not to eat mommies while their boo-boos watch," she called as we sailed. "It's bad for my digestion!"

"What a nice grandmother you have, Prince Neelkamal." Ma beamed. We'd been sailing for a while into the Ruby Red Sea, and everything seemed relatively calm.

Baba had stopped hugging Ma, and now was just wiping tears away and thanking Neel. "Yes, a very nice ... erm ... woman." Ma elbowed him, making him cough. "Most charming."

I shook my head and smiled as I looked out over the calm, dark waters. People—even demon people—really surprised you sometimes.

"How is my brother?" Ma asked Neel. "And my lovely niece, how is she keeping up with her stable-hand duties?"

"Wait, Neel knows your brother?"

"The prince didn't tell you, darling?" Baba was rowing us into the dark night, with Tuni perched comfortably on his shoulder. "We were knowing something unexpected might happen around your twelfth birthday, so we took some precautions."

Ma patted my arm. "It was your uncle Rahul, the stable master, who suggested that the Princes Lalkamal and Neelkamal might be dispatched to help you."

"Wait," I said, "let me get this straight. Lal and Neel's stable master is your brother?"

My mother nodded.

Neel had just finished explaining the Queen's unfortunate decision to eat Lal and Mati, and their subsequent transformation into inanimate objects.

I pointed at the humming silver object in Neel's sling. "So that bowling ball is my cousin?" No wonder Mati felt so familiar to me.

"Oh, yes," Baba agreed. "But as you know, where we come from, even the most distant cousin is called a sister."

My cousin Mati, I thought. *My sister Mati.* After having had so little family for so long—and then recently discovering some less-than-desirable family members—it was nice to know I had some normal relatives. If you count someone who was trapped inside a silver bowling ball—and occassionally turned into a solar phenomenon—normal.

"I can't believe we still don't know how to get them b-a-ck." Neel kind of sputtered that last word, because just then, the boat lurched to the right.

"Oh, I think I have an idea," I said. "The golden branch in the poem must mean . . ." I stopped mid-thought, because the boat swayed again.

"What was that?" Ma looked over the edge. "The water seems so calm."

"Oh, nothing," said Tuni drowsily. "We're almost—"

But he couldn't finish his sentence because the next lurch of the boat sent him flying off Baba's shoulder and onto the floor of the barge. We all collapsed to the left.

"I'm getting a bad feeling about this . . ." I drew an arrow from my quiver.

But before I had a chance to shoot it I was coughing up water from a wave that rushed over the entire boat. We were knee-deep and the boat was still tossing on the newly rough seas.

"Bail! Bail!" Neel yelled, his hair streaming into his face. We all grabbed whatever we could to chuck water overboard, but all of our hard work was meaningless when the next big wave swept over the peacock barge in a few minutes.

"Are we all okay?" Neel shouted. I took a glance around. Except for being drenched, and the terrified expressions, we all seemed to be in one piece.

But the respite was half as long as the last time. I'd only just scooped a couple quiverfuls of water out of the boat when another wave hit.

"Gaak!" Tuni went overboard, but Baba grabbed a feathery wing and yanked him back.

"I'm afraid this doesn't seem like an altogether natural storm," Ma ventured, ever grammatical, even in a crisis.

There was a weird sucking sound coming from somewhere. A hole in the boat? I looked around at our soggy barge, but couldn't find one.

"What makes you say that?" I shouted over the now rushing winds.

Wordlessly, she pointed at the sea. I felt my heart drop.

"Neel!" I yelled. He was still bailing water from the back of the boat with my boot. "I think you'd better see this!"

All around our boat rose a wall of spinning water, inclined like the steep seats at an auditorium. Only, this was theater in the round, and we were the performers.

"We're in the middle of a whirlpool!"

The sucking sound was the water below us getting pulled downward. To make matters worse, on the top edges of the giant water tornado were what looked like gigantic rakkhosh fangs.

"Yum! Yum! In my tum!"

The all-too-familiar voice echoed weirdly from within the unnatural torrent of water.

"Oh gods! He's more powerful than I thought!" yelled Neel. "This isn't a whirlpool; it's that demon brat's open mouth—and he's going to eat us all!"

CHAPTER 31

The Man Behind the Baby

That snot-nosed newborn demon transformed himself into a *whirlpool*?" I screamed furiously at Neel. "Is there more stuff you people can do that you didn't tell me?" I rowed like a wild thing, as did all of us, but our boat was going nowhere.

"He shouldn't be able to! A newborn practice that kind of complicated magic? I've never heard such a thing," Neel protested. "There has to be someone helping him!"

There weren't enough oars, and he was bent over the side trying to muscle us physically up the mountain of water. But it wasn't working. For every few inches we moved forward, we moved more back down toward the whirlpool's center.

"Well, he's obviously smarter than we gave him credit

for!" I could barely see, there was so much water rushing into my eyes.

"Stop arguing, for goodness' sake," Baba said, putting his shoulder into his oaring. "It's not very royal behavior on either of your parts!"

"Oh dear, I'm afraid we are traversing backward," Ma piped in.

She was right. Despite our best efforts, our barge was sliding inevitably down the demonic drain. Or demonic digestive system, as the case may be.

"Yum! Yum! Snaky King is a big dum-dum!"

"What did he say? Oh no, what did he say?"

The boat went almost vertical and tumbled backward.

"Yaaaa!" I wasn't sure who was shouting, but the last thing I saw before we got pulled down into the center of the whirlpool were people—and a bird and two magical spheres—that I didn't want to lose.

It was a long way down—history-test long, humiliating-moment-in-the-locker-room long, Alice-falling-down-the-rabbit-hole long. And dark. And loud. And terrifying.

When we landed—with a hard thunk, I might add—it wasn't in the demon's stomach, but in a relatively dry under-sea cavern. The peacock barge, luckily, *was* equipped with airbags, and they seriously broke our fall. (Go magical crash-test systems!)

We climbed out, leaving the gold and silver balls in the barge for safekeeping, and looked around. I could hear the water of the whirlpool still swirling above us. The scene was all too familiar. The demon baby was nowhere to be seen. But someone else was.

"Hello, Sssissster," said a set of seven nasty voices.

I whipped around to see that last-place winner for brother of the year—Naga, the seven-headed snake.

"Oh, booger-nosed snot fest, where did YOU come from?"

"Daughter, your *mouth*."

"Yesss, indeed, your mou-sss," hissed the cobra heads in unison. In a flash, Naga wrapped Ma, Baba, and even poor terrified Tuntuni in his coils. As a last flourish, he slapped his nasty tail over all their mouths. They were effectively bound and gagged.

"Let them go!" Neel brandished his sword. Even in the dark cavern, it glinted with an inner light.

"Now!" I aimed my arrow at the largest of his seven hooded heads. The snake lunged at me, flicking seven forked tongues.

I saw Baba's eyes widen at something behind me even before I heard the chilling voice. I whirled around, my arrow still raised. I should have known who was behind all this.

"Children, children, why all the fuss?" The Serpent King slithered into the room—his top half human, but his bottom half in his terrible serpentine form. "Do you like my new undersea residence?" he oozed. "It's a rental, and I'm still waiting on the interior decorator . . ."

"You!" Neel ran at the Serpent King, his sword aimed at my birth father's throat.

"Impudent demon-ling!" The Serpent King held up his hand, sending Neel's sword clattering to the floor with a bolt of green lightning. "Did you actually think you could destroy my glorious kingdom and get away with it?"

"Stop!" I whirled back around and aimed my arrow at the largest of the cobra's seven heads. "Let them all go—it's *me* you want. Otherwise . . . I shoot Naga!"

The Serpent King waved a callous hand, mocking Naga's snakey lisp. "Oh, shoot him, what do I care? You'd think those ssssseven ssssstupid heads would make him sssssmarter. But he let you get away last time, didn't he?"

If it was possible for a magical seven-headed cobra to look hurt, he did. But it's not like my snake-brother got all warm and fuzzy as a result. In fact, he squeezed his prey even harder. Ma and Baba sputtered, their faces red, and an alarming number of yellow feathers discharged from where Tuntuni must be—almost invisible in the folds of cobra muscle.

"Stop!" I shrieked, turning to the Serpent King. "Please! He'll kill them!"

"So what?" snarled my biological father. "Did you show my poor snakes any mercy? Hmm? Did you?"

"Let them go!" I sent an arrow flying at the Serpent King, but he stopped it mid-flight with a green bolt. As I aimed a second arrow, the Serpent King shot another bolt of green lightning, this time directly at my hands. My beautiful bow exploded in green flames. I dropped it, before falling to the ground myself. Where the green fire hit me, my arms felt like they were burning, only from the inside out. It was agony.

Neel had picked up his sword again, and ran screaming at the Serpent King. "Aaaa!"

"Oh, will you never learn?" He shot a bolt of green, this time a flaming sphere that imprisoned Neel within it. The prince screamed in pain—a sound that made my blood run cold. He writhed around within the glowing orb, his body twisting in unnatural contortions, as if he was being tortured.

"Neel!" I shrieked, running toward him. The heat of the sphere was scorching, and it shot out green flares. It burned me even at a distance, like the molten surface of some alien sun. "Neel, hang on! Hang on!"

"You'll join him soon enough, you pathetic waste of a daughter." The Serpent King aimed his hands high.

"No!" Everyone I loved was going to die. And it was all my fault. My legs couldn't hold me up anymore, and I collapsed. I was screaming and crying so hard, my tears were tumbling from my face. I didn't try to control them. I had much more important things to worry about. But where the tears hit my arms, something strange happened. They eased the burning feeling of the green bolt.

My tears. In a flash, I remembered how Tuni had seemed dead, but how he'd come to life in my arms. I'd been crying then too. And why was it exactly I'd spent so many years training my own tears not to spill? Had I somehow known the power they contained?

Unless the pearly waters of the fountain can flow free.

Were my tears the salty pearls that needed to flow free too?

And then I heard her voice, as clean and pure as a bell. *The tears of the moon's daughter are as powerful as the tides.* I felt her strength within me, my moon-mother. I had always had it—the strength of the night, the strength of the tides, the strength to reflect the light of others. The strength to weep without weakness.

"You're not going to kill them."

I rose from the ground, my arms outstretched. I was my father's child. I was my mother's daughter. My face was still wet, and my heart beat in rhythm with the music of the oceans.

"And you're not going to kill me."

The jagged green light shot at me, but I met it with a

searing white light of my own. Where they clashed, the green glowing softened, became liquid, and fell to the floor like rain.

"No!" the Serpent King cried, his eyes burning orbs. "How is this possible?"

"I guess there's no getting around it. I am your daughter, at least biologically," I said. "I can't hide from who I am. But it doesn't mean I can't choose my own destiny."

He shot bolt after bolt of green fire, but I met them all with the shimmering, diamond light of my own. The intensity of its power grew each time I aimed my hands.

When unleashed, there is no more powerful force than the will of nature.

I was a part of nature, a moon-child, and I wanted desperately to live, to have my loved ones live. Not die in this horrible dark cavern, but walk together into the light.

My body felt possessed, as if I was channeling all my moon-mother's energy through me. My eyes were wet and felt like they were glowing white-hot. My hair shot out around me—shimmering as if with electricity. And the moonlight—not soft, but terrible, and beautiful too—shot like dancing fire from my upturned palms.

There was a rumbling, and I knew that I was somehow

shifting the tides in the sea above our heads. I heard a familiar groaning.

"Where din-din go? Snaky King, you steal Bogli's din-din?"

The cavern started to shake, and streams of water poured down from cracks in the ceiling. Then I heard a drumbeat that could only be the rhythmic sound of demonic footsteps.

The rakkhosh baby, Bogli. Somehow, the Serpent King had recruited him to get us to this cavern. And now Bogli was coming to collect his reward. The thought of facing both the Serpent King and the baby demon should have terrified me. But I wasn't scared. I knew exactly who I was.

I turned to the seven-headed cobra and said, with both sympathy and hard honesty, "You better run, Brother. All heck's about to break loose, and our father's not going to save you."

The seven forked tongues flickered for only a moment as Naga considered my words. Then the seven heads nodded as the cobra unwound himself from his victims. Ma, Baba, and Tuni fell in a collapsed heap on the ground. All injured, but all breathing.

"Thisss isssn't the end, Sssisssster." Naga shot his

muscular tongues in my direction, but I fended them off with a bolt of white light.

"Oh, I'll count on it," I called as the cobra slithered down a passage and disappeared.

"Good riddance to old rubbish," the Serpent King snarled, aiming his claws at me. "Now to take out the rest of the trash!"

I was tired, but exhilarated. I aimed my hands, willing the white light with all my might, but before I could, something happened. From the streams of water pouring out of the cracking ceiling, a woman in misty white appeared. She was translucent, as if she existed only as a reflection in the water.

"Mother," I breathed.

"I have let this go on for long enough!" Her voice boomed through the cavern with an unearthly force. "I let my love for you blind me to your darkness, but no more!"

"You are my wife," the Serpent King snarled. "You are bound to my darkness. You don't have strength to kill me!"

But this was the moon's most fierce face. Her light glowed a thousand times brighter than mine. It was glorious and terrifying at the same time. Confronted with such power, the Serpent King went from scoffing to disbelieving to actually a little worried.

Even still, he raised his hands, sneering at her. "You don't have the guts!"

As he launched the crackling lightning from his hands, the moon shot a white-hot beam at the Serpent King. He glowed an incandescent green, but then began to writhe and decay, his energy going from green to brown to gray to black.

As his power dissipated, so did the swirling orb holding Neel. Neel was free—panting, eyes closed, on the ground. But free.

When I turned back around, the Serpent King was a pile of char. She had done it. The moon maiden had freed me, and herself.

I could barely look at her; her aspect was so awesome and powerful. I ducked my head in a grateful bow.

"He is gone for now, but not forever," she said, her voice shimmery like the ocean.

"Thank you, Mother," I whispered.

For a moment, she touched my head with a silvery hand. I felt the cool liquid of her touch fill me with energy, power, and love. She slipped something strong and yet pliable in my hands—my bow, magically intact.

"You are the daughter of the moon. But you are also the daughter of those good people who raised you. And yes, you are the daughter of the dark Serpent King too." Her voice rang like a bell in the echoing cavern. "Everything is connected to everything, Kiranmala."

I nodded. My eyes were too full of tears to do anything else. It was only when I admitted to myself all of who I was that I was able to find my deepest power.

Then my moon-mother withdrew, becoming faint and distant again.

Her last words to me were ones of warning. "And now, you must run, my daughter, for the demons are coming."

CHAPTER 32

But How?

The ceiling was collapsing, and the underground cavern was filling with seawater. The thumping footsteps of the baby demon were fast upon us, and everyone was half unconscious from the attack of my serpent relatives. Just another average day in the alternate dimension.

"Neel, get up!" I didn't have time to be super sympathetic right now. He was a demon prince and a fast healer, and I needed his help with the others. I hauled him up by the armpits and yelled into his half-focused face. "Come on, daycare demon's on his way, and we've got to get out of here!"

I was thinking about slapping him across the face, but he got it together about the third time I shook him. The water in the cavern was already waist-high.

"Let's get the others in the boat."

Neel and I half dragged, half carried Ma, Baba, and Tuntuni into the peacock barge. The golden and silver spheres rolled around as if glad to see us. My parents were holding up okay, but the small bird had really gotten the worst of it. He sputtered and coughed, his face and body badly bruised.

Ma wrapped the bird in the frayed end of her sari, but her troubled eyes were on me. "Are you all right, my golden one?"

I couldn't say anything. Fat tears fell out of my eyes. Now that I'd turned on the faucet, I couldn't seem to shut it off.

Ma and Baba were horrified at the sight of me crying. "Are you hurt? Oh, what can we do? Is it your bowels?" They looked as if they thought I was going to die.

"No, it's not that," I sniffled. "It's just that you didn't ask to get involved in this. All you did was take care of me. You tried to tell me—but I never believed your stories. Can you ever forgive me?"

Their faces cleared.

"Shona, none of this is your fault." Ma wiped my tears with her fingers. "We are your parents; it's our job to take care of you. We will always love you, no matter what."

"We humans may not be powerful or magical," Baba added, holding me close. "But the stories we pass on to our children can be."

"I hate to break up this touching moment," Neel interrupted, "but we've got to find a way out of here before the cavern is totally flooded."

As if on cue, we heard a familiar voice bellow.

"Where you go, din-din? Here, little din-din, come to Bogli belly!"

We all started rowing like crazy.

As we hauled the boat as fast as we could down a stony passage, I noticed my parents were looking a lot more sprightly. My tears seemed to have cleared up the bruises on their faces and hands. And even the few tears that hit Tuntuni, in my mother's lap, had done him a lot of good. The little bird ruffled his feathers, and then flew over to help Baba row.

The narrow passages made everything echo. Now the baby demon's voice seemed to be coming from everywhere.

"Come to Bogli, little din-din."

And then we heard the most disturbing sound. Like someone was slurping a thick milk shake through a tiny straw.

"What is that?" I began to ask, when I realized what I was hearing. Oh gods, we were moving backward. That imbecilic demon brat was sucking the cavern water dry—and in the process pulling us toward him!

"Row! Row!" I yelled, and my parents obeyed. Neel, bizarrely, did not.

"What are you doing?" He'd pulled out his sword and was standing at the back of the boat, like some kind of advertisement for a one-leg-lifted-in-the-air pirate.

"I'm tired of this snot-nosed rakkhosh baby calling the shots," he yelled. We were getting sucked back so fast now, Neel's hair was swirling around his head.

"I think I'm retiring as a demonic pacifist." Neel's teeth flashed. "I'm going to kick some rakkhosh baby butt!"

We were back in the main cavern again and could see Bogli at one end. The demon was crouched low to the ground, sucking the water like some kind of deranged elephant. His beady red eyes glowed at the sight of us.

"Come to belly! Come to belly!" he squealed.

"I'll come to your belly, all right," Neel shouted, jumping off the boat into the ankle-deep water. "I'll come to your belly to cut it in half!"

With a ferocious yell, Neel charged the demon.

"We'll be fine, don't worry," I called to my parents as I jumped out right behind him, my weapon raised. The magic bow vibrated in my hands as I volleyed arrow after arrow in the demon's direction. My moon-mother must have done something to my quiver as well, because, no matter how many arrows I shot, it kept refilling on its own.

My arrow tips glowed with white-hot moonlight, and where they hit the rakkhosh, they burned. The confused creature batted at the stinging missiles.

"Ow! Mean girl has mean pointies! Why you so mean?"

Neel was on him now, slashing at his ankles with his sword. Bereft of the Serpent King's magical backup, the baby rakkhosh seemed to cower.

"*Ow!* You mean too! Why hurt Bogli?"

"Bogli needs to *back off*!" Neel shouted. "Stop chasing us, got it?" He was right up in the baby demon's face, pointing his sword at Bogli's eyeball.

The rakkhosh sat down with a plunk on the wet cavern floor.

"Mama! Mama!" Bogli wailed. "Boy yell at Bogli!"

"Mama?" I moaned.

"Let's get out of here!" Baba yelled from behind me. "We don't want to meet his mother!"

Unfortunately, we already had. Because, in a puff of acrid-smelling smoke, who should be standing there but . . .

"Ma?" Neel yelled. "Are you kidding me?"

I stared. "Are you trying to tell me that Bogli is your . . ."

"Adopted daughter? Yes, as a matter of fact, she is just that." The Demon Queen picked her front teeth with a sharpened nail. "Say hello to your little sister, darling."

Sister? I choked back a snort.

"Bogli's a girl?" The odd revelation seemed to take the anger right out of Neel's sails.

"Do you have a *problem* with that?" The Queen crossed her taloned hands over her chest, her nostrils spewing flames. "Have I raised some kind of demonic sexist? A purveyor of rakkhosh patriarchy?"

Huh. Maybe I liked Neel's mother more than I realized.

Behind the Queen, Bogli stuck her giant thumb in her even more giant mouth. "Big Bwother!" she bellowed.

Neel shook his head. "Enough stupid tricks." He pointed his sword at his mother's throat. "You tell us how to turn Lal and Mati back. You tell us now!"

"They're still trapped?" The Demon Queen belly-laughed hard and long, only stopping when she burped. "Vah! Some big demon prince you turned out to be—you haven't even figured that out yet?"

"Tell us, Ma!"

The rakkhoshi rolled her eyes, "Oh, come on, Moon Moon Sen, you haven't the faintest idea?"

"Well." I looked apologetically at Neel. "I did have *one* thought . . ."

"Let's have it, then!" the demoness urged.

Neel pulled me aside. "Are you seriously having this conversation? Did you forget she tried to *eat* my brother and Mati?"

"Well, she didn't kill them, did she? And don't you want to know how to bring them back?"

I turned again to the demoness. "Well, Your Highness . . ."

The Queen puffed up, raising one hairy eyebrow in her son's direction. "At least *some* people know how to show respect, eh?"

Neel snarled, still clutching his sword.

I ignored him. "That line in the poem—" I started.

"Poem?" the Queen interrupted.

"Tuntuni's poem . . . it said—"

"That interfering birdbrain of a minister? Is he still up to his tricks?"

I heard a faint squawk from the peacock barge behind us. I hoped that one of my parents had sat on the bird to keep him quiet.

"Are you going to let her talk or not?" Neel snapped.

"Fine, fine." The demoness waved her hands at me. "Go on, Stella Luna."

"'Let golden branch grow from the silver tree,'" I quoted. "So I was thinking: Prince Lal is golden—of royal blood. The stable master's daughter—though loyal and honorable—is not. How could a golden branch grow from a silver tree?"

Now that she was in her mother's care, Bogli seemed to have all the bite—and intelligence—of a trained house pet. She clapped happily for my efforts. "Mean girl smart!"

"I don't get it," interrupted Neel.

"Such a disappointment!" the demoness moaned, rubbing her stomach. "Oh, my reflux! My kingdom for an antacid!"

Neel was looking murderously at his mother. I jumped in to distract him. "Lal's the golden branch, but he needs Mati, the silver tree, around him to grow into his full potential as a ruler."

"Okaaay," Neel said slowly. "It's true. Lal and Mati are friends and she is a good influence on his confidence, or whatever. He's definitely less flaky when he's around her."

"Right, but the Raja and the queens will never allow Lal and Mati to continue to be friends, right? Not now that he's the crown prince. Not as they get older."

"No way, chickie!" The Rakkhoshi Queen cackled.

"Since they've been spheres, they've been so happy. Humming and buzzing and hanging out together. But once they become human again, then Mati goes back to the stables and Lal to the palace."

"I guess."

"So we've got to convince the Raja otherwise."

Neel looked at me, the truth dawning in his eyes. "So we have to take them home again."

I nodded.

"Everything is connected to everything," drawled the Demon Queen in a bored voice.

Neel and I both snapped around to face her.

She arched a wicked eyebrow. "Haven't you figured out the *how* part yet?"

I shook my head. To which she belched. Then, rolling her eyes, she shouted, "By love, you morons, by *love*!"

We stared at her. She moved her gruesome head side to side, cracking her neck with a gesture that reminded me of her son.

"You're lucky you have Loonie-Moonie here." She pointed a talon at Neel. "I for one am going to try to raise a real rakkhosh this time!"

As we talked, Bogli had fallen asleep right on her

mother's foot. The Queen shook her off, and the baby demon woke up, bawling. The Queen slapped her hand to her forehead.

"Am I to be forever cursed with imbecilic offspring?" the Rakkhoshi Queen snapped, and the two demons were gone in a puff of smelly darkness.

Her voice cackled through the vapor. "Don't call me, dum-dums, and I won't call you!"

CHAPTER 33

Home Again, Home Again

The Raja wanted to banish Neel.

"We told you not to come home without your brother!" he bellowed.

"Well, that's just too bad," Neel snapped. "Because half rakkhosh or not, I'm still your son too."

I was proud of Neel for saying that and not just stomping out of the throne room in a huff. I wasn't quite as proud of the shouting match the father and son then had.

It took my parents, Tuntuni, and me a lot of effort to calm them both down. We all tried our best to explain to the Raja what had happened, but it was Tuntuni who actually saved the day with a song.

"The Demon Prince and Moonbeam Girl, each a royal
    child
One father of the dark, the other loving and mild
To save a brother and a sister
To serpent land descended
With shadow's force they drowned the snakes
And the python jewel defended
Crossed ruby seas full of jewels beneath the dark red
    moon
Survived Demon Land in Ai-Ma's arms but not a
    minute too soon
In the Mountains of Illusions there sang a golden bird
In the well of demon-birth, loving parents heard
With sword and bow and bravery, the darkness they
    did hold
Tears' magic did appear as nature's power bold
Now home again to plant a seed for friendship's ever
    near
The branch grows from the tree of gold and silver
    spheres."

"Loving and mild," the Raja murmured. "We like that." He'd been eating during most of the song, so I wasn't sure how much of the rest he actually understood.

Neel stole a glance at me. I nodded.

"Father, for Lal to come back into his human form, you have to guarantee something."

The Raja narrowed his eyes. "Kings don't make guarantees."

"Do you want him back or not?" Neel practically shouted, and was about to say more until I stepped on his foot. Hard.

"Please, sire," I wheedled. "If Lal and Mati want to spend more time together, you would surely not stand in their way?"

"If we had our son and heir back in human form, that's all we care about," said the Raja, wringing his hands. "Yes, yes, best friends since childhood, friendship knows no class, race or creed, blah blah blah. We don't like it, but we suppose that would be fine." He waved his hands vaguely in the direction of the golden and silver spheres. "Just bring our boy back to us!"

Neel and I crossed the palace gardens and went back out to the forest. Tuntuni was waiting for us at the base of his tree. There were two shovels propped up against the base.

"Go to it!" the bird squawked.

Neel and I dug two holes next to each other. The sorts of holes we dug at school on Arbor Day to plant a little memorial tree or something. Only, Neel and I didn't stick bulbs into the holes; we placed the golden and silver spheres inside. They hummed and glowed, even halfway under the dirt.

"You're sure they won't . . . like, suffocate or something?" I asked, rubbing at my forehead with a dirty hand.

"They're glorified bowling balls right now, Kiran, except for the brief time they were part of the star cycle, so unless you have a better plan as to how to make them human again, I suggest you cover them up with dirt."

Once we filled in dirt over the spheres, Neel watered the spot. Then there was nothing to do but brush the dirt off our clothing and go check on the horses.

Princess! You made it! Snowy exclaimed when we walked into the stable.

"So did you!" I hugged the horse around his neck. "Was it a long flight?"

Neel looked at me curiously. "Are you talking to the horse?"

"Yeah." I crossed my arms across my chest. "You got a problem with it?"

"Is that supposed to be an imitation of me or something?"

I laughed. Even if it wasn't home, it felt good to be back.

In the morning, we ran down to the forest to see what had happened and found a beautiful sight. Lal and Mati, sitting up in a shimmering, silvery tree that had sprouted from the ground overnight. Although most of the branches were silver, it was the long glittering branch of gold on which the best friends were sitting. With them was Tuntuni. Lal and Mati were swinging their legs to his music, and looking pretty happy to be back in human form.

"Brother!" Lal exclaimed, jumping down from the branch.

The two princes bro-hugged. They didn't, however, cry.

"Cousin!" Mati ran over to throw her arms around me. Unfortunately, she did cry. A lot. Which made me kind of tear up too. Oh, the heck with it, I totally boo-hooed like a baby in her arms. It was awesome to find out I had a cool horse-wench for a cousin.

We left them there then—they didn't seem to need us

anyway. At the stables, I turned right, toward my uncle Rahul's apartments, where my parents were waiting, while Neel turned left, toward the palace.

"Kind of what it's always been like for Lal and Mati, I guess," I said.

"Only, you're a princess, and she's the stable master's daughter."

"Well, for all intents and purposes, I'm the stable master's niece, the daughter of Quickie Mart owners," I corrected.

"That's not entirely true . . ."

"It is true." I kicked a clod of dirt with my toe. "Look, it's not like I don't know who I am. But in the end, they're not the parents I choose. I mean, which would you rather be, a snake princess in a dark cave with a bunch of homicidal relatives you don't even want to know—or part of the nice, warm, non-royal family that brought you up?"

Neel bit his lip, squinting into the distance. "You're lucky, you know."

"I can't believe I used to always get bugged about how weird my parents were. How different they were from everyone else's parents in New Jersey. They only ever wanted me to be proud of who I am."

"That," said Neel, "and to get enough fiber in your diet."

I gave Neel a smack on the arm even as I laughed.

"Hey, I've got one for you. Why couldn't anyone see the bird?"

"I don't know." Neel grinned. "But I suspect you're going to tell me."

"It was in da-skies!" I whooped.

Neel frowned. "Is that supposed to be funny?"

"Da-skies? Da-skies?" I insisted. "What does that sound like?"

"Look, seriously, it's all right. It's the thought that counts."

"Disguise! It was in disguise!" I said, waving my arms. "Get it? It was in disguise!"

"That's okay, Kiran." Neel patted my arm. "Not everybody has to have a good sense of humor. You have other qualities that are really nice."

But he was laughing, and I was laughing, and everything felt right and good.

Later, when we came back to the palace, everybody's happiness was a teensy bit squelched by the Raja totally jacking up and refusing to remember his promise.

"We said no such thing," he insisted.

"Sire, do you want your son and heir to return to his other form?" Tuntuni snapped.

And so, despite the queens wailing and beating their not-inconsequential bosoms and smashing their bangles against the floor, the Raja officially promised not to stand in the way of any friendship between Lal and Mati. Tuntuni actually produced a document from somewhere called a "Treaty of Royal-to-Non-Royal Friendship Noninterference" and made the Raja sign it, there and then. The handsome human prince and his loyal stable maid couldn't seem happier at this. It was strange, but I could swear they still hummed and vibrated in each other's presence.

As for Neel, he was still acting pretty mysterious. Finally, he admitted what it was. "I'll have to go soon and fulfill my word to the shadow merchant."

We were standing in a quiet corner of the throne room, where the festivities for Lal's return were going on full blast. I'd dressed in my mother's red wedding sari, with the same jewels I'd once hated wearing. Ma had styled my hair so that it swept off my neck, and the scar on my arm was completely visible too. I didn't care. They were a part of who I was. Anyway, I looked—and felt—like a total princess.

Mati stuck by Lal's side through the whole party, as the people of the kingdom showered their crown prince with love and affection. It was strange to see how easy it was for Neel to slip away unnoticed. Because he was a half demon, it was as if he didn't count, that people seemed to think he was hardly worth counting.

Of course, what I was realizing was that Neel counted to me. He counted very much. I remembered that ominous promise he made to the seller of shadows and how upset Lal was to hear his brother make it.

"How could you promise to give her your soul?" The thought made me sick. "Of all the insane, irresponsible things to do—"

"Wait a minute, wait a minute," Neel cut me off. "Why do you think that? I didn't promise Chhaya Devi my soul." He had a little smile on his lips. "But it's nice to know you worry."

"You didn't promise her your soul? Then what is it?"

"Chhaya Devi used to be our nanny, a long time ago, before she got into the shady world of shadow selling."

"Very punny."

"Seriously, she's not as young as she used to be, and she's always trying to convince us to stay with her for a couple of months and help her catch shadows."

"Then why was your brother so upset when you promised?"

"Really?" Neel pointed at Lal and Mati, who were gazing at each other all glowy like. "He didn't want to be separated again from Mati."

"Oh." I looked down at the purple boots that I'd worn under my sari, which had made me feel all sorts of awesome and rebellious when I'd put them on. Now I just felt seriously stupid.

"So . . ." Neel stared at my shoes too, like I had the secrets of the universe written on them. "I guess, after all this is done, you're going to go back, huh?"

"To Jersey?" I nodded. "I think my parents always thought they'd move back here some day, but now that we're here, it's not at all the way they remember it. More demons, I guess," I laughed. "I don't know. I mean, I don't know if the place has changed or they've changed, but Ma says she can't bear to think of her house as a disaster zone, and Baba gets seriously choked up at the thought of all the spoiling store inventory."

"Your parents want to go back, but what about you?" Neel said in a lower voice.

I bit my lip. My eyes were getting a little hot. "Well, I've still got to finish the sixth grade," I babbled. "I've missed a major Spanish test while I was gone, not to mention a ton of homework. And my math teacher will probably beat me with her protractor for how behind I am, and besides, Zuzu'll be totally worried . . ."

There was a pause, and neither of us looked directly at the other. My face glowed with heat.

"Well, you sneak through wormholes all the time, don't you?" I finally asked. "I mean, like, to see movies and stuff?"

Gah, would he think I was asking him out to a movie? *Was* I asking him out to a movie? I wanted to ask him out to a movie, I realized.

I mentally kicked myself. I'd made it through some pretty life-or-death situations recently, and yet, why was this one the most tricky to figure out?

Neel stared off at a weird angle behind my head, chewing a nail. "Yeah, yeah, I like to see movies, but mostly stuff you probably wouldn't like. Old vampire flicks and science fiction, weird stuff."

"No, I love that kind of thing," I said quickly. Maybe too quickly.

"Oh, okay. Then I guess we'll have to go see something really bloody and scary next time I'm over in your realm. Maybe something in 3-D."

I grinned. "Is that a promise?"

Neel squirmed. So did I. We didn't meet the other's eyes.

"And maybe I can come visit, stay with Mati and her dad," I said finally.

"Yeah, that would be great."

"Bye, Demon Prince," I said in a low voice.

"See ya around, Moon Girl," Neel said before he turned around and walked away. As he did, I realized that he too was blushing.

Author's Note

The Serpent's Secret is an original story that draws from many traditional folktales and children's stories from West Bengal, India, which have been told by grand-parents, parents, aunties, and uncles to generations of children. I've used many of these stories as a basis for inspiration while writing *The Serpent's Secret*—and as a way to tell my own story as an immigrant daughter. In the same way that Kiran has to discover the land of her parents in order to really understand herself, I spent many summer vacations in Kolkata, India, getting to know not just my language and family, but getting immersed in Bengali cultural stories. My grandmothers and aunts would tell me these tales, usually before bed. My cousins and I would curl up together under the mag-ical protection of a mosquito net, while the whirring overhead fan made the netting dance gently about us. In hearing these stories of talking birds, flying horses, brave princes, clever princesses, and evil rakkhoshi queens, I felt like I was entering an amazing new universe of imagination. When I was writing this novel, it only made sense to have Kiran return not to a real country, but to a place populated and inspired by these traditional stories themselves.

Thakurmar Jhuli and Rakkhosh Stories

Folktales involving rakkhosh are very popular in West Bengal, as they are in many parts of India. The word is sometimes spelled *rakshasa* in other parts of India, but in this book, it is spelled like the word sounds in Bengali. Folktales are of course an oral tradition, passed on verbally from one generation to the next, with each teller adding spice and nuance to their own version. In 1907, Dakshinaranjan Mitra Majumdar collected, wrote down, and published some classic Bengali folktales in a book called *Thakurmar Jhuli* ("Grandmother's Satchel"), and the introduction to that book was written by Nobel laureate Rabindranath Tagore. This collection, which involves separate stories about the Princess Kiranmala and the brothers Neelkamal and Lalkamal, is also full of tales involving rakkhosh and khokkosh, as well as stories about the Kingdom of Serpents and the magical land of Maya Pahar. Pakkhiraj horses are plentiful in *Thakurmar Jhuli*, as are evil snakes, stupid kings, and peacock barges. The demon queen hungry for Lalkamal's blood appears in the original Neelkamal and Lalkamal story, as does the lovably goofy rakkhoshi grandmother, Ai-Ma. Lalkamal and Neelkamal never meet Kiranmala in their original stories, but brave Kiranmala does have two brothers named Arun and Barun, whose lives she must save. A version of the Serpent King appears in this collection as well, although not exactly as he appears in this book. And the dumb khokkosh who get fooled into thinking Kiran and Neel are rakkhosh by a sword, some arrows, and an oil lamp? All inspired by *Thakurmar Jhuli*. *Thakurmar Jhuli* stories are still immensely popular in West Bengal and Bangladesh, and have inspired translations, films, television cartoons, comic books, and more. Rakkhosh are very popular as well—the demons everyone loves to hate—and appear not just in folk stories but also Hindu mythology. Images of bloodthirsty, long-fanged rakkhosh can be seen everywhere—even on the back of colorful Indian trucks, as a warning to other drivers not to tailgate or drive too fast!

Abol Tabol and Sukumar Ray

Sukumar Ray can be considered the Dr. Seuss or Lewis Carroll of the Bengali literary tradition. His illustrated book of nonsense rhymes, *Abol Tabol*, was first published in 1923, but like *Thakurmar Jhuli*, it is an evergreen Bengali children's favorite. The character Mr. Madan Mohan in this book was inspired by two nonsense poems from *Abol Tabol*—the first about a man with a bizarre contraption on his back that dangles food in front of his face ("Khuror Kal"), and the second about an office worker who is convinced that someone has stolen his very hairy and very much present moustache ("Gopf Churi"). The snake-charming poem that Tuntuni recites, "Baburam Sapure" also appears in *Abol Tabol*. Two other characters in *The Serpent's Secret* were also inspired by Sukumar Ray's brilliant poems, that of the rhyming transit officer, who appears in a poem called "Bhoye Peo Na" ("Don't Be Afraid"), and Chhaya Devi, purveyor of shadows, who was inspired by a poem called "Chhaya Baji."

Tuntuni

The wisecracking bird Tuntuni is another favorite, and recurrent, character of Bengali children's folktales. The father of Sukumar Ray, Upendrakishore Ray Chowdhury (also known as Upendrakishore Ray), collected a number of these stories starring the clever tailor bird Tuntuni in a 1910 book called *Tuntunir Boi* ("The Tailor Bird's Book").

Panchatantra

The thirsty crow is a story that appears in many cultural traditions. The Indian version appears in the *Panchatantra*, an ancient collection of interrelated animal tales thought to have first appeared around the third century BCE.

Astronomy

There are a number of references to astronomy in this book, most notably to black holes and the life cycle of a star. This is because, like in every culture, traditional Indian stories are often infused with stories about the stars and planets. Like ancient peoples in Egypt or Greece, long ago Indians wondered what controlled the sun, moon, and stars, and made up many stories and myths to explain their behavior. When writing *The Serpent's Secret*, I was inspired by scientific writing about dark matter, dark energy, string theory, Einstein's ring, and the star cycle, but much of what comes in between in this story is entirely fanciful and fictional! Please don't take anything in this book as scientific fact, but rather use the story to inspire some more research about astronomy and, of course, His Brilliance, the Guru-ji Albert Einstein!

Other Random References

There are a lot of other Indian references in the story. Moon Moon Sen is a well-known actress. Kati rolls are a popular Kolkata street food snack, while luchi, sandesh, and rasagolla are all very classic Bengali foods. The absurd signs in Demon Land and Maya Pahar were inspired by the often hilarious, usually misspelled Indian signs on roadsides, highways, and even the back of trucks. The idea that there is a universal soul, and our bodies are but temporary vessels that on our death return our essence to that universal stream, is a central—if simplified—idea of Hindu philosophy. The German nursery rhyme the star-babies sing in Dr. Einstein's class is a real German song, with slightly altered lyrics thrown in.

And I have no doubt that almost every daughter of Indian immigrants, like me, was forced to dress up like a "real Indian princess." Every. Single. Halloween!

If you'd like to read more Bengali folk stories, here are some books in English:

- **The Demon Slayers and Other Stories: Bengali Folktales** by Sayantani DasGupta (that's me) and Shamita Das Dasgupta (that's my mom). New York, NY: Interlink, 1995.

- **The Ghost Catcher** by Martha Hamilton and Mitch Weiss. Atlanta, GA: August House, 2008.

- **The Buri and the Marrow** by Henriette Barkow. London, UK: Mantra Lingua, 2000.

- **Tuntuni, the Tailor Bird** by Betsy Bang. New York, NY: Greenwillow Books, 1978.

Acknowledgments

Kiranmala would never have been successful on her quest without the help of her friends and family, and the same goes for the publication of this book. First and foremost, I must heartily thank my agent, Brent Taylor, who championed this story with clear-eyed enthusiasm, stalwart belief, and mad skill. And to his colleague Uwe Stender—vielen vielen Dank für Alles! I'd like to humbly thank Abigail McAden and Patrice Caldwell—the best editorial demon slayers around, who not only helped me write better and dream bigger but also made every moment of this process a delight.

Thank you to Vivienne To and the entire art department at Scholastic, particularly the visionary Elizabeth Parisi, for this beautiful cover and art, and Abby Dening for her clever interior design. To Rachel Gluckstern, my production editor; Rebekah Wallin, my copyeditor; Talia Seidenfeld, my eleventh-hour proofreader; and the rest of Team Kiranmala including intergalactic marketing and publicity heroes Rachel Feld, Lizette Serrano, Tracy van Straaten, and Jennifer Abbots—thank you again and again for helping me share these beloved stories from Bengal with a global audience of readers.

Thank you to the best critique group around—Sheela Chari, Veera Hiranandani, and Heather Tomlinson—who believed in my stories even when I forgot how and continue to help me grow as a writer and reader. Eternal love and gratitude to my writing sister, Olugbemisola Rhuday-Perkovich, who plies me with wisdom, inspiration, and gluten-free treats, and to my oldest sister-friend, Kari Scott, who shared my love of stories in childhood and does still. (I wouldn't be writing stories now if not for all those summer afternoons reading them, watching them, and acting them out with you.) I'm also indebted to my sis and dance partner Mallika Chopra and her brother Gautam for their invaluable support and advice on this project and so many others.

Endless gratitude to the entire We Need Diverse Books, Kidlit Writers of Color, and Desi Writers families. I am proud to be a part of such a visionary group of artists who are writing a more just future into reality every day. Thank you to my local creative moms posse, Kerri, Viv, Liv, Laura, Meg, Jill, and the real Jovi—who is nothing like the mean girl named after her—for reminding me all the time that parenting and art go hand in hand. Lots of love too to my Bengali community from childhood and now for helping me celebrate the rich, funny, wacky, and powerful reality of being a Bengali immigrant daughter in New Jersey.

Thank you to my narrative medicine/health humanities colleagues at Columbia and around the country, who taught me that stories are the best medicine. Lots of gratitude as well to my former pediatric patients and my current undergraduate and graduate students, who teach me, inspire me, and fill me with hope for the future of this planet.

To my loving parents, Sujan and Shamita, and my entire extended family of storytellers, I am so grateful to have received these stories at your feet. To my husband, Boris, and my beloved partners in crime, Kirin and Sunaya—thank you for cheering me on every step of the way. You are the joy, you are the magic, you are the feeling of flying through the sky. I'd slay all the demons for you, my darlings, in this universe and all the rest.

About the Author

Sayantani DasGupta grew up hearing stories about brave princesses, bloodthirsty rakkhosh, and flying pakkhiraj horses. She is a pediatrician by training but now teaches at Columbia University. When she's not writing or reading, Sayantani spends time watching cooking shows with her trilingual children and protecting her black Labrador retriever, Khushi, from the many things that scare him, including plastic bags. She is a team member of We Need Diverse Books and can be found online at www.sayantanidasgupta.com and on Twitter at @sayantani16.

————— FROM BOOK 2 —————

KIRANMALA AND THE KINGDOM BEYOND

Sequel to The Serpent's Secret

The first time the Demon Queen appeared in my bedroom, I tried to decapitate her with my solar system nightlight.

I was fast asleep, but got woken up by the freaky sound of buzzing. Then I smelled that rancid, belch-y, acid-y odor I'd come to associate with the rakkhoshi during my adventures in the Kingdom Beyond Seven Oceans and Thirteen Rivers. As soon as I opened my eyes, I saw her tell-tale outline: pointy crown on her giant head, sharp horns peeking through her dark hair, and evil talons reaching from her long arms.

I reached for my magic bow and quiver under my bed, but when my hand came up empty, I remembered I'd left them in my locker at school. So instead, I laced my fingers through the plastic rings of Saturn, yanked my old night-light from the socket, and spun the entire solar system like a flying discus right at the Rakkhoshi Rani's head.

Unfortunately, the sun and orbiting planets never managed to hit her. To my shock, the plastic solar system just sailed through her see-through, sari-clad body, crashing on the front of my Princess Pretty Pants dresser, part of the disgustingly princess-themed bedroom set my parents had bought me when I was, like, six.

"Honestly, Moon-girl! Is that any way to greet the mother of an old friend?" The rakkhoshi's fangs glinted in the moonlight that streamed through my curtain-less windows. Then she stretched her claw-like hand toward the fallen night-light, making the plastic explode with a fiery bang.

"Stop that!" I ran out of bed, throwing my bedside glass of water on the place my bubble-gum pink carpet was burning. It did basically nothing to squelch the flames, though. "You're going to burn the whole house down!" The smell of melting plastic gagged me as Mercury and Venus started ooblecking right before my eyes.

"Spoil sport!" The Demon Queen drawled, but she did lean over and breathe an icy gust of wind onto the burning planets—a little mini hailstorm—leaving a charred and smelly solar system on my bedroom floor.

"You're not real." I blinked my eyes, trying to wake myself up. "I'm imagining this."

The demoness belched. Loudly. "You don't have enough imagination to conjure the likes of me!"

Hoping to catch her off-guard, just in case I was wrong about the whole being-a-nightmare thing, I launched myself at the rakkhoshi with a ferocious yowl. But she just yawned, and let me go flying right through her vaporous form.

I slammed into my dresser, hitting my head hard on a tiara-shaped drawer knob. "I knew you weren't real!"

"Oh, fie on your underdeveloped cranium, you pea-brained tree-goat!" The queen picked her teeth with a long nail. "Listen up, I have something important to tell you. A matter of life and death. About…"

"What?" I prompted from my position sprawled out on the floor.

"Oof!" The demoness made a choking sound, grabbing at her throat. She repeated the nonsensical word, fluttering her hands like she wasn't getting enough air. "Oof! Eesh! Arré!"

Then, her image flickered, like she was a broken movie reel.

It went on like this, night after night. The Rakkhoshi

Rani showing up in her smelly but see-through form, insulting me, trying to tell me something, but then disappearing.

If the demoness were real, I would have guessed this was some kind of trick. But since she obviously couldn't be, I could only surmise I should stop sneaking so many chocolate chip cookies before bedtime. Because man, was this a super weird dream. Every time we got to the part where she wanted to tell me her secret, the rakkhoshi would open her mouth and flap her lips, like some kind of landed demonic fish. She would claw at her throat. Her mouth would move, but no sound would come out. Eventually, her image would flicker and fade altogether.

The closest she got to telling me her secret was one night when she managed to tell me some kind of riddle poem that made absolutely no sense when I first heard it:

> *Elladin belladin, Milk White Sea*
> *Who seeks immortality?*
> *A drum and flame, eternity*
> *Life and death in balance be*
> *My heart in chains where my soul sings*
> *The prison key a bee's wings*
> *With father's tooth you crack the case*
> *Humility must wash your face*

Sacrifice is love's reward
The path of truth is ever hard
Justice can't be stopped by a wall
Purity is not the end-all
Without the dark, the light will fail
Gods and demons both will rail
Elladin, belladin, Milk White Sea
Who seeks immortality?

"What is all that supposed to mean? What's that elladin belladin stuff anyway?"

"Oh, this pancreatic pain! This gaseous gallbladder!" The queen groaned. "Try to listen between the lines, khichuri-brain!"

"I'm trying!" It was hard to win an argument with a figment of my imagination. "If I figure out your riddle, will you leave me alone?"

"Oh, the intestinal agony of your stupidity!" The rakkhoshi grew so big in her frustration, her crown grazed my old-fashioned popcorn ceiling. She blew green smoke out of her ears and nose, and burped like she was lactose intolerant and had just eaten a cheesy burrito chased by a dozen milkshakes.

"You can't understand, can you Loonie-Moonie?"

"Of course I can't understand! Because you're. Not. Real!" I shouted so loud I actually woke myself up.

Coming back from the bathroom, though, I couldn't help but stare at the dents in the popcorn ceiling, the flakes of plaster on the foot of my bedspread, the half-melted solar system on my dresser, and the charred spot on my carpet. Plus, my bedroom smelled all gaseous like it was at the receiving end of an exhaust vent straight from a garbage dump.

But that was all just my middle-of-the-night imagination. Or maybe some cookie-induced sleepwalking. The nightlight was obviously so old and decrepit it had just spontaneously combusted. And the smell was probably a lingering combination of melted plastic and some nasty gym clothes that I'd forgotten to wash. Or so I tried to convince myself.

But the thing about subconscious dreams that aren't actually subconscious dreams? Eventually, they come back to bite you in the chocolate chip.